THE FORTUNATE ONES

ALSO BY ED TARKINGTON

Only Love Can Break Your Heart

The Fortunate Ones

||||

a novel by

ED TARKINGTON

ALGONQUIN BOOKS
OF CHAPEL HILL   2021

Published by
ALGONQUIN BOOKS OF CHAPEL HILL
Post Office Box 2225
Chapel Hill, North Carolina 27515-2225

a division of
WORKMAN PUBLISHING
225 Varick Street
New York, New York 10014

This is a work of fiction. While, as in all fiction, the literary perceptions and insights are based on experience, all names, characters, places, and incidents either are products of the author's imagination or are used fictitiously.

LIBRARY OF CONGRESS CATALOGING-IN-PUBLICATION DATA

Names: Tarkington, Ed, [date]– author.
Title: The fortunate ones / a novel by Ed Tarkington.
Description: First edition. | Chapel Hill, North Carolina : Algonquin Books of Chapel Hill, 2021. | Summary: "When young Charlie Boykin gains entry into the wealthy society of the most exclusive part of Nashville, he falls under its spell. But he soon learns what he'd have to give up in return in this novel that asks why we envy and worship a class of people that so often exhibits the worst excesses"—Provided by publisher.
Identifiers: LCCN 2020025221 | ISBN 9781616206802 (hardcover) | ISBN 9781643751078 (ebook)
Classification: LCC PS3620.A735 F67 2021 | DDC 813/.6—dc23
LC record available at https://lccn.loc.gov/2020025221

10 9 8 7 6 5 4 3 2 1
First Edition

For Margaret Renkl and
Haywood Moxley

"And what we students of history always learn is that the human being is a very complicated contraption and that they are not good or bad but are good and bad and the good comes out of the bad and the bad out of the good, and the devil take the hindmost."

—ROBERT PENN WARREN, *All the King's Men*

THE FORTUNATE ONES

Prologue

Casualty Notification

The mother was standing behind the screen door when we stepped out of the car. She knew what we were there to do. This was my third such trip in a month. Fort Campbell had averaged about one a week since the surge. Casualty notification assignments were supposed to rotate, but Command kept giving them to me. Mike told me I was too well suited to the task.

"You've got a sweet face, Charlie," he told me. "A sad face. They feel better when they think you're sad."

"I am sad," I said.

"We're all sad," Mike said. "Some people just don't know how to show it, that's all."

He was talking about himself.

Mike and I got on well, perhaps because he was always game for a few drinks afterward. The Protestant chaplains were all teetotalers. I hadn't been out with the rabbi. Mike Bailey, however, liked his Irish whiskey. And he had no interest in counseling me. "Find us a nice, quiet spot, Charlie," he would say when it was over, and before long, we were someplace dark where you could still smoke inside. Catholics understand the healing power of a stiff drink.

The dead boy's parents lived in Bellevue, at the end of a quiet, shady street lined with red brick '50s ranch houses and split-levels with well-kept yards. There were kids throwing balls and riding bicycles, elderly women sitting on front porch chairs and lawn furniture, a few men riding mowers. Manicured flower beds resting at the bases of mailboxes decorated with eagles and flags. Pickup trucks and minivans and motor homes and pontoon and bass boats on trailers parked at the ends of the driveways. America the beautiful, forever and ever, amen.

"Didn't you grow up around here?" Mike asked. "You and this kid's family might know some of the same people."

"I doubt it."

"Come on. You Southerners are all cousins, right?"

"And I assume you're related to the Kennedys."

A trio of old men congregating around an ancient Ford pickup turned from their conversation to watch our car roll past. They exchanged a few words and dispersed, heading toward their respective homes, no doubt to inform their wives of our arrival.

"There they go," Mike said. "Tuna casserole, on the way. I'll bet you a hundred bucks the first one shows up before we leave."

I couldn't say whether or not Mike Bailey was a good priest. He was a product of one of those big Irish Catholic families, the kind with a dozen kids, most of which give at least one son to the Army and one to the church. Mike had somehow managed to satisfy both requirements. I got the sense that he'd opted into the chaplain thing when he was still young and romantic, maybe under the influence of a charismatic Jesuit who'd filled him with dreams of emulating the heroic missions of Saint Ignatius and his followers. His idealism did not seem to have survived Fallujah.

I slowed to a stop in front of the appointed address, and the dread came on.

I reached back for the folder I'd set on the rear seat before we left. I looked up at the house, and there she was, standing behind the screen door, as if she'd sensed we were coming, as if she'd felt the life she'd brought into the world go out of it from thousands of miles away, and we were just there to confirm what she already knew.

"Let's not keep her waiting," I said.

She opened the door before we even reached the front porch steps. Her eyes were damp.

"Hello, ma'am," I said. "Are you the mother of Private First Class Cody James Carter?"

"His daddy's in the back," she said.

We followed her through a small entry hall into a dim wood-paneled living room. On the wall over a gas-log fireplace hung a large flat-screen TV tuned to Fox News.

Mr. Carter stood when he saw us. He picked up the remote control and pressed MUTE. Maybe he was afraid he'd miss something.

Mrs. Carter came to her husband's side. They stared at us, their faces anguished, waiting. In the language of the Casualty

Notification Officer Module, I informed them that their son was dead.

Mrs. Carter's face slackened. She drooped to the couch. Her husband sat down and wrapped his arm around her but remained rigid, his eyes fixed on some point between the television and the fireplace as I finished reciting the script.

Mike sat down next to Mr. Carter. I rounded the coffee table and sat close enough to touch the mother.

"Did he suffer?" she asked.

"We won't have the full incident report for another day or two," I said.

The father removed his glasses and set them on the table, his arm still wrapped around his wife. His face went pale, and the tears began to form, but they did not fall, as if he had somehow willed himself not to cry.

"Would you folks like to pray?" Mike asked.

They nodded.

Mike removed a rosary from his uniform pocket and began. Above them, the talking heads on Fox News, silenced by the MUTE button, felt both comical and profane. While they debated whether this or that multimillionaire Republican candidate was sufficiently conservative, kids like Cody Carter were still dying in a place most Americans couldn't find on a map. The world had moved on to a new movie.

As Mike finished, I opened up my dossier and explained the protocol for their son's homecoming.

I have delivered casualty notifications to parents to whom the Army meant nothing at all—people whose sons had joined up because of the GI Bill, or because they played too much *Call of Duty* on the Xbox, or because they thought it might be fun to get paid instead of arrested for shooting at brown people or just wanted out of their shitty circumstances and away from the very folks to whom I was delivering the news of their death. Some, like me, joined up in the vain belief that the service would afford them the chance to atone for past sins— or, at least, to flee the scenes of our crimes. This was not the case with the parents of PFC Cody Carter. For the Carters, the Army was a calling. I knew without asking that they would go to Fort Campbell, and then to Dover, or anywhere else, to greet the remains of their son. They would leave that very second if they could. The Carters were True Believers.

"As part of the Dignified Transfer," I said, dutifully reciting the script of the CNO Module, "Cody will arrive in a coffin draped with the flag of the United States of America."

Dignified Transfer. The sound of it made me feel like a vacuum cleaner salesman. But I knew when I recited those words the Carters could hear the twenty-one-gun salute and see the honor guard folding the flag into a tight triangle and presenting it to Mrs. Carter with the thanks of a grateful nation. Who was I to say or even to think otherwise? So I did my duty.

My eyes drifted over to a wall decorated with family photos. Beneath the pictures stood a bookshelf full of trophies and medals and photographs of Private Carter and his brothers and sisters—the boys in wrestling singlets and baseball uniforms; the girls in choir robes, Sunday dresses, one posing in a pink leotard, another holding a violin. I recognized Cody Carter from his class A uniform portrait. He was the youngest.

"If you'll excuse me," I said, "I'll contact your Casualty Assistance Officer and make the arrangements for you."

I left Mike with the Carters and walked out into the entry

hall and toward the open front door to call the base on my mobile phone. Outside, the old men we had seen were standing in the front yard under a big hickory tree wrapped with a fading yellow ribbon, along with a small group of neighbors, some of them smoking, the lot of them looking back and forth between themselves and the door. I started to duck back into the house, but they'd already seen me. So I stepped out onto the sidewalk and removed my mobile phone from my uniform jacket pocket. One of the old men shuffled over.

"Afternoon, sir," I said.

"You boys drive over from Fort Campbell?" the old man asked.

"Yes, sir," I said.

"Served there myself, a long time ago. Airborne," he said, pointing to the patch on the shoulder of my uniform. "Hundred and first. 'Nam. Three tours."

"My father was in 'Nam."

"He must be proud of you."

"He didn't make it back, I'm afraid," I said. "I never knew him."

"I'm sorry to hear that. All the same, I know he's watching."

The man tilted his head and pointed to the sky.

"Yes, sir," I said.

"Is it Cody?" he asked.

"Yes, sir."

"What happened?"

"I can't say, sir."

"Understood," the man said. "How they holdin' up?"

"As well as anyone could," I said. "Better than most."

"They're good people," the old man said. "Some of the best I know. Cody was a good boy. He's a big deal to the kids around here. Wrestled over at Sacred Heart. State champ his senior year at one thirty. Little fireplug. He wasn't the strongest or the fastest, but, boy, he just kept coming. Made the other guy want to quit. I bet he was a good soldier."

Was Cody Carter a good soldier? For all I knew, he'd been an absolute shithead; unlikely, given what I'd seen of his life thus far, but, God knows, the Army was full of them. It didn't really matter anymore. He was a hero now.

"Excuse me, sir," I said. "I need to take care of some arrangements for the Carters."

"Beg your pardon."

"No need to apologize," I said. "Thank you for speaking with me, sir."

"You tell Pete and Martha we're here for them when they're ready," the old man said.

I nodded. The old man straightened his back as if standing at attention and held his hand out for me to shake. I knew what was coming.

"Thank you for your service," he said.

These moments happened to all of us, everywhere. Walking through an airport concourse, we'd meet the wistful gazes of hundreds of well-meaning citizens, and we'd know they were wondering if we were headed home or instead back to one of those far-flung deadly lands, with parents and spouses and children—some still unborn—waiting for us on front porches and stoops in all the Bellevues of America. Men patted us on the shoulder or gave us a soulful nod or a solemn salute. Some wanted to tell us that they also served, that they, too, had done their part, that they were different from the hordes of civilians who did not understand the concept of valor.

I knew these people meant well—that their respect was genuine and their gratitude sincere. Nevertheless, every time this happened to me, I felt like I was going to fucking puke.

I took his hand and shook it.

"Thank you, sir," I said, returning one of those sad smiles that Mike thought made me such a popular Casualty Notification Officer.

I held up my phone.

"Excuse me, sir," I said.

"Remember," the old man said. "You tell 'em we're out here."

He rejoined the others gathered under the hickory tree with the big yellow ribbon around it. After I called the CAO, I retreated into the house, where the Carters still sat on the couch beneath the silent television while Mike tried to act comforting.

"Mr. and Mrs. Carter," I said, "Lieutenant Garrett will pick you up in the morning, at eight a.m. He will travel with you to Dover. We've reserved a room for you at the Courtyard Marriott near the airport. You'll stay overnight and then accompany your son home to Fort Campbell the following morning. They've notified your eldest son as well. His CO will do what he can to get him home for a few days."

"Will we be able to see Cody?" the mother asked.

"No, ma'am," I said. "Not at Dover. But you'll be with him, to bring him home."

Mrs. Carter rose from the couch. Finally, she broke. Her

husband lurched up and reached for her. I heard a muffled moan, high and keening. Her husband stroked her back.

"I'll be damned," Mike blurted.

He pointed at the television. The Carters turned toward the screen.

Because I had seen Arch Creigh's face on the news so many times before, it took me a moment to grasp the reason why I was looking at it now.

"What happened?" the mother asked.

"The son of a bitch shot himself," Mike said.

There they were—Arch and Vanessa, in old footage from the day Arch declared his Senate candidacy. The camera cut to a live image, in front of the house on the Boulevard, surrounded by men with cameras, Vanessa's face pale and slack with shock and grief.

"Charlie," Mike said.

Vanessa was giving a statement to the media, which we could not hear. Mr. Carter picked up the remote and turned on the sound. The police had found him out at the family hunting camp—I was sure I knew exactly where. There didn't appear to be any doubt about how it had happened. He'd left a note.

"That's a hell of a thing to do to your wife and kids," Mr. Carter said.

"They don't have any children," I said.

The television vultures were feasting on what lay before them: Charismatic Southern Republican Senator commits suicide in the midst of a tight race. Potential for upset in the reddest of red states. Who would the party tap to replace him? What scandal would emerge? Could the Dems seize this moment of crisis to narrow the gap in the Senate? Who would fill Arch

Creigh's shoes in the eleventh hour? Would the grieving widow take up the mantel herself?

I felt a hand on my shoulder.

"Charlie?" Mike asked. "Are you all right?"

I was crying. The tears just came. I couldn't stop.

"Charlie?" Mike repeated.

I looked away from the television and over at Mike and the Carters, who were staring at me.

"I'm so sorry," I said. "Forgive me."

Mr. Carter looked back toward the television. His wife glanced down at the floor.

"What on earth is wrong with you?" Mike whispered.

I wiped my eyes.

"I knew him," I said.

"You knew Arch Creigh?" Mr. Carter asked.

"Yes," I said.

"Like, you knew him," Mike said, "or you *knew* him?"

How could I even begin to answer such a question?

PART ONE

||||||||||||||

Princes in the Tower

ONE

When I learned what had happened to Arch, what he'd done—when I saw him there on the TV screen in the living room of a dead soldier's family and wept—I thought not of what he'd become, but, rather, of a boy I once knew, with a mop of golden hair and a golden smile and a sense of certitude so strong it spilled onto everyone around him. And I thought of the boy I had once been, aimless and timid, and how when that magnificent boy turned his light toward me, I fed on that light, and in doing so, became transformed.

I was born in Nashville, but I got my start in the mountains of Western North Carolina, on the last day of the second session at Camp Hollyhock for Girls, August 1969, in the back seat of an old Buick parked on a deserted fire road above the camp lake. My mother, Bonnie, fifteen years old, between her sophomore and junior years of high school, had fallen for a handsome stable boy named Johnny Larue, recently drafted and bound for Basic Training. Her parents were strict Upstate

South Carolina Presbyterians, who firmly believed that God hates liquor and sex and loves rich white people, so long as they at least pretend to hate liquor and sex. But my mother never listened in church.

Three months later, back home in Greer, when she could no longer hide her condition and was forced to confess, my grandfather vowed to make this Johnny LaRue take responsibility. But by then, he was on the other side of the world fighting communists. My mother's letters to him went unanswered. Years would pass before she found out he'd been killed in action. She did not know if he'd learned that he was going to be a father before he disappeared. She knew only that she was about to become an unwed mother in a town where such a designation was a disgrace. My grandfather resolved to send her off until I was born and could be given up for adoption. He knew of a home for unwed mothers in Virginia that placed infants born to wayward daughters in good Christian homes. Everyone in Greer would be told that Bonnie had gone off to boarding school, which would soon enough be true: my grandfather had arranged to send her to a girls' school notorious for breaking the spirits of privileged girls who had turned out willful or wild or "fast."

My grandfather had not accounted for the fact that Bonnie had inherited both his temper and his stubbornness. One morning, she woke before dawn, packed a suitcase, stole all of the money her mother kept stashed in a coffee can, and hitched a ride to the Greyhound station. She had a cousin who had run off to Nashville to become a country singer—Beverly Poteat, who called herself Sunny Brown. A few months later, at Vanderbilt Hospital, I made my inglorious entry into the world.

These were the days when they stamped BASTARD on the birth certificates of fatherless children. Still, my mother decided to name me Charles, after her father, in the hope that this sign of respect would soften his heart, and that, perhaps, he might beg her to come home. When she called to give him the news, he said only two words to her—"Good luck"—and hung up.

Unwed mothers and absent fathers were not unusual in the Montague Village Apartments. In school, I suffered far less persecution for being a bastard than for being one of the few white boys in a black neighborhood and school. When I got old enough to start asking who and where my daddy was, my mother told me he was a soldier who never came home from the war. When I asked more questions—why we had no photographs of my father, where were my grandparents, where did we come from—my mother looked at Sunny.

"Well, honey," Sunny said, "your daddy knocked your momma up, and your granddaddy kicked her out."

By then, Sunny's dreams of stardom had stalled in an airport bar, where she sang for tips. Her stage was a small riser equipped with a microphone and a PA system running a loop of country classics like "Crazy," "D-I-V-O-R-C-E," and "I Will Always Love You."

When I was old enough to be left with one of the neighbors, my mother started waiting tables. She worked at a diner until she turned eighteen, whereupon she moved up to cocktailing in a honky-tonk on Lower Broadway, which back then was all strip clubs, junkies, and hustlers. Eventually, she migrated to Café Cabernet, a dim restaurant in Midtown, also known as Café Divorcée for its popularity as a pickup spot. Every time I visited the place, the stereo seemed to be playing something by Steely Dan or Supertramp. My mother was a beauty, both sensuous and demure, with a curvy figure just on the right edge of plumpness. She was a bit heedless, but smarter and tougher than she looked. Tips were good enough for the three of us to upgrade to a three-bedroom apartment at Montague Village.

We children of Montague were passed around from mother to mother, depending on who wasn't working at the time. None of them appeared to notice where we were or what we were doing. I spent most of my time with Terrence Robie, who lived across the hall with his grandmother Louella, a maid for a pair of families across the river in Belle Meade. We were raised from infancy in such close proximity that we might as well have been brothers. Though we were only a few months apart in age, by the time we reached middle school, Terrence had grown six inches taller and at least thirty pounds heavier than I. He began to protect me as if I actually were his brother. Terrence could not save me from all of the abuse I suffered for being the smallest and meekest of the few white students in the halls of W. E. B. DuBois Middle, but he made things less miserable than they might otherwise have been.

My mother never showed much interest in my education until, when I was in eighth grade, she received a hospital bill for eight hundred dollars after one of my regular beatings outside school resulted in a broken collarbone.

"We've got to get you out of that school," she said.

One morning not long after, she woke me up early and ordered me to dress in the clothes usually reserved for Christmas Eve and Easter morning church visits.

"Where are we going?" I asked.

"There's something I want you to see," she said.

The Yeatman School lay at the end of a narrow drive lined by hickory trees, such that it couldn't be seen from the road; the only markers of its presence were two weathered stone columns, each with the letter *Y* engraved on flat concrete panels. The obscurity of this entrance suggested that one wasn't meant to be able to find the school without being told where to look. The forest surrounding the campus—the Grove, they call it— was so dense that I felt, after passing through the shadowy woods and coming upon the white columns bathed in sunlight, that if I left and came back to the same spot, I might not find it there.

Coach Baldwin, a blond, lantern-jawed statue of a man with the stiff, erect posture of an antique nutcracker, toured us around. My mother blushed when he held the door for her and called her "ma'am." It took me a while to process the fact that Coach Baldwin was, for lack of a more accurate expression, *courting* us, trying to persuade us of the school's worthiness.

What I remember best about that day was not the school's beauty or its expensive amenities, but how different my mother seemed while we were there. At home, she still wore jeans and T-shirts, short skirts and sleeveless tops, cowboy boots or spike-heeled shoes. In her work attire, she looked like what she was: a sexy cocktail waitress with a keen grasp of what an extra inch of exposed thigh or cleavage could be worth in tips. That day at Yeatman, however, she wore a prim short-sleeved, knee-length blue dress and a pair of tan patent leather flats I'd never seen before. Her hair, usually sprayed out, lay flat and neatly brushed. All of the men we encountered—Coach Baldwin, the teachers who stopped to greet us in the hallways, the coaches in the gym—treated her with polite deference. I'd never heard my mother referred to as "ma'am" before. The whole picture was jarring, and, I thought, more than a bit deceiving. But I had only ever seen one side of her—the waitress, the unwed single mother, the drinker and smoker. I had forgotten, or perhaps never really understood, that she had grown up around the kind of people who sent their boys to places like Yeatman. Indeed, in her life before my arrival, she'd been one of them.

At the end of our tour, Coach Baldwin led us back to the admissions office. My mother sat at a desk, filling out a form, while I flipped through a copy of the alumni magazine. When my mother was through, Coach Baldwin handed me a cellophane bag full of Yeatman Y-embossed knickknacks: buttons, stickers, a T-shirt, pencils and a sharpener, and a foam finger.

"How would you like to go to a school like that?" my mother asked as we began the drive home in her Chevy Cavalier.

Truth be told, I didn't give the first thought to how out of place I would be at Yeatman. Nor did I question the expense involved, or why the opportunity had been extended to me. I could only think how lovely it all was—the brightness of the white columns—how clean everything seemed, how peaceful, how stately and noble.

"Sure," I said.

If not for that day, I would never have left East Nashville for Belle Meade, nor would I have understood how much the conditions of life in one world depend on the whims of those who live in another.

TWO

A note on stationery embossed with a gilded Gothic Y arrived in the mail at our apartment a few weeks later, inviting me to join the Yeatman class of 1988. Admission letter in hand, I went to tell Terrence.

"My cousin went there for football," Terrence said. "Those folks Grand-Lou used to work for sent their boys there. That's a rich white boy school, Charlie."

"It's not all white," I said. "You could go there too."

"You think I want to go to school with a bunch of rich white boys?" he asked. "Besides, who's gonna pay for that? You rich now, Charlie? Last time I checked, you still lived in the hood like the rest of us."

I felt my face flush hot with both shame and indignation.

"I don't know," I stammered.

"You tell me when you figure it out," he said.

When I asked my mother about it, she let out a long sigh.

"Have you ever heard of need-based scholarships, Charlie?"

I hadn't.

"Well, you qualify for one," she said. "So would Terrence. He'd probably get a better deal than you. Maybe he'd like to apply."

I said nothing. Terrence had made his feelings about the Yeatman School very clear.

"You let me worry about money," my mother said. "You just work hard and do well, okay?"

A WEEK BEFORE the beginning of school, my mother and I returned to Yeatman to attend a reception for new high school students and their parents, which revolved around an audience with the headmaster and the introduction of each new freshman to a sophomore designated to be his "big brother." We gathered in the lobby outside the headmaster's office, around a pair of long tables loaded with cookies, and pitchers of orange juice and ice water. Most of the rising freshman class had come through the Yeatman junior school; hence, there were only twenty new students. The boys who were familiar with one another all had tousled hair, Sperry Top-Siders or Clarks Wallabees, web belts from Brooks Brothers and L.L.Bean, and the tanned, healthy look that comes from tennis and swimming lessons and summer camps. The other group was smaller and motley: boys with cheaper clothes and shoes and buzz cuts; a few Asian and black boys to satisfy the recently implemented diversity quota. My mother and I stood at the front of the room, afraid to part from each other. I wanted to join the larger group of tanned, tousled boys and be absorbed into their ranks. But I knew that I belonged with the other group.

I was rescued by the headmaster's assistant, Mrs. Barnett, who led me up the hallway. Through a door to my left, I heard the chatter of voices—the sophomore big brothers, lounging in the chairs around the boardroom table.

"Go on in, honey," Mrs. Barnett said. "They're waiting for you."

Inside the frosted doors, Dr. Dodd, the headmaster, leaned against the front edge of his desk. To his left sat a large man in pressed chinos, an open-collared white shirt, and a navy blazer. Dr. Dodd stood and extended his hand. The other man remained seated.

"Hello, Mr. Boykin," Dr. Dodd said.

I grasped his hand and shook it.

"This is a friend of mine, Mr. Haltom," Dr. Dodd said.

"Hi," I said.

Mr. Haltom smiled. "Hello, Charlie."

"Have a seat." Dr. Dodd gestured to one of the club chairs arranged in front of his desk. "Don't be nervous. We're just going to get to know each other a bit."

"Yes, sir," I said.

Dr. Dodd asked me a short series of questions that made clear he already knew the answers. He talked about the importance of applying oneself, staying on top of things, showing up for extra help in the mornings. I was distracted—by the pictures on the walls and the windowsills, and the various other objects decorating the office; by the peculiarity of Dodd's appearance, with his longish silver hair and glinting gold rings and dress watch; perhaps most by Mr. Haltom, whose presence remained unexplained.

I was jerked back to attention as Dr. Dodd shifted off his desk and extended his hand again.

"We know you're going to thrive here," Dr. Dodd said.

"I'll do my best, sir," I said.

Dr. Dodd pressed a button on his office phone.

"Carolyn?" he said. "We're ready."

A moment later, the door opened and closed. I looked up from the floor. There he was: strong jaw and broad shoulders, studiously sloppy sandy-blond hair.

"Hey, bud," the boy said. "I'm Arch Creigh."

Arch held out his hand for me to shake.

"I'm your big brother," he said.

"Archer's one of our best," Dr. Dodd said. "You're very fortunate."

Dr. Dodd stood; this time, Mr. Haltom came to his feet as well.

"Well then. You boys get acquainted," Dr. Dodd said. "Archer, take good care of Charlie, won't you?"

"Yes, sir," Arch said.

I shook Dr. Dodd's hand for the third time. Mr. Haltom offered his hand as well. I tried not to wince at the strength of his grip.

"We're glad you're here, Charlie," he said.

"Thank you, sir," I replied.

I followed Arch out of the office, and we descended the stairs and walked out into the quad. The air was hot and scented with ginkgo blossoms.

"So what do you think of Yeatman so far?" he asked.

"It's great," I said.

I didn't want to tell the truth—that I felt frightened and woefully out of my depth.

"Wait until school starts," he said. "You ever take Latin before?"

"No," I said.

"It's an absolute bitch. I think Yeatman might be the last school on earth that still requires Latin. It's supposed to boost your SAT score, but I think they mostly hold on to it for the sake of tradition."

I'd not yet heard of the SAT, but I nodded as if this benefit was something I'd already considered.

"That's a big thing around here, you know," he said. "Tradition."

He spoke the word in a tone both mocking and sincere.

Arch had been given my class schedule; the ritual, it seemed, was for each of the big brothers to tour his protégé from room to room. As we walked, he spoke to me with genial familiarity, pausing on occasion to point something out or wave to someone across the quadrangle. I was too captivated by his allure to remember anything but the sound of his voice, the way he walked, the casual confidence with which he carried himself, how he inhabited the navy blazer and regimental tie as if he had been the model for which all prep school uniforms had been designed.

When we were finished, Arch led me back to the reception area outside the theater.

"It's great to meet you, bud," he said. "I'll be in touch."

"Thanks," I said.

Again, we shook hands. The touch of his hand felt like an electric charge.

I found my mother sipping a cup of coffee and nodding along as one of the well-dressed mothers prattled about what made Yeatman superior to Montgomery Bell, Nashville's other elite boys' school. Even then, my mother may have been plotting her own escape from the low-down life of Montague Village. But I knew none of this, distracted as I was by my own ascension.

Heading home, my mother waited until we'd reached the highway before lighting a cigarette.

"I saw you through the window, talking with that boy," she said.

I nodded.

"Who was he?"

"Arch," I said. "My big brother."

Two narrow funnels of smoke unfurled from her nostrils and wafted out the crack in the window.

"He's cute," she said.

THREE

The spell cast by that first hour with Arch took little time to break. The various cliques in my grade had all been established long before my arrival. The school's idiosyncrasies and traditions only made me feel that much more the outsider—an impostor bound to be exposed at any moment. I was a year behind every other boy in my grade in math and Latin, and had to take both of those courses with junior schoolers. I went from being first in my class in almost everything to fighting to stay off the bottom among boys a year younger than me.

My greatest humiliations took place under the tutelage of my Latin teacher and advisor, Dean Varnadoe. In his late sixties, Walker Varnadoe was an elegant man, slim and rangy, with a sonorous baritone and pale-blue eyes that seemed to glimmer both when he recited a favorite aphorism and when he leveled his disapproval upon us. He carried a black cane with a polished brass head, which he used not to help him walk but, rather, to point and gesticulate at the board or around the classroom and to rap on the desks of drowsy students, startling them back to rigid, chastened attention.

Varnadoe referred to his classroom as "the harbor." We never saw him outside his harbor during the school day, not even in his office or in the dining hall for meals; he brought his lunch from home and preferred to dine alone while grading or reading from one of his numerous books of poetry, all of them aged, many in the original Latin or Greek. He was the only teacher granted a regular audience with Dr. Dodd—not in Dodd's office, but in Varnadoe's classroom, as if the headmaster needed the teacher's blessing over the most vital matters that came across his desk.

The bookend of my day, my sole refuge, was an hour in the art room. The new art teacher, Miss Whitten, had been hired at the last minute after a severe stroke forced her predecessor into retirement. Young and plainly inexperienced, Miss Whitten appeared baffled by the school, with its hypermasculine traditions and persistent whiff of testosterone. She had difficulty managing the classroom; neighboring teachers popped in a few times a week to complain about the noise.

Miss Whitten didn't smile often; she bore herself with a persistent air of mild melancholy. But she was kind, and encouraging. Drawing and painting in her classroom served as a salve on the battering my ego took everywhere else. In a period of profound disorientation, I lacked the vocabulary to express what I was experiencing in words; I channeled it all into pictures. Miss Whitten received me each day with both eagerness and relief. I would like to think she recognized in me the beginnings of an artist. More likely, she just appreciated having at least one student who took the work seriously. Or maybe she sensed, without knowing why, that I, too, like she, was a stranger in a strange land.

NEAR THE END of the first week, as I came up the stairs, headed toward Dean Varnadoe's room, I found Arch Creigh waiting outside the door, leaning against the wall, flipping through a copy of Richard Wright's *Black Boy*.

"Hi," I said.

"Hey, bud," he said. "Thought you'd never get here."

"What are you reading?"

He glanced down at the book.

"Propaganda," he said. "Hey, what are you doing tomorrow afternoon?"

"Nothing."

"Coach is giving us a day off from practice. Want to hang out?"

"What do you want to do?" I asked.

"I don't know," he said. "Drive around in the truck. Maybe get together with some people."

"You can drive already?" I asked.

"I'm sixteen," he said. "My parents held me back."

"Did you have bad grades?" I asked.

Arch laughed.

"No," he said. "It's just a thing people do. Most of the kids here get held back before kindergarten."

"Cool," I said.

Where I came from, no one was held back; on the contrary, the mothers were eager to get us into school as early as possible; reaching school age meant nine months of free childcare and lunch.

"So do you want to come or what?"

"My mom has to work tomorrow night."

"I can give you a ride home," he said.

"I don't know," I said. "It's kind of far away."

"It's not that far."

"You know where I live?"

"Yeah," he said. "East Nashville."

Overhearing conversations about summer camps and beach vacations and country clubs, I had dreaded the moment when everyone would discover that I lived in a cheap apartment off Gallatin Pike. But I wanted to know him—to be near him— badly enough to risk the shame.

"Okay," I said.

"Good," he said. "Meet me in the quad after school tomorrow."

LIKE MANY OF the Yeatman boys, Arch drove a truck. Arch's was a black Ford F-150 with oversized tires and a white fiberglass camper top on the bed, a Grateful Dead STEAL YOUR FACE sticker placed in the center of the rear window.

We drove out of the lot, down the long, dark driveway, and out into Belle Meade.

"You live alone with your mom?" he asked.

"My aunt lives with us," I said, as if my mother had taken in Sunny and not the other way around.

"What about your dad?" he asked. "Where does he live?"

"He died."

"Oh, man," Arch said. "What happened?"

"Vietnam."

"Man, that's tough," he said.

"Yeah," I said.

"He was a hero."

"I don't know if he was a hero."

"Sure, he was."

Arch asked me more questions—about where my parents were from, how we'd arrived in Nashville, and so forth. I shaped my answers to hide the seedier aspects of my history. Instead of a runaway, my mother became an orphan, and Sunny, her only living relative. My mother had left college to get married. We'd once lived in a house. With each half-truth and outright lie, I realized how easy it was. Just as my mother always presented herself at Yeatman in what seemed to me a costume, I could write myself a role and act it out. I couldn't hide where I lived or what sort of life I'd come from. But I could recast my story in a manner that made me seem less inferior than I felt. I was sure my mother would have no problem with Arch and the rest of the Yeatman people believing her to be a forlorn war widow, scratching and clawing to give her only child a leg up in the world. And I could be the son of a fallen hero instead of a bastard whose father had never known he existed.

Arch's house, on Glen Eden, was a Colonial Revival with a slate roof, three dormer windows, two brick chimneys, and a white-columned side porch facing out onto a large yard that sloped gently down to the street.

He pulled around the back, in front of a two-car garage. I followed him through the back door into a kitchen with a ten-foot ceiling and a large island with tiled countertops. At the end of the counter sat a woman. She looked up and smiled.

"Charlie," she said. "What a pleasure to meet you."

Mrs. Creigh had bobbed silver hair. She wore no makeup.

The pink reading glasses at the end of her nose made her seem too old to be Arch's mother. Her shirt and wrists were faintly soiled; a pair of gardening gloves and a straw hat lay beside her teacup and newspaper.

"There's some chicken salad and pimento cheese in the fridge," she said. "Do you like chicken salad, Charlie?"

"Sure," I said.

"I'll make some sandwiches," she said.

"Thanks, Mom," Arch said.

What a thing it would be, I thought, to come home every day to such a house, to find your modestly elegant mother sitting at the kitchen table perusing the newspaper or the latest issue of *Southern Living*, waiting to ask you about your day and make you a chicken salad sandwich.

I followed Arch through a hallway where the walls were covered with family photos: Arch and his older sisters at every age; his mother holding an infant, his eldest sister's child; the whole family dressed in matching chinos and white shirts on a beach. The offshore wind blowing their hair just so. Arch's mother looked more or less the same; his father looked much younger than his wife, with a thick head of golden hair and a smile identical to his son's. The sisters were striking, in the way people with breeding can be.

The hallway opened up onto a sun-splashed room with a sectional couch and a glass-top coffee table with a bright flower arrangement in a ceramic urn. A pair of bookshelves flanked an enormous television. On the opposite wall by the windows stood a pool table. Arch racked the balls and handed me a cue.

"You want to break?"

"You go ahead," I said.

He cracked the cue ball and set to work clearing the table. After a few minutes, Mrs. Creigh appeared in the doorway with plates holding sandwiches and little ramekins of fruit salad. She set the plates on the coffee table. Arch leaned his cue against the wall and opened up the cabinet beneath the television set to reveal a hidden bar refrigerator.

"Want a Coke?" he asked.

I nodded.

"Hey," he said. "You want to go swimming later?"

"Where?" I asked.

"A friend's house," he said.

"I don't have a suit," I said.

"You can wear one of mine."

"All right."

After a few games of pool, Arch led me upstairs and down another corridor decorated with family photos, to his bedroom. He had a desk set strewn with books and school supplies, a queen-sized bed, a cabinet filled with awards and trophies, Pink Floyd and Grateful Dead and Rolling Stones posters on the walls. He disappeared into his closet and came back out holding a pair of yellow swim trunks.

"My old Birdwells," he said. "Size medium. Try them on."

"Where's the bathroom?" I asked.

"What?" he said. "Scared to get naked in front of me?"

It felt like some sort of dare. I took off my shoes and pants. Eyes fixed on the floor, I slid off my underwear and stepped into the yellow trunks.

"Fit all right?" Arch asked.

"Yeah," I said. "Thanks."

He stripped before searching his drawers for his swim

trunks and a T-shirt. I was unused to being around another boy so at ease in his nakedness. This turned out to be the case for many of the Yeatman boys, conditioned as they were, from years in country club and private school locker rooms, to be unashamed of their bodies. It was easier for Arch, no doubt. He was tan and lean and muscled. I took my time tying my shoes.

I followed him back downstairs into the kitchen. He grabbed his keys and sunglasses off the counter and walked out the back door.

"Bye, Mom," Arch called.

"Where are you going?" she asked.

"To the Haltoms'," he said.

Haltom—that was the name of the man sitting in the office during my interview with Dr. Dodd, watching over the whole proceeding like some sort of auditor.

We drove through the leafy lanes until we came out onto Belle Meade Boulevard. Both sides of the street were lined with houses too grand to be called such. I had difficulty imagining anyone actually lived in such places—that to someone, these places were home.

"The Haltoms are old friends. Family, really," Arch said. "You probably know Jamie. He's a freshman too. His twin sister, Vanessa, goes to Steptoe. We've known each other all our lives. Jim Haltom is like a dad to me, especially since my own dad died."

"Your dad died?" I asked.

"I didn't tell you that, did I?" he said. "I forget sometimes that people don't already know. Yeah, my dad died, when I was twelve. Brain cancer."

"I'm sorry," I said.

"At least I had him for twelve years, right? You never got to know your dad at all."

"I didn't know what I was missing."

"I guess you could look at it that way. Anyhow, Uncle Jim was my dad's best friend since college. He promised my dad he'd look out for my mom and me. He's pretty much my best friend, to tell you the truth."

Even then, it did not occur to me that Arch Creigh being assigned as my big brother might have been more than a happy accident.

Near the end of the Boulevard, not far from the country club, he turned onto a pea gravel driveway that led through a moss-covered stone gate and wound up past a lawn dotted with tall trees. At the top of the slope stood an enormous stucco manor home with a steep-columned porch and a slate roof lined with copper flashing turned a luminous green. We parked and walked up to the side door. Arch rapped on it. A light-skinned black woman in a white short-sleeved blouse opened it.

"Hi, Shirley," Arch said. "This is Charlie."

"Pleased to meet you, Charlie," Shirley said. "Jamie's out back. Y'all walk on through."

I can still see the great house on the Boulevard as I did on that first day: the drawing room, with the toile settee and the velvet Empire sofa and armchairs, and oil paintings of landscapes, and portraits of prize-winning horses and hunting dogs and distant ancestors, and the crystal chandelier descending from the high vaulted ceiling. The dining room, with its broad teak table, the inlaid sideboard with the silver tea set, the hand-painted wallpaper depicting scenes from medieval China. Outside the windows, the bright blooms of heirloom roses.

I followed Arch out the French doors, onto the stone porch, and down through the rose garden, toward the pool and the small white house next to it. Across from the diving board stood a fountain trimmed with a tile mosaic. On the other end, a slate path led to the open doors of the pool house. Inside, someone hidden by the back of a large couch was playing *Punch-Out!!* on the TV.

"Typical," Arch said as we came in. "Beautiful day, sweetest backyard pool in Tennessee, and Jamie Haltom's inside playing video games."

Rounding the couch, he snatched up a remote control from the coffee table and pressed the POWER button. The screen went dark.

"Goddamn it, Arch!" a voice cried.

Arch picked up a can of Coors Light from the tabletop and shook it.

"Give me that," the boy said.

He stood up and snatched at the beer, which Arch dangled in front of him like a dog's chew toy. I recognized him from school; we had two classes together—math and history. Jamie Haltom straightened himself and cocked his head.

"Hey," he said.

We must have been thinking the same thing—that we were being set up, like a playdate.

"Charlie, Jamie," Arch said. "Jamie, Charlie."

He emptied the beer into the bar sink and tossed it into a garbage can.

"Damn it, Arch," Jamie said.

"Shut up, dumbass," Arch said. "Come on, you need a little vitamin D."

We had just come out of the pool house when she appeared: the loveliest girl I'd ever seen, emerging from the rose garden and traipsing across the yard in an oversized white T-shirt and a pair of white-framed Wayfarers, a thick paperback book under her arm.

"Is this Charlie?" the girl asked.

"I told her about you," Arch said. "Charlie, this is Vanessa. Jamie's twin sister."

"Nice to meet you, Charlie," she said.

"Hi," I replied.

Vanessa pulled her T-shirt over her head to reveal a two-piece seersucker bathing suit. She walked around to one of the lounge chairs and settled in to read her book.

She was still very much a girl—just shy of fifteen—but she had emerged from the chrysalis. Were it not for their matching blond hair, no one would ever believe she and Jamie were twins. The only features that betrayed her youth were the braces on her teeth and a stray pimple near the corner of her mouth, which could have easily been mistaken for a beauty mark.

"Whatcha reading?" Arch asked.

"*Sense and Sensibility*," she said. "Last of my summer reading books. The quiz is on Monday."

"Can't be any worse than *Black Boy*," he said.

"It's actually pretty good," she said. "Did you do all of your summer reading, Charlie?"

I nodded. I'd read the books the first week of summer and

had scanned back over them every night, thinking about what kind of questions I might ask about them on the first day of class to show how carefully I'd read.

"Which did you like best?" Vanessa asked.

"*A Separate Peace*," I said.

"Oh, please," Jamie said. "I've never been so bored in my life."

"I thought it was good," I said.

"You're a terrible liar," Jamie said.

I did like *A Separate Peace*. It was about a prep school for boys. Every page seemed pregnant with precious intelligence. I regarded it less as a story than as a user's manual.

Jamie grinned and gave me a playful punch so I would know he hadn't intended to embarrass me, or if he had, he wanted to walk it back.

"Just messing with you," he said.

We didn't do much of anything that afternoon, but it was all a dazzlement to me—splashing around in the pool, lounging on recliners, listening to the radio. Arch performing jackknife dives and backflips. Vanessa reading on her recliner. I was marveling at the fine shape of Vanessa's calves when a shadow falling across the pool startled me out of my daydream. Mr. Haltom loomed over us in his shirtsleeves.

"Hey, Uncle Jim," Arch said.

We climbed out of the pool to greet him.

"Hello again, young man," Jim said.

"Hello, sir."

Feeling his powerful fingers squeezing my own, I found it unfathomable that Jim Haltom could ever have been a boy himself.

"How are you liking Yeatman so far?"

"It's great," I said.

"Arch here taking care of you?"

"Yes, sir."

He slipped his hand into the pocket of his suit pants. I heard the sound of jangling keys.

"Hey there, son," Jim said. "Good day at school?"

"Yeah," Jamie said. "I guess."

"Great. Say, kids, I'm meeting a few fellows downtown to go over a deal. Your mother wants to order in tonight. Would you mind calling the club, Vanessa? Ask Carl to run it over."

"Okay, Daddy," she said.

He turned and strode across the lawn. The moment his father disappeared through the French doors on the other side of the rose garden, Jamie went back into the pool house and emerged holding a beer. Vanessa let out a long, low sigh.

"It's just a beer," Jamie said.

Vanessa closed her book. "I'm going inside to call the grill," she said. "Arch, are you and Charlie staying for dinner?"

"Do you mind?" Arch asked.

"Not at all. Charlie, what would you like?"

"They have good cheeseburgers," Arch said.

"That sounds good," I said.

"Order some seasoned fries," Jamie said.

She slipped her T-shirt back over her head and started off toward the house.

"I'll be back in a few," Arch said.

He toweled himself off and jogged after Vanessa. Jamie went back into the pool house. I walked in after him.

"They'll be a while," he said. "You want a beer?"

He held the can out toward me.

"Okay," I said.

I sat down on the couch next to him. Jamie turned on the television.

"So, Arch and Vanessa," I said. "Are they—"

"What?" Jamie said. "Boyfriend and girlfriend? Not yet. Arch just recently got interested, now that it looks like Vanessa's going to turn out hot. I mean, we're practically related. Technically it's not incest, I guess, but it's pretty close."

"Well, we are in Tennessee," I said.

Jamie let out a harsh, barking laugh.

"So what's your deal?" he asked.

"What do you mean?"

"You know. Your *deal*. Where are you from, what do you do, what brought you here to my humble abode? You're clearly not a ringer."

"What's a ringer?" I asked.

"You know. A ringer," he said. "A stud athlete meant to bring glory to the empire."

The fact that most of my nonwhite classmates were talented athletes had not escaped my attention. I remembered what Terrence had said about his cousin.

"So what's your special talent?" he asked. "All the scholarship kids are good at *something*."

"How do you know I'm on scholarship?" I asked.

"Come on," he said. "Where'd you get your shoes? Payless?"

My face flushed hot. I took a big gulp from the beer.

"I'm just curious," Jamie said. "Are you a mathlete? A violinist? Did you build a nuclear reactor in your closet? You must be bringing something to the table."

"What do you bring to the table?" I asked.

He rolled his eyes.

"Look around," he said.

Jamie, at least, was always honest with himself. Most Yeatman boys—many who lived in similarly opulent surroundings—maintained the delusion that they had earned their places through their intrinsic merits. Jamie knew exactly what *he* brought to the table. He was neither proud nor ashamed; it was just a fact.

"So what do you do?" he said.

I thought about it. Did I have a gift? I'd considered myself a promising student, but after only a week at Yeatman, I had discovered myself to be decidedly mediocre. What else was I good at?

"I'm pretty good at drawing," I said.

"So you're an artist," he said.

"Yeah."

"Cool."

We sat together playing *Punch-Out!!* for what seemed like a very long time, Jamie draining beer after beer. By the time Arch returned with the takeout, the evening had grown cool and fragrant with the scent of the magnolia trees surrounding the pool. No one asked what had become of Vanessa; I assumed she was having dinner with her mother.

Arch flipped on the pool lights, turning everything cornflower blue. On the other side, across the lawn, the house was lit up like the Magic Kingdom at Disney World. Indeed, the whole effect of the evening was quite magical, save for Jamie's crack about my cheap shoes and the collection of spent beer cans he was accumulating on the pool deck.

At some point, Jamie wandered off toward the trees behind the pool, returning with three beers in his hands.

Arch stood. "No, thanks," he said. "Gotta drive Charlie home. Come to think of it, we probably ought to get going."

I said goodbye to Jamie with a timid wave and followed Arch back across the lawn. Just inside the kitchen door, he came to an abrupt stop. Standing before the refrigerator, the door open, was a slim blond woman who looked to be about fifty, holding an open bottle of white wine by the neck in one hand and a half-full glass in the other. Her long white bathrobe had fallen open, revealing a silk nightgown beneath. She gazed at us with a benumbed expression.

"Oh," Arch said. "Hi, Aunt Cici. We were just leaving."

Aunt Cici, Mrs. Haltom. She teetered a bit. I worried that she might drop the bottle or the glass and step into the shards with her bare, tender feet.

"Where's Vanessa?" Arch asked.

Mrs. Haltom muttered something as she tipped the bottle and splashed wine into her glass.

"Vanessa!" Arch called back into the house.

Mrs. Haltom shuffled forward toward the island counter-top. Without thinking, I took the bottle and placed it on the marble surface and grasped her hand. She turned toward me and opened her mouth to speak, but no words came out.

"This is Charlie, Aunt Cici," Arch said.

Vanessa appeared in the doorway. "I thought you'd gone to bed," she said.

She reached for the wineglass. "Come on, Mother," she said. "Let's go upstairs."

Mrs. Haltom jerked her hand back, splashing wine on her nightgown.

Arch stepped forward and slung her arm around his shoulder.

"Go wait in the truck," he said to me.

A few minutes later, Arch came out of the house, climbed into the truck, and started the engine.

"I'm sorry you had to see that," he said as we rolled down the long driveway.

If anything, I felt relieved. In Montague Village, someone's mother staggering around blind drunk didn't arouse much notice. It was somehow reassuring to learn that such things also happened on Belle Meade Boulevard.

When we reached Montague, Arch parked and cut the engine, perhaps waiting to see if I would invite him in. I had no intention of doing so. But neither was I eager to part from him.

"I guess I should be going," he said. "See you Monday."

"Okay."

I stepped out and shut the door, and stood watching as Arch navigated out of the parking lot, following his taillights down the narrow side street until he made the turn onto Gallatin and disappeared.

FOUR

On Monday morning, Arch waited for me outside Dean Varnadoe's harbor with two grocery bags, filled with pairs of used Top-Siders and duck boots just half a size too large; some faded shirts with the little alligator on the lapel; khakis and button-down shirts only slightly frayed at the collar; and a nearly new navy blazer.

"Jamie can be a real asshole," Arch said. "But he's right about your shoes."

I put on Arch's Top-Siders and tossed my shoes in the garbage.

Abandoning my old life took no effort whatsoever. I woke and left the apartment an hour before the other kids in Montague went out to the bus stop, and returned after dark. No one seemed to miss me. Terrence had varsity football and a new set of friends. On nights when both Sunny and my mother were working, I might hear the rap of Louella's cane on the door, inviting me over to have supper with her and sometimes Terrence, or offering a plate of hot food covered in tinfoil. Terrence hadn't turned on me completely, but when we saw each other, neither of us could pretend that things had not changed between us. Hence, when I was home, I kept to myself, doing homework, yearning to be on the other side of the river in the lavish houses of Belle Meade.

Arch began to offer me rides home in the afternoon and kept nudging Jamie and me together. I didn't object. Few childhood friendships begin through any kind of sincere linking of souls; people mostly cling to whatever they can grasp. I was a good choice of companions for Jamie. I was a better student than he was, but nowhere near the top of the class. Nor was I an athlete, or a star debater, or a musician. Being good at drawing and painting didn't win you any popularity contests at Yeatman. So I had no advantages over Jamie, and every reason to be impressed, even awed, by the trappings of wealth that were commonplace to most of the other boys. I was eager and earnest, just happy to be there.

Jamie told me things I wasn't meant to know—about his mother's drinking and pill-popping, for instance, and about his father's ruthlessness.

"Don't buy his whole gentleman act," Jamie said. "My dad is a pure son of a bitch. He destroys anyone who crosses him. He always gets what he's after. The guys who don't like it just have to sit there and suck on it."

I said nothing. But I had no trouble believing Jim Haltom got what he wanted.

"It's hilarious, really, watching all of those 'old Nashville' snobs bowing to kiss his ring," Jamie said. "It must kill them, having to suck up to a hick from the sticks like my father."

"What are you talking about?" I asked.

"You don't know? My dad's no blue blood. He's a hillbilly. I've got cousins who are married to each other. Dad's disowned his whole family, but everyone who's been around long enough knows he's new money trash. He never would have gone to college if he wasn't good at football. Then when he got to Vandy, he latched on to Uncle David, and the rest is history."

"Uncle David?" I asked.

"Arch's dad," he said. "He was a snob like all the rest of them, but even snobs get starstruck by the starting fullback. And once Dad saw the way people like Uncle David lived, he went after it like he was running the ball against Alabama. Which is why people who don't know any better assume he's a fifth-generation Belle Meader, not a guy who grew up going barefoot nine months of the year."

Jamie's revelations about his father did not disillusion me; instead, they engendered even greater admiration and empathy. I knew exactly how Jim must have felt to come from nothing and find himself surrounded by people who had everything.

"You know who hates him the most?" he said. "Fucking Varnadoe. He can't stand it that my dad chairs the board at his precious Yeatman School. All the old guys are delusional about Yeatman, but Varny's the worse, because of his fancy degrees and all of that Greek and Roman bullshit. He thinks he's Marcus-fucking-Aurelius and my dad's like some barbarian invader defiling the empire."

I told Arch what Jamie had said about his father and Varnadoe.

"Jamie's so full of shit," Arch said.

In the library, I dug the old Vanderbilt yearbooks out of the stacks and found Jim Haltom's pictures there. There were shots of him clutching a football, gazing off into the distance, his brow furrowed with determination. The years had made him a bit heavier and grayer, but he still had the same look in his eyes—the intense gaze, always probing, looking for the next guy to knock on his ass.

Later that fall, I was often the Haltoms' guest at Vanderbilt games. I watched Jim Haltom huddled with business acquaintances, paying no attention to what was going on in the stadium; half of the time, he never left the tailgate. (Admittedly, the Commodores didn't offer anyone much to get excited about.)

The more I learned about Jim Haltom, the more I watched him, the more I began to see him as a role model. He had taken his opportunity and made the most of it. This, I thought, was how one rose in the world. I wasn't from the hills of East Tennessee, but my father was born and raised in Appalachia, just like Mr. Haltom. I began to draw conclusions. Without football, Mr. Haltom would never have left the woods of East Tennessee. Without Mr. Haltom, I'd never have left the streets of East Nashville. Having climbed out of his meager circumstances, he'd deigned to lift another like him, though perhaps less gifted, into the position of advantage he'd needed to achieve his remarkable rise. It was obvious, I thought. Jim Haltom was my fairy godfather. To deserve it, I merely had to follow the lead of his true son—Arch Creigh.

As often as I could, I went home with Jamie after school until my mother or Sunny could get there to pick me up. The Haltom house was big enough to get lost in; you could go a week without having to see anyone you wanted to avoid. I rarely saw Mr. and Mrs. Haltom in the same room together. They were both very busy, Mr. Haltom with his business ventures, Mrs. Haltom with her social calendar and her philanthropy and the various regimens she undertook in her war against the twin tolls of time and booze.

One afternoon, I left the game room and went into the kitchen for a Coke. Mrs. Haltom was at the club playing golf; Vanessa wasn't home yet. Shirley was downstairs vacuuming. Jamie, I knew, was immersed in his video game. I left the Coke sweating on the glass-top table at the foot of the landing and tiptoed up the stairs and into Vanessa's bedroom.

The room had matching bedding and wallpaper, all in the flowery prints popular among people who took their decorating cues from *Southern Living*. Above the desk was a corkboard festooned with photographs.

I couldn't help myself; I slid the top drawer of the dresser open to gape at her underwear. I noticed something peeking out from beneath a sheet of floral contact paper—a wallet-sized school portrait of Vanessa, taken a few years earlier: braces and glasses, her hair pulled back into a tight ponytail. I should not have been surprised; I'd already learned from Jamie that Vanessa had only recently grown out of her awkward phase. Still, the picture transformed her in my imagination. Up to that point, she had hardly been real to me—more like an icon of idealized Southern womanhood in bloom. I tucked the picture into my front left pocket so I could take it home and look at it later, promising myself

I'd return it the next time I visited and could slip upstairs unnoticed.

I left Vanessa's room and walked down the hallway toward the master bedroom. The door was cracked. I pushed it open and stepped inside. Against the wall stood an enormous canopy bed. In the corner sat a chaise lounge, and a table holding a stack of magazines and a single empty wineglass. A red-and-blue Persian rug covered most of the floor. In the corner nearest one closet door, a men's valet stand. In the opposite corner, Mrs. Haltom's white bathrobe hanging from a hook on the back of the door.

"What are you doing in here?"

Mrs. Haltom stood in the doorway, dressed in a white golf skirt and a polo shirt the color of a fresh-cut lime. How had I not heard her coming up the stairs?

"Where's Jamie?" she asked.

I stood frozen as Mrs. Haltom took her measure of me. I felt as if I might wet my pants.

"He could play those goddamned games for hours and not notice if the sun had gone down and risen again," she said.

I nodded.

"Where are you from, Charlie?" she asked.

"Nashville," I said.

"I mean what part," she said. "I know you're one of Jim's projects, but I don't know where you live."

"East Nashville," I said.

"I see," she said. "And do you live with both of your parents?"

"With my mom," I said. "And my aunt."

"And what do they do?"

"My mom works at a restaurant," I said. "My aunt's a singer."

"A singer?" Mrs. Haltom said. "Have I heard of her?"

"I don't know," I said. "Her name's Sunny Brown."

"Sunny Brown?" She grimaced, as if the words tasted sour in her mouth.

I was silent. I'd never thought about the name; she was just Aunt Sunny.

"Has she recorded anything?"

"No," I said. "I don't think so. She sings at . . . a bar."

"I'm sure she's very good," Mrs. Haltom said. "She was probably the best singer in her little town and came to Nashville thinking she was going to be a big star one day. This town is full of Sunny Browns, you know. None of them imagines that the peak of their career will be singing for tips in some shitty bar."

Perhaps Mrs. Haltom had heard Sunny singing in the airport back before her husband bought them their own plane. I did not ask her.

"Is your mother a singer too?" she asked.

"No."

"What about your father? What does he do?"

I recited the amended version of my father's demise and my mother's struggles as a young single mom getting by with the help of a kindhearted cousin.

"Sounds like a good story for a country song," Mrs. Haltom said, her tone mercilessly dry. "Maybe Sunny Brown should write it. It might be her ticket to the top."

Mrs. Haltom's face darkened. She looked me over, glancing up and down, examining me the way you might a painting you suspected might be counterfeit.

"Empty your pockets," she said.

"Why?" I asked.

"It's not every day that I catch someone snooping around in my bedroom."

I glanced at the door.

"Pull them out," she said. "I want to see the lining."

Head bowed, I pulled out the cotton pocket liners, lamely trying to palm the picture of Vanessa.

"Give me that," she said.

I picked up the picture and handed it to her.

"Where did you get this?" she asked.

"In Jamie's room," I said. "On the floor. I just picked it up to give it back to him."

"You're a terrible liar."

I stuffed my pockets back in and kept my hands there. I looked at the door again. I wanted to run, not just from the room, but out the door and down the driveway and onto Belle Meade Boulevard to Harding Pike and all the way across the river.

"Not a very flattering picture," she said.

She held it out to me.

"Here," she said. "You can have it."

I kept my hands in my pockets.

"Go ahead, take it," she said. "Don't worry. I won't tell her. Run along, now, Romeo."

Later that night, back home, I took the picture out and

placed it on the desk in front of me, reliving the shame I'd felt when Mrs. Haltom ordered me to empty my pockets. I put the picture into a shoebox filled with baseball cards and swore I'd never look at it again.

FIVE

The week before Thanksgiving, my mother announced that Nancy had phoned and invited both of us to the annual "leftovers party" the Haltoms held on the Friday after the holiday.

"That's nice," my mother said. "Don't you think?"

Every time Sunny or my mother picked me up from the Haltoms' or the Creighs', I ran out the door, anxious to leave before anyone could see my aunt with her bottle-blond bouffant in her mustard-yellow '73 Cutlass Supreme or my mother behind the wheel of her old Chevy Cavalier.

"You have to work, right?" I asked.

"I have the night off," she said.

"But you have plans," I said. "Don't you?"

She glanced over at me with a purse-lipped smile.

"If you're going to spend so much time with these people," my mother said, "I ought to get to know them a little bit."

I HELD MY breath as we rolled through the Haltoms' gate. Cars were parked along the driveway. In front of the house stood two valets in red windbreakers. To my relief, my mother parked her Cavalier behind the last car down the hill and out of the reach of the floodlight mounted atop the garage.

As we approached the house, I led my mother to the kitchen door, where I always entered with Jamie when we arrived after school. But before we reached it, I heard Jim Haltom's voice.

"Charlie!" he cried, his voice sharp, almost angry.

We rounded the corner to find him standing on the porch, Arch behind him, holding the door open.

"Y'all come on in the front," he said, a tad out of breath. "Please."

Later, Arch explained to me why Mr. Haltom had made such a fuss. To people of Mr. Haltom's generation, Arch said, the kitchen door was for servants.

The party turned out to be a larger gathering than I'd expected. There were at least twenty people milling around in the entrance hall underneath the big chandelier, even more in the drawing room.

"Would you like a drink, Bonnie?" Mr. Haltom said. "There are cocktails and wine. And we've just opened some nice champagne."

"Champagne sounds lovely," my mother said.

I never quite got used to watching my mother transform herself back into the debutante-in-waiting she'd once been. Then again, I, too, had become adept at dissembling. Perhaps it was an inherited trait.

"Hello, Miss Boykin," Arch said.

Arch asked my mother about our Thanksgiving. He

commented on the weather, complimented me on how well I was doing at Yeatman. Mr. Haltom handed my mother a flute of champagne. My mother thanked him and took a dainty sip.

"Come on," Arch said. "Everybody's in the pool house."

I glanced over at my mother, now surrounded by both Mr. and Mrs. Haltom and Mrs. Creigh. She looked both elated and a bit helpless.

"I should probably stay with my mom," I said. "She doesn't know anybody."

"She'll be fine," Arch said. "Come on."

In the pool house, we found Jamie and Vanessa, along with the Barfield sisters, Alice Hudson, a few kids from Arch's class, and maybe half a dozen other kids I didn't recognize. A football game was on the television.

"I thought you'd never get here," Jamie said. "Vanessa keeps trying to leave me alone with Alice Hudson."

I looked over my shoulder at sweet Alice, who had long been branded as disagreeable by Jamie and the rest of the Yeatman boys, for reasons I could not discern but did not contradict. Vanessa had persuaded me to ask Alice to the homecoming dance a few weeks prior. We'd had a fine time. Alice was gracious and funny and clever, easy to talk to, amiable, and apparently sincere. Furthermore, her father was a radiologist, her mother was heiress to a substantial insurance company fortune, and her grandmother was board chair at Steptoe. But no one pointed this out to me until much later; hence, to me, she was just poor Alice, a "good girl," pretty enough in most company but plain when compared to the likes of Vanessa.

"Come on," Jamie said. "I'm dying for a smoke."

I followed him around the pool and back into the woods,

where he had found a tree with a knot that curved down into a bowl shape, into which he deposited his butts.

"Behold," he said. "My ash tree."

He lit up, while I glanced around to see if anyone might notice us there.

"There are a lot of people here," I said.

"It was bigger last year. This time, Mother wanted something more—what was the word she used? Intimate."

I gazed back through the woods at the amber rectangles of the pool house windows. Vanessa was chatting with a tall boy, distinguished by his coat and tie (everyone else wore sweaters or button-downs) and a prominent Adam's apple.

"Who's that talking to Vanessa?" I asked.

"Rhys Portis. He goes to Deerfield. It's a boarding school."

"Is he from Nashville?" I asked.

"Yeah," Jamie says. "He lives right down the block, in the yellow house with the fountain in front."

"Why doesn't he go to Yeatman?" I asked.

"Believe it or not, there are people who think they're too good for Yeatman."

I watched Rhys Portis's arm extend out onto the back of the couch, inching closer to where Vanessa's pale-blond hair met her white sweater.

"I think he's after your sister," I said.

"Rhys Portis has been in love with Vanessa for forever. Even back when she wasn't so much to look at."

"Should Arch be worried?"

"Well, it would serve him right if she did make it with Rhys Portis. But get real," Jamie said. "Would any girl in the world take a douche like Portis over Arch? Look at him. Overdressed for the occasion, as usual. Like he thinks only boarding school kids ever wear neckties. You want a drink?"

Jamie reached behind his "ash tree" and pulled out a half-full fifth of Jack Daniel's. I shook my head.

Jamie unscrewed the bottle and turned it up. He winced and gasped.

"Where'd you get that?"

"From the catering table," he said.

He took another pull.

"I better check on my mom," I said.

"What, you're going to make me drink alone?"

"She doesn't know anybody," I said. "I just want to make sure she's okay."

"Suit yourself."

I left Jamie and walked through the woods out to the lawn. A scattering of stars lit up the sky over the bright windows of the great house. When I reached the patio, I peered inside, scanning the faces of the guests, holding cocktail tumblers or champagne flutes and little plates of canapés in hand or perched on knees. I spotted my mother at the center of a long couch, flanked by Mrs. Creigh and a man who looked to be about my mother's age, a little thick around the middle, hair slicked back, with plump cheeks and thick eyebrows. My mother looked as if she was having a terrific time listening to this fellow, his fat face animated with the rare good luck of showing up to a holiday party and ending up next to a woman like her.

I heard the sound of laughter. I turned and saw Miss Whitten, smoking a cigarette, talking to Arch, of all people.

"What are you doing here?" I blurted.

The two of them turned with a start.

Miss Whitten exhaled a funnel of smoke and smiled. "We were just talking about you."

She seemed very different, and not just because of the cigarette. Whenever I imagined Miss Whitten away from the classroom, I saw her in some austere room, seated in front of a canvas, brush in hand, eyes focused and intent—not hanging around at a holiday party in Belle Meade.

"What were you saying about me?" I asked.

"Arch caught me indulging in this dirty little habit of mine," Miss Whitten said. "He told me you were around somewhere."

"And here you are," Arch said. "Where's Jamie? You ditch him?"

"I thought I should check on my mother."

"She seems okay," Arch said, nodding toward the window.

"Who's that guy she's talking to?" I asked.

Miss Whitten smirked and took another drag on her cigarette.

"That," she said, "is my date."

"How are things back at the kids' table, Charlie?" Arch asked.

"When I left," I said, "Rhys Portis was making a pass at Vanessa, but other than that, everything's fine, I guess."

Arch chuckled.

"I better go rescue my girlfriend," he said.

"You won't tell on me, will you?" Miss Whitten said. "Dean Varnadoe would be appalled if he found out I'd been drinking and smoking with the boys at the board chair's holiday party."

"My lips are sealed," Arch said. "Come on, Charlie, let's go."

"In a minute," I said.

He paused for a beat, no doubt affronted that, for the first time, I wasn't obeying his commands like a loyal terrier.

"Okay then," Arch said.

He walked off into the dark yard.

"And you?" Miss Whitten said.

"What do you mean?" I asked.

She held up her still-smoldering cigarette.

"I won't tell," I said. "But it's no big deal, you know. My mom smokes. So does my aunt."

"Terrible habit. Good for concentration. Please don't try it."

She turned back toward the windows.

"Your mother's very pretty," she said. "I missed meeting her at parents' night."

"She had to work."

"What does she do?"

"She's a waitress. At Café Cabernet."

Perhaps revealing my mother's humble occupation would make Miss Whitten feel better about what we were looking at, I thought. She, at least, was a teacher, and an artist. My mother had only one thing going for her—never mind that it was the thing that mattered most to almost every man I'd ever known.

"I've never been there," Miss Whitten said. "but I've heard . . . good things."

"People call it Café Divorcée."

"Who told you that?" she asked.

"Jamie Haltom."

"How would he know?"

"You'd be surprised what Jamie knows."

"I'm sure I would."

She dropped her cigarette on the slate patio, stamped it out with the toe of her shoe, and nudged the butt into the ivy.

"Sorry," I said.

"For what?"

I nodded toward my mother and Miss Whitten's date. "I could go get her," I said. "Tell her I'm not feeling good so she'll have to leave."

"He's not my boyfriend," she said. "This was a fix-up. He can talk to anyone he wants."

"Good," I said. Miss Whitten deserved someone better, I thought. Despite my limited experience of polite society, I knew that abandoning one's date to pursue another woman qualified as "ungentlemanly."

"This is our first date, actually," she said. "Dalton works for Mr. Haltom. *Jim*, I mean."

The way she said the name sounded vaguely insulting.

"Does your mother socialize much with the Haltoms?" Miss Whitten asked.

"Nope. We're from East Nashville. My mom ran away from home before she turned sixteen. Because she was knocked up with me."

"Charlie," she said.

"What?"

"You don't have to— I don't care, you know."

I don't know why I wanted Miss Whitten to know these truths, which I would never dream of mentioning to anyone else at Yeatman besides Arch.

"I'd better go back inside," Miss Whitten said. "Thanks for keeping me company."

"Any time," I said.

I waited until she was gone, and watched to see if she entered the room and approached her date, but she did not. After a few minutes, Mr. Haltom appeared, and my mother and Mrs. Creigh stood up from the couch and followed him out of sight, leaving Miss Whitten's companion on the couch with no one to talk to.

By the time I returned to the pool house, Arch had his arm around Vanessa, whispering something in her ear as she nodded and giggled.

"Where's Jamie?" I asked.

As if answering a cue, Jamie appeared in the doorway. He rounded the corner of the couch and fell in a great heap of drunken flesh into the plush cushion next to Vanessa.

"I love you, sis," he said.

Arch looked over at me. "How'd you let him get like this?"

I led Arch back to the ash tree and showed him the bottle of Jack Daniel's. It looked empty but for a bit of spittle backwash.

"How much was in here when he started?" Arch asked.

"I don't know. Half, maybe?"

"Idiot," he said. "Well, we can't let him go into the house. Come on."

From the dining room, we saw my mother, this time outside the kitchen, standing between Mrs. Haltom and a woman I didn't recognize.

"Why have you been hiding your lovely mother from us?" Mrs. Haltom cried.

"I didn't know I was hiding her," I said.

Mrs. Haltom laughed as if I'd said something clever.

The buffet was spread out on the dining room table and two sideboards. At the center sat a large stewpot full of steaming gumbo, surrounded by gold-rimmed china bowls. On one of the sideboards: platters heaped with turkey, slabs of beef tenderloin, and roasted vegetables. On the second sideboard: pies and cookies and tarts. These were the leftovers?

"Fix yourself a plate," Arch said. "I'll take care of Jamie."

When we returned to the pool house with the food, Jamie's eyes were red and stained with tears. Vanessa sat beside him on the couch, arms folded, her eyes dark with fury.

"Fixed a plate for you, Jamie," Arch said.

"I can fix my own fucking plate," he said, but when Arch set the food in front of him, he grabbed the tenderloin sandwich.

"Come on, Van," Arch said.

Vanessa stood and smoothed her dress. I followed the two of them out onto the pool deck.

"I'll be back in a bit," Arch said. "Don't let him go anywhere."

"How's Mother?" Vanessa asked. "Did she ask about Jamie?"

"I think she's having too much fun to care," Arch said. "She's showing Charlie's mother off like she's some sort of acquisition."

"Oh God," Vanessa said, turning toward me. "I'm so sorry."

"It's fine," I said. "Mom's having a good time, I think."

"And Daddy?" Vanessa asked.

"Didn't see him," Arch said. "He's probably in the study having man talk with the big dogs."

"That's good, I guess," Vanessa said.

I enjoyed the idea of teaming up with Arch and Vanessa, conspiring to preserve the illusion of domestic bliss in the Haltom household. I tried not to smile.

"What if Jamie tries to go inside?" I said. "I don't think I could stop him."

"Just turn on a video game," Arch said. "He'll stay out here all night."

"Good idea," I said.

Arch could see how excited I was about being entrusted with what I took to be a vital and significant responsibility.

"We should go," Arch said.

Vanessa leaned forward and kissed me on the cheek.

"Thank you," she said. "You're such a good friend."

I watched the two of them walk back toward the house, my body thrumming, a faint breeze from the open door cooling the spot where Vanessa's damp lips had touched my skin.

Back inside the pool house, Jamie was making a mess of himself.

"I'm such a fucking loser," he moaned.

"No, you're not."

"Yes, I am. I'm a fucking joke. Right now, all those assholes are in there laughing at me. I should just kill myself already. No one would care."

"Don't talk crazy," I said. "Come on, let's play some vids."

As usual, Arch was right. Once I turned on the Nintendo, Jamie calmed down into a benign state of inebriation.

In retrospect, Jamie's self-loathing made perfect sense. By the time he'd reached high school, the weight of expectations had ground his ego into grist. His father was charismatic and commanding. His mother was frosty and supercilious. His twin sister was blond and blue-eyed and leggy and clever. Jamie, on the other hand, was awkward and ungainly. He was neither an athlete nor a scholar. He was not hale or beautiful. If we'd all been born pigs, Jamie would have been the runt of the litter, denied the sow's teats and left to starve. And in a way, Jamie had been starving, for a very long time—more so since Arch's father's death had made it possible for Jim Haltom to shift his attentions to Arch.

As someone who had never known his father nor grown up in luxury, I'd have been entitled to hate Jamie. But I felt sorry for him.

He had sobered up somewhat by the time Arch returned.

"Your mom's looking for you, bud," Arch said to me. "Folks are starting to leave."

I set my game controller on the table.

"I better go," I said.

Jamie paused his game but did not sit up from the couch.

"Thanks for chilling with me," he said, as if it had been a typical evening. I suppose for him it was.

I followed Arch back across the lawn.

"Sorry for leaving you out there babysitting," he said.

He stopped in his tracks and gazed across the lawn at the house.

"About sixty percent of the people in that house right now are complete assholes," he said. "And about thirty-five percent are total imbeciles."

"What about the other five percent?"

"Well, two of them are standing right here," he said.

You can imagine how it felt to hear that.

We found my mother in the entrance hall with Mr. Haltom and Dr. Dodd. People were putting on their coats and heading out to their cars, talking and laughing and waving to one another. Everyone looked "a little tight," as polite people liked to say.

"Thanks for letting us steal Charlie so often, Miss Boykin," Arch said. "He's a great kid."

"You really are too kind, Arch," my mother said.

Too kind.

My mother and I shook Dr. Dodd's hand and waved to Mrs. Creigh and thanked the Haltoms. We walked silently down the driveway, passing out of the light into the shadows, the only sounds the crunch of our feet on the stone pebbles and the fading voices of partygoers. When we reached our car and climbed in and shut the doors, we both drew in a deep breath, as if the journey from the house to the car had been an underwater swim.

Driving home, my mother breathlessly chattered about the people she'd met, the things they talked about. I mentioned Miss Whitten; she said they'd spoken. She made a few dry remarks about Dalton, Miss Whitten's date. She told me about Dodd, and the Haltoms, and Mrs. Creigh, who had been "just lovely." She gushed about the house, and the food, and the general grandness of it all.

"You are so fortunate to have made these friends, Charlie," she said. "So fortunate."

SIX

After her debut at the leftovers party, my mother became a kind of mascot to a small coterie of society women, led by Ellen Creigh. Given that Arch's sisters—both married and moved away—were not much younger than my mother, it was only natural for Mrs. Creigh to turn her attentions toward this fallen angel, rescuing her from Café Divorcée and surrounding her with a less outwardly dubious caste of people. Within a week, Mrs. Creigh had arranged a job for my mother as a personal assistant for the elderly Mrs. Kenton Tate, whose late husband had been a prominent insurance company executive, and a second job as a salesperson at an appointments-only dress shop. How could my mother turn these down? What woman would prefer schlepping drinks in a shady bar for a bunch of leering creeps to helping a genteel matron host tea parties in her manse on the Boulevard? And thanks to Mrs. Creigh, my mother soon found herself being extended every imaginable courtesy by women who would otherwise have looked down their noses at her.

"Watch yourself, honey," Sunny told my mother. "Those Belle Meade folks might seem nice, but you're trash to them."

Sunny did not envy the country club set, nor did she believe in miraculous escapes from hard living and hard times.

"They're not like you think," my mother said.

Sunny took a long drag on her cigarette.

"We'll see about that," she said.

A WEEK OR two before exams and the end of my freshman year, Mrs. Haltom invited my mother and me over for family dinner. I'd been around long enough to know that "family dinner" was not really a thing in the Haltom home. But when we arrived, Mrs. Haltom behaved as if the four of them held hands and said grace six nights a week over wholesome meals prepared by her own design, if not her own hand. The twins and I exchanged a few curious glances. But we played along.

My mother seemed more comfortable with the fiction. There were no "family dinners" in Montague Village either; she seemed neither affronted nor surprised when the occasion shaped up into a de facto interview.

"Now, Bonnie," Mrs. Haltom said. "Remind me where you came from."

"South Carolina," my mother said. "Greer. It's a little town just outside of Greenville."

"I've heard Greenville's lovely," Mrs. Haltom said. "What made you leave?"

"After Charlie's father died, I thought it might be good for us to have a fresh start," my mother said.

"So far from your family?"

"I have a cousin here."

"Oh, yes," Mrs. Haltom said. "The singer."

My mother offered no further explanation beyond a polite nod.

"You and Ellen Creigh have become quite close," Mrs. Haltom said.

"She's been very kind," my mother said.

"How do you like working for Kenton Tate?"

"Mrs. Tate is wonderful," my mother said. "Just lovely."

"She adores you," Mrs. Haltom said. "She told me you've come along so quickly. Isn't that right, Jim?"

Mr. Haltom lifted his head. "Yes," he said. "Very quickly."

Vanessa touched my arm. "Will you help me clear the plates?"

I all but leapt from my chair.

In the kitchen, we found Shirley putting away the last of the pots and pans, two hours after the end of her normal shift. When she saw us come in with the plates, she sighed and reached for her apron.

"Please don't, Shirley," Vanessa said. "We'll take care of it."

Shirley ignored her, strapping on her apron and stepping up to the sink with a curt efficiency.

"I'm so sorry, Shirley," Vanessa said, her voice weary with shame. "Can I give you a ride to the bus stop?"

"No, thank you, honey," Shirley said. "Y'all just get back in there. Don't leave that poor girl alone for too long."

By the time we got back to the dining room, however, they were already up from the table—all but Jamie, who sat waiting for us, looking both bemused and annoyed.

"Where'd they go?" Vanessa asked.

"They're giving Charlie's mom a tour of the carriage house," he said. "What the fuck's going on?"

"Let's go find them," Vanessa said.

In the carriage house, Mrs. Haltom was explaining all of the work that had gone into the recent remodel. She described each phase of the project as if she'd done the job herself.

"The original floors weren't at all what I asked for," she said. "So I had them ripped up and replaced."

"I'm sure these are much nicer," my mother said.

"For twenty-six thousand dollars, they ought to be," Mrs. Haltom replied. "Right, Jim?"

"Mm-hmm," Mr. Haltom said.

"There are two bedrooms in the back," Mrs. Haltom said. "Would you like to see?"

We followed her down the hallway. The master bedroom had a queen bed and a wall full of windows facing out on to the rose garden and a big private bathroom with a claw-foot tub and a shower. The second bedroom was smaller, with a double bed and a single window facing the boxwood grove in the backyard, but it had its own half bath and a desk and an empty bookshelf and a chest of drawers.

Mrs. Haltom turned toward me.

"How would you like to live in a place like this?"

"It'd be great, I guess," I said.

"Quite an upgrade from where you are now, right, Bonnie?"

"Nancy," Mr. Haltom said, "please."

"I don't understand," my mother said. She gave Mr. Haltom a winsome glance, which seemed to plead for some gesture of mannerly intervention.

"Oh, I'm so sorry," Mrs. Haltom said. "Did you think I meant to insult you? On the contrary. We have a proposition for you. For you both, as a matter of fact."

"Jesus, Mom," Jamie said. "Would you spit it out already?"

"Jamie," Mr. Haltom said.

"As you probably know," Mrs. Haltom said, "it's going to be a very busy year for me. I'm chairing three different galas in addition to my normal slate of obligations. To make matters worse, the girl I've had for five years has decided to go and get pregnant, and I'm going to need someone more than three days a week given all of the big things that are coming."

"It sounds like you'll be very busy," my mother said.

"The long and short of it is this," Mrs. Haltom said. "I need a new assistant, and I'd like it to be you. I know you're working by the hour for Kenton Tate, but I'll need much more of your time, and it will be fairly flexible. So I'd like to put you on salary—say, thirty thousand, plus we'll take care of whatever you owe Yeatman after financial aid. And I'd need you closer than East Nashville. So we'd like the two of you to live here."

Mrs. Haltom swung her hand back in a long, circular wave around the room.

"I don't know what to say," my mother murmured.

"Say yes," Mrs. Haltom said.

"But Mrs. Tate," my mother started.

"I've already spoken to her. I'll loan you out when she needs you until she can find a new girl of her own. She doesn't really need you, you know. She just likes the company. Same for your deal at Serenity. That was just a favor to Ellen. They'll get on fine without you."

"So you would want me to start right away?" my mother asked.

"You can move in tomorrow if you like."

My mother bowed her head. Her cheeks had turned crimson. Mr. Haltom and Vanessa seemed even more embarrassed.

I should have felt ashamed, or affronted, but I was giddy. I didn't give much thought to the reasoning behind the invitation. If anything, I assumed it was just another case of competition between Belle Meade grande dames. All Mrs. Haltom wanted, after all, was to be Mrs. Creigh—to be revered as an icon of genteel grace and largesse. I had no real consciousness of humility, or humiliation—of that sort, anyway.

Even if she knew what she was in for with Mrs. Haltom, my mother couldn't refuse. She'd never even graduated from high school; it would have taken her years to get anywhere close to what Mrs. Haltom was offering her overnight. And Mrs. Haltom knew, by making the offer in front of me, that if my mother refused or demurred, she'd have to justify turning down a chance to get us both out of Montague Village, where the sound of gunfire and breaking bottles drifted through the walls at night and the few people who had ever greeted me with kindness now looked on me with a resentment bordering on hatred.

My mother had to take the job, but not just for me. Ever since she'd brought me to Yeatman, I could sense her longing for the kind of life she'd given up. She saw women her own age who had never been forced to work to survive, whose hardest choice seemed to be whether to spend spring break on a private Gulf Coast beach or on the slopes in Vail, whose biggest worry seemed to be whether their sons would get into Vanderbilt. By living in the Haltoms' carriage house and working for Mrs. Haltom, my mother knew she would not be equal to any of those women, but she'd at least enjoy some proximity to their privilege.

"Children," my mother said, addressing Jamie and Vanessa, "would *you* approve of our living here?"

"Of course, Miss Boykin," Vanessa said.

"Yeah," said Jamie. "I think it would be cool."

I nodded.

"Jim?" my mother asked.

"Absolutely, Bonnie," Mr. Haltom said, recovering himself somewhat. "Charlie's practically a member of the family now. I know it seems very sudden, but we feel like you'll be happy here, and we know you'll do a fine job."

"Thank you," my mother said.

"So you accept?" Mrs. Haltom said.

"I do," my mother said, with all of the enthusiasm of a mail-order bride.

"Grand," Mrs. Haltom said.

SUNNY SAT ON the couch smoking while we carried our boxes out. The Haltoms' caretaker, Scott, had driven over to help us move.

"I won't be holding your room," she said. "So don't come crawling back when that old bitch kicks you out on the street."

My mother didn't say a word. She might have felt guilty about ditching Sunny, who had taken us in when no one else would. She probably also worried that Sunny was right—that our elevation would be cut short by a change of heart or a misstep.

In any case, our last moments as a makeshift family were depressingly unceremonious. Sunny refused to get up off the couch; my mother had no interest in appeasing her.

"I'll give you a call when I find out our new number," my mother finally said.

"You do that," Sunny said.

"Bye, Aunt Sunny," I said.

"See you around, kiddo."

We must have seemed so ungrateful. But what could we do? Sunny couldn't possibly have thought my mother would be better off staying at Café Divorcée with nothing to show for it but gray roots and a gin blossom.

We walked out to the parking lot. Scott had already started back toward Belle Meade. My mother and I climbed into the Cavalier and followed him.

SEVEN

Ours was not an especially unusual arrangement. In recent years, the wealthier Yeatman families had taken to sponsoring financial aid boys and rehabilitating their families' circumstances. De'Ante Gillette, a football star who ended up going to Furman on a full athletic scholarship, had lived with Graham Burke's family since the eighth grade. After De'Ante started at Yeatman, his mother transitioned from selling Avon to managing the cosmetics department at one of Graham's father's department stores. Jarrett Hutcherson had his own bedroom at Haynes Reynolds's house and stayed there at least three nights a week.

When I pointed out that most of these boys were ringers who'd dramatically improved the fortunes of the football team, Arch assured me that countless lavish acts of generosity were dispensed without anyone ever noticing, simply because the beneficiaries were not minorities or star athletes. Sometimes, he said, they were even from the same zip code as the Haltoms and the Creighs.

"You have no idea how many people driving around Belle Meade in new Beemers don't have two nickels to rub together," Arch said.

So I was afforded the illusion that my good fortune resulted solely from beneficence.

In her new position, my mother's main tasks were running errands, managing Mrs. Haltom's appointments and checkbook, making phone calls, and writing thank-you notes, letters of invitation, and the occasional bit of personal correspondence. My mother had lovely handwriting. She wrote perfect cursive on evenly spaced lines so precise that they would have seemed machinelike if not for their softness and femininity. I could practice for a thousand hours and still be incapable of producing a single line of cursive like my mother's.

"If only you knew calligraphy," Mrs. Haltom sighed.

Among my mother's new amenities was the use of the Haltoms' Jaguar. Sometimes I rode along. It was easy to see why they'd named the car after a cat—the engine positively *purred*.

One afternoon, we were driving home on Highway 100, a long stretch of road running parallel to the Harpeth River.

"Watch this," my mother said.

She threw the gearshift into second. The car lurched; that gentle purr turned into a roar, dropping and rising again as she moved through the gears up to fifth. The trees along the roadside became a hurtling blur. As we neared a turn in the road, my mother shifted back into fourth and eased off the accelerator. The car drifted back down to normal speed, and the engine resumed its quiet hum. My mother giggled like a schoolgirl, her eyes bright with exhilaration.

The hard part of the job was not the work itself. Mrs. Haltom wanted to be a good person, I think—or at least, she wanted to be seen as such. Looking back now, the thought of her in those years fills me with a far greater measure of pity than resentment. Was she entitled, selfish, manipulative, spiteful? Yes, she was all of those things. But could it be the case that those outward flaws were merely symptoms of a deeper malaise? I think they were.

Most of us imagine that, were we to be as fortunate as she was—to have millions in the bank, to live in a sprawling manse on Belle Meade Boulevard, to have servants at our beck and call, to fly around in a private jet and buy whatever we liked without even looking at the price tags, to have a social calendar filled with grand events in opulent settings—most of us imagine this would be more than enough to make us happy, or, at least, content. But what if we were to have all of these things and discover that they weren't enough?

I, for one, could not then conceive how anyone could have all the Haltoms did and be unhappy. But I have never known anyone as unhappy as Mrs. Haltom—at least, no one who seemed to have less reason to be so.

It might have been easier if she were simply awful. But she had moments of what felt like real tenderness, and would precede or follow an eruption of temper with gestures of touching generosity. Once, the day after calling my mother "useless" for neglecting to pay a bill (my mother swore she'd never seen the bill in the first place), Mrs. Haltom surprised her with a "girls' day" at the spa. Another time, she gave my mother an expensive clutch purse she'd bought in Paris ("It doesn't match anything I own," she said), only to berate her the next day for taking too long on a trip to the bank. My mother never learned to shake off the feelings of worthlessness that followed phrases like "After all I've done for you."

Still, my mother remained loyal. "I think she just gets lonely when Jim's out of town," she would say, or "She doesn't mean the things she says when she's tipsy."

"You just remember, honey," Shirley told her, "half of what she's paying you for is the right to treat you like trash."

Since my mother also dropped off and picked up Mrs. Haltom's prescriptions, we knew the variety of drugs she kept at her disposal—Valium, Seconal, Xanax, Percodan, Lortab, Dexedrine, Ritalin. It was no wonder Mrs. Haltom couldn't remember whether she'd handed a credit card bill over to my mother, or that she was so irritable between noon and five, when she was stranded in the fog between one night's indulgences and the next.

Sometimes, I heard my mother weeping quietly in her room. The drain was often clogged with the clumps of hair she was losing.

But Mrs. Haltom always countered her cruelties with kindnesses. She passed on the bulk of her wardrobe to my mother and paid to have it altered. She schooled my mother in her own version of the rules of etiquette and the minutiae of party planning and social arrangements. She taught my mother how to play bridge and took her along on shopping trips to New York and Los Angeles and, once, to Paris. It beat the hell out of carrying a tray for a living. Wasn't it all worth the occasional insult?

I thought so, when I thought about it at all, which wasn't often.

Sometimes at night, after Jamie gave up and went off to play video games or listen to music, I sat at the kitchen table with Vanessa while she studied, doing my own homework or drawing in my sketchbook. By sophomore year, I'd had pieces featured in the school art show and a painting chosen as the cover of the literary magazine. So it no longer seemed inappropriate for me to draw Vanessa right in front of her. I sketched her face at least half a dozen times, first in pencil, then in charcoal and pastel, sometimes abstractly in imitation of Matisse and Picasso's line drawings, but more often realistically, so I could take my time memorizing her features.

There were many other sketches in my notebook, some better than others: Dean Varnadoe, holding his cane aloft at the head of the classroom; Miss Whitten poised in front of one of her own canvases. As my technique improved, I moved beyond the problem of realistic representation and became entranced by the mysteries suggested by a particular gesture or pose.

One morning, during the spring of our junior year, I sat down in Dean Varnadoe's classroom before the beginning of first period and opened up my book to work on my most recent drawing of Vanessa, taken from a photograph—the two of us standing next to each other at the Association of Fundraising Professionals gala, where Mrs. Haltom was honored as Philanthropist of the Year. Vanessa wore a sleeveless gown the color of mint cream; I had on a rented tuxedo with a silver ready-tied-tie-and-cummerbund set. In the photograph, I am grinning stupidly, but Vanessa's expression is sanguine, her hair pinned up in a delicate chignon, a few loose strands tickling her eyes, her cheeks sprinkled with freckles.

My eyes moved back and forth between the photo and the paper, trying to make the face on the page speak to me the way the real one did. The intensity of my concentration was such that I did not notice Varnadoe stand up from his desk and come around behind me to examine my work.

"Very nice, Mr. Boykin," he said. "May I have a look?"

I handed him the sketchbook.

"The young Miss Haltom?" he asked.

I nodded.

"Quite a fine likeness," he murmured.

He flipped through the sketchbook. I felt a mild twinge of fear, but also one of pride. When he reached the drawing of himself, he raised his brow and let out a low whistle.

"You don't mind, do you?" I asked.

"Not at all," he said. "On the contrary. I'm flattered."

He flipped back to the picture of Vanessa and set the sketchbook back down on the desk in front of me.

"She's an intriguing girl, isn't she?" he said.

"You know her?" I asked.

"I've seen her on the stage. She was Olivia in *Twelfth Night* last spring, no? I remember it well. That's not a face one easily forgets. Very cool. Easily misread for arrogance, I suspect. Look closely, however, and you notice that the mood is more melancholy. You capture that well."

"Do you think she would like it?" I asked.

"I think she would admire it," he said. "I'm not sure she'd like it."

"Why not?"

"Some people don't want to be seen so clearly," he said.

Two other boys came through the door, carrying on a loud debate about Vanderbilt's prospects in the SEC basketball tournament. I shut my sketchbook and stuffed it into my backpack.

The night we posed for that picture had been my first black-tie dinner. I did not know at the time what a farce the gala had turned out to be. Determining that the association had hired what she considered to be an inferior catering company, Mrs. Haltom had had my mother cancel the original contract and enlist another at nearly twice the expense. The association had originally agreed to have a local performer donate his talents, but Mrs. Haltom wanted dancing, so a soul band was flown down from New York and paid a considerable fee so that Mrs. Haltom and her pals could shake it to covers of "Mustang Sally" and "Sittin' on the Dock of the Bay."

The gala was a great education for my mother, not only in the fine points of event planning but, moreover, in how people will flatter and appease to secure a donation. Unsurprisingly, Mrs. Haltom's charities were not soup kitchens or shelters or homes for abused women, but the ballet and the opera, the art museum, the symphony, and the Yeatman and Steptoe Schools. Who am I to judge? I was hardly one to put the welfare of the homeless above the value of a Yeatman education.

My mother hustled around the tables in her lavender evening gown, making sure everyone was getting enough wine, chatting with Ellen Creigh and Mrs. Haltom's various bridge and tennis friends, and charming the old men, including a few of her old patrons from Café Cabernet. I felt so proud of her. She seemed to have found her niche.

Jamie managed to force a smile for the family photos. Afterward, he waved me over.

"Let's hit the head," he said, raising his eyebrows so I would know he meant to go out for a smoke.

"You go," I said. "It might look bad if we go at the same time."

Jamie wandered off, leaving me to stand next to Vanessa, watching the ballroom staff clear the dais for the band. Arch was out of town at a lacrosse tournament. I had her all to myself for once.

"Your mom did an amazing job," Vanessa said. "I don't think it could have gone off better."

"Where is she?" I asked.

"Right over there," Vanessa said.

She lifted her lovely arm and gestured toward the side of the stage. My mother stood next to Mr. Haltom, looking on as Mrs. Haltom had her moment in the spotlight. Mr. Haltom turned toward my mother and tilted his head. My mother lifted her eyes to his.

You'd have had to be watching closely to see it. They were in the shadows. The focus of the attention was elsewhere, on Mrs. Haltom, who at that moment could not have known or cared if either of them was even in the same room. I saw, but I did not consider the implications. I was too stupidly joyful to be at a fancy party, standing next to my dream girl to feel any undercurrents swirling below the shimmering surface of the masquerade. But Vanessa saw it. She knew.

"Hey, you two—smile!"

Our heads turned abruptly toward a photographer taking pictures for the society pages. The camera flashed. When we glanced back, Mr. Haltom had rejoined his wife, and my mother was gone.

EIGHT

Sometime in the '70s, Mr. Haltom and Arch's father had gone in on a large tract of land near Rock Island, Tennessee, about two hours' drive from Nashville. The two friends wanted a retreat of their own, where they could teach their sons about the great outdoors. After David Creigh died, Jim Haltom had carried on alone, teaching the Creigh and Haltom kids to fish and shoot. But Jamie had allergies and preferred video games, and Arch's sisters were nearing college age and disinterested. Vanessa was more earnest, and showed some aptitude, but Mrs. Haltom didn't want a tomboy. Consequently, Arch became the sole focus of Mr. Haltom's attentions.

By the time I came along, Mr. Haltom was mostly too busy to get out to the hunting camp. He'd bought a retreat closer to Nashville, in Leiper's Fork, a farmhouse, where he could keep horses. Once he could drive, Arch started going out to the hunting camp on his own. Half of it was his, after all. His father was buried there. The cabin could be called a "cabin" in the same sense that the Haltom residence could be called a house: a big stone A-frame the size of a basketball gym, with exposed wood beams, a great room, and a huge hearth. Two flights of stairs on opposite sides of the room led up to a long balcony and four bedrooms. Beneath them on the first level were two master suites. Above the mantel hung the head of an enormous elk.

Meat on the grill and fish in the cast-iron skillet; coffee from a thermos in the early morning dark; whiskey served neat with dinner. Long walks out in the fields, silent but for the swish of the bird dog's tail across the high grass as she sniffed at the air, then the breathless moment when she stopped and pointed at the covey hidden in the brush, followed by the flurry of wings and the roar of gunfire echoing off the distant trees. The twitch of the line, followed by the pull and the bend of the rod and the tense dance of the reel and run.

Up early in cold darkness, Arch and I sat silent, sometimes for hours, watching the air become illuminated as the sun crept over the hidden horizon and filtered down through the canopy of trees or burned off the mist over the pond. In those quiet moments, I thought of the poster on the door of my English teacher Mrs. Shackelford's classroom, printed under an old painting depicting two men atop a rocky overlook in the wilderness, a stream beneath them, green mountains in the distance. NOTHING CAN BEFALL ME IN LIFE WHICH NATURE CANNOT REPAIR, the poster read, quoting Emerson. The painting, I later learned, was named *Kindred Spirits*.

In the deep silence of those still mornings, the world's vastness became present and visible. I understood what people meant when they talked about having a "religious experience."

In my imagination, it was Arch, not God, to whom these things belonged, who showed them to me, who made me feel both sublime peace and joy.

ON MY FIRST visit to the camp, Arch led me out past the pond, which stood in a small clearing at the center of a copse of poplar trees.

"I'll be buried here too one day," he said.

It was a beautiful spot, wide enough so that the sun shone down through the gap between the branches of the trees above us. The headstone was a simple marble slab engraved with Arch's father's name and the years he'd been born and died above a Celtic cross. A border of flagstones marked off the grave itself. In front stood a bench Arch had built with Jim years before in what now seems a rather heavy-handed bonding ritual but which I thought of then as deep.

"I wish I'd known him," I said. "He must have been a great man."

"Not really."

A darkness came over Arch. I can now see that darkness for what it was, though at the time, I thought only of myself: how the confidences Arch shared with me drew me closer to him, deepened our connection, proved that I meant as much to him as he did to me—that we were, in fact, kindred spirits, like the men in the painting from English class.

"My dad was no saint," he said. "Not by a long shot. He was mean as hell. Uncle Jim says it was because he was depressed. Not depressed like he got the blues sometimes— the serious kind of depression, the kind you need medication for. He tried to kill himself in college. Did you know that? Of course you didn't. He washed down a bottle of sleeping pills with a fifth of Jack Daniel's. Uncle Jim found him and took him to the hospital. They had to pump his stomach. He went off for a while after that. Everybody thought he was just in a spin-dry clinic for booze. Not that he didn't need that too, by the way. He went to rehab three times before he finally got sober, and that was only because of the cancer. You know what else? He was cheating on my mom when he got sick. And not with some random woman either. It was the wife of one of his best friends. They were all friends—Mom and Dad, Uncle Jim and Aunt Cici, and the Potters. It was a big scandal. The Potters actually moved to Atlanta to get away from the gossip. My mom was humiliated. Then dad got sick. That changed the subject, I guess."

Arch stood up from the bench and walked slowly around the headstone.

"Everyone in Belle Meade considered my dad a first-class asshole," Arch said. "People pitied my mother. Then along comes cancer, and just like that, Dad went from spoiled loser to saint. It's amazing what a lethal illness can do for your reputation."

"How do you know all of this?" I asked.

"I heard things. Saw things. My sisters told me some of it. They tried to hide the affair, but we knew there was something weird when the Potters just disappeared after being around our parents nonstop for most of our lives. They didn't ever visit. Didn't even come to the funeral. And the Potters were my oldest sister's godparents. When I got older, I asked Uncle Jim about it, and he came clean. Said he hated to do it, but he'd promised he'd never lie to me."

Arch sat down next to me.

"He really was brave at the end," he said. "But I think if he'd lived, he'd still be thought of as the guy who cheated on my mother and nearly broke up the marriage of two of their dearest friends. Even if he'd quit drinking, he'd still be remembered for all the times he got plastered in public and shot his mouth off or had to be carried out to the car at the end of the night. Instead, he got to go out as a martyr."

I noticed that his hands were shaking.

"That's the thing," he said. "Down deep, most people are pretty awful. Still, we spend half our lives pretending we're better than we really are. I'm the worst, I know. I guard my reputation like my life depends on it. Because it sort of does. Once you screw up, you have to go through hell to get your honor back."

I felt like Arch's honesty deserved a comparable disclosure.

"Remember when I told you about my dad being a hero in Vietnam and everything?" I said. "Well, he died in Vietnam, but I don't know a thing about him. I've never even seen a picture. My parents were never married. My mom got knocked up when she was fifteen years old and ran away from home. My dad was a stable boy at my mom's summer camp. He shipped out for the Army before she even knew she was pregnant. They never saw each other again. Aunt Sunny took my mom in before I was born. My mom's parents know I exist, but I've never met them. Never seen a picture of them either. I'm not even sure they're still alive, though I figure they are, since my aunt keeps in touch with the people back home. I think she'd have told my mom if something had happened to them. Or maybe she wouldn't."

Arch shook his head.

"Damn, bud," he said.

"I should have told you."

"I understand why you wouldn't."

"I wish I had."

"You can tell me anything, Charlie," he said. "You're my bud—my brother. You know that, don't you?"

"I know," I said. "It's just . . . you understand, right? You and the Haltoms—everyone at Yeatman, really—you're all so nice. I didn't want you to think I was poor white trash."

"You know how Uncle Jim got his start, don't you?"

"Jamie told me."

"You think he gives a shit if people know where he came from?"

"Yeah," I said. "I do."

"Well, they all know," Arch said. "And what are they going to do about it? He can buy and sell the lot of them. And he came from nothing. Started with nothing but a shit-ton of determination. Now he's the big dog. You could do that too, you know."

"I doubt it."

"I don't."

"You mean it?"

"Damn right I do."

I wanted with all my heart to believe him.

"Are you really named after your grandfather?" he asked.

"Yes," I said.

"You ever think about him, or your grandmother? Ever wonder why they've never tracked you down?"

"I used to ask Mom about it all the time. She always

changed the subject. Eventually, I caught on that she didn't like the questions."

"Did your mom have any brothers or sisters? You got any aunts and uncles out there wondering what became of you?"

"Mom was an only child."

"That makes sense," he said. "If I was your mom's brother, I'd have found her by now."

"I don't know," I said. "I think my grandparents were pretty pissed at Mom. They were going to send her off and have me put up for adoption. That's why she ran away."

"Damn," Arch said. "I knew I liked your mom, but now I sort of love her."

"What do you mean?"

"She could have let you go and pretended it never happened," he said. "Instead, she gave up everything to keep you. You shouldn't be embarrassed. You should be proud."

"I never thought of it that way."

Arch put his arm around me.

"No secrets between us anymore, right?"

"Right."

He stood up from the bench.

"Let's go fishing," he said.

AT HOME, ARCH didn't drink much; he was always exceedingly conscious of how easily even a minor indiscretion could blot his sterling reputation. At weekend parties, when he had a beer can in hand, more often than not, it was full of water from the bathroom tap, so he could maintain control without coming off as prudish. That night at the hunting camp, however, we both got plastered. Mr. Haltom kept a lot of high-end bourbon out at the cabin, and we both knocked back shots the way cowboys do in Westerns.

After dinner, both of us good and drunk, we collapsed onto the couch in front of the hearth. Arch started unpacking his history of conquest, boasting of exploits with a plethora of girls in a multitude of settings. In the woods outside a dance at the sister camp, with a debutante from Atlanta. With a few girls from Steptoe before he'd turned his attentions to Vanessa. With the bored young wife of one of Mr. Haltom's business associates, who had led him away from the Independence Day celebration at the country club and straddled him in the middle of the eighteenth fairway, just as the fireworks show began. It seemed like an awful lot of experience. But I believed it all, partly because of the conviction with which Arch told his tales, and partly because he seemed like the kind of guy to whom things like that actually happened. If Arch had gone all the way yet with Vanessa, he didn't say and I didn't ask. Even drunk, I did not want to hear Arch describe the liberties he may or may not have taken with Vanessa.

"What about you?" he asked. "You done it yet?"

"No," I said.

"Why not?"

"I don't know," I said. "Just haven't had the chance, I guess."

"Do you jerk off?"

I felt my face turning crimson.

"No," I lied.

"Really?"

"Yes, really."

"You need to start. Break it in good, so when you get your chance you don't make a fool of yourself. My first time was with an older girl. She knew I was a virgin, so she sort of expected me to come fast. You might not get so lucky. You don't want to be a premature ejaculator, do you, bud?"

"No."

The room had gone dark but for the fire in the hearth. In the silence, I looked back at him and found him staring at me, grinning, his face and his eyes lit up by the firelight.

"So do you know how?" Arch asked.

"I don't know," I said. "I guess."

He stood up and stumbled around the table toward me.

"Come on," he said. "I'll show you."

What happened after remains both vague and vivid in memory. Even the next morning, my head throbbing from too much whiskey, I recalled it all clearly but could not square what I remembered with reality. When I came out of the bedroom, Arch was already cooking eggs and bacon. He poured me a glass of tomato juice.

"Here," he said. "That'll help."

We never spoke of it, ever, even after it happened again, and again. I did not allow myself to consider what it might have meant, for either of us. I knew if anyone ever found out about it that Arch and I would both be ostracized for all time by our schoolmates. But I never considered the possibility that what we were doing defined either of us in the way such a thing might, or perhaps should. Arch had slept with all of those girls, after all, and he was probably sleeping with Vanessa. As for me, I was sure I wasn't gay. I liked girls—Vanessa first, but I wasn't so devoted that I didn't notice other girls, and my fantasies always only involved women. It was just Arch. He had mastered my heart almost from the first second. He was the pillar upon which my entire identity rested. After what he'd shared with me by his father's tombstone—after he'd called me his brother—if there had been a shred of doubt before that, it was long gone. I loved him, as I had never loved anyone or anything before; as I have loved only one other since.

NINE

One afternoon, Jamie and I came home and found Sunny's mustard-yellow '73 Cutlass Supreme parked in front of the door to the carriage house.

"Whose car is *that*?" Jamie said.

Nothing that ugly had come up the Haltoms' driveway since my mother's Cavalier, which had been replaced by a used two-door Beemer.

"Shit," I said.

"What?" Jamie said. "Is it like some angry ex-boyfriend or something?"

"Worse," I said.

I was afraid to face Sunny. My mother and I had both treated her very poorly. The first year we'd been with the Haltoms, we drove across town on Christmas Eve—we gave her a poinsettia and a Wal-Mart gift card; Sunny gave my mother a pair of fuzzy pink bedroom slippers and me a cartridge for the Game Boy I no longer used. We left before she'd had a chance to serve us the pecan pie she'd baked.

"I better go by myself," I said.

"Fine by me," Jamie said.

That Jamie had no desire to meet the woman who had helped raise me, and that I was even less inclined to introduce him to her, said a lot about both of us, I think.

"Hi," I said.

"Hey, baby," my mother said.

I could see that both of them had been crying.

"What's wrong?" I asked.

"It's Louella," my mother said.

"Who?" I asked.

"Terrence's grandmother," my mother said.

"Is she sick?" I asked.

"She's gone," Sunny said.

"Gone where?"

"To heaven, honey," she said.

THE FUNERAL WAS held that Saturday, in the Lighthouse Church in East Nashville. The room was full. My mother and I sat with Sunny near the back. We almost hadn't come. My mother had to supervise the caterers at Mrs. Haltom's annual party in the Haltoms' box at the Tennessee Breeders' Cup. Jamie and I had planned to go down into the infield and cruise the fraternity tailgates, where we would find Arch and the older boys who had recently graduated from Yeatman. But we still had a shred of decency left. Mrs. Haltom had reluctantly agreed to let my mother attend as long as she headed straight to the race park afterward.

"Not a minute after twelve," Mrs. Haltom had said.

My mother had never been to a black church before. I'd

gone a few times with Terrence and Louella years before, but I'd forgotten how much longer and more passionate the services were—even the funerals. We weren't the only white people in the room; there were three elderly couples I spotted, one of them with their adult children, whom I presumed to be Louella's former employers. They looked as out of place as I felt. I wondered if they, too, would be hastening off to the horse races as soon as they could get out of the church. Only Sunny seemed at ease. She'd been helping Terrence bring Louella to church since we were boys, and was almost a member of the congregation, though she'd kept her membership in the Church of the Nazarene out in Inglewood.

On the front pew sat Louella's children—two sons, one living in Memphis and the other in Louisville; a daughter who had married a soldier and eventually settled in Cincinnati; and Terrence's mother, who had been found by her siblings and brought back home to see her mother buried. We sang hymn after hymn, from "Blessed and Highly Favored" to "Take Me to the King," broken up by a long of line of speakers who gave remembrances of Louella. Each of her children came to the pulpit and spoke a few words. Terrence's mother made a few halting remarks before becoming too overwhelmed to continue.

Terrence walked past her as she descended the stairs, as if she were invisible. Instead of speaking from the pulpit, he took the microphone from its stand and walked down to the floor in front of the congregation.

"I want to say a few things about Grand-Lou," he said.

Terrence paced the floor, his body humming with energy, the congregation urging him on in the pauses, his voice rising and falling. It occurred to me that this was something he'd done before, something they'd all seen.

When he was finished, Terrence called Sunny forward and handed her a microphone. She got up from beside us and strode to the front of the congregation as if she'd sung there a thousand times. She nodded at the drummer and the organist, and they began. It was a song called "Wayfaring Stranger." I'd heard the bluegrass-country version when I was a kid, but I'd never heard it done in a gospel style. Sunny's voice sounded different than I remembered it—deeper, more soulful, maybe wiser.

> *I am a poor, wayfaring stranger*
> *Traveling through this world alone*
> *And there's no sickness, toil, or danger*
> *In that bright land to which I go.*
>
> *And I'm going there to see my mother*
> *And I'm going there no more to roam*
> *And I'm only going over Jordan*
> *And I'm only going over home.*

When she was finished, she put the microphone back in the stand. The congregation rose to its feet in rapturous applause as Sunny returned to her seat.

We sang a final hymn, and the preacher gave his benediction, and we spilled out of the stifling heat of the sanctuary onto the sidewalk and stood in silence as the pallbearers—mostly football and basketball teammates of Terrence's—carried the coffin out to the hearse. The family followed, stepping into a white limousine.

"Who's paying for all of this?" my mother whispered.

"Lou had insurance," Sunny said. "I think those folks Lou worked for helped. Plus Rev Joseph gave them a special."

"A special?" my mother asked.

"He's also the undertaker, honey."

"Oh."

My mother and I stood by as parishioners crowded around Sunny, thanking her and praising her performance. We walked around the building to the reception hall, where we were to eat and socialize and wait until the family returned from the burial. We were halfway down the sidewalk when my mother stopped.

"I have to go," she said.

"Where?" Sunny asked.

"Work," my mother replied.

"It's Saturday."

"I don't really get days off," my mother said. "I told Mrs. Haltom I'd be away for an hour, maybe two. She has a big thing going on. I was supposed to be there an hour ago."

"Terrence will be sorry to have missed you," she said.

I badly wanted to leave with my mother, to get away from my shame and back to Jamie and Arch and the tailgates. Sunny squeezed my hand.

"I think I'll stay if that's all right," I said.

"Are you sure?" my mother asked.

"I can't leave without seeing Terrence."

Sunny lit a cigarette and held the pack out. My mother shook her head. She hadn't quit, but she'd cut back. Mrs. Haltom had taught her that a lady wasn't seen smoking in public, and never unless she was sitting down.

"How are you going to get home?" my mother asked me.

"I'll drive him," Sunny said.

"That won't be necessary," I said. "I bet I can get a ride."

"From who?" my mother asked.

"Arch can pick me up," I said.

"That's a lot to ask, Charlie," my mother said.

"He'll do it," I said. "That is, if I can catch him at home before he leaves. Is there a phone I can use?"

"Sure, hon," Sunny said. "Just inside that door over there."

I slipped away to the church office and called Arch's house.

"Hey, bud," he said. "Where the hell are you? The traffic's going to be ridiculous."

I explained the situation. "I'm sorry to ask," I said.

"Forget it," he said. "It's important that you stick around. I've been to plenty of tailgates. How long do you need?"

"An hour or so, I guess. Thanks, Arch," I said. "I owe you one."

"More than one, bud," he said. "But who's counting?"

By the time I came back out, my mother was already gone. Sunny stood waiting for me, smoking another cigarette.

"Good thing I got a ride," I said.

"She sure left in a hurry," Sunny said.

"Yep."

I was going to defend my mother, but thought better of it. Sunny would never understand.

"Come on, honey," Sunny said. "I bet you're hungry."

There were at least half a dozen serving trays of fried chicken, beef, and pork ribs, dozens of casseroles, deviled eggs, green beans, and buttered mashed potatoes. We found our way to a table covered with a pale-blue paper cloth. I ate while Sunny

continued to receive compliments on her singing and thanks
for the attentions she'd shown Louella over the years. I thought
of afternoons in Montague Village, spread out on the couch
under a blanket, watching soap operas with Sunny while my
mother was at work. Here was my second mother, the woman
who had rescued my mother and taken her in and made us a
little family, only to be left alone again while my mother and I
had taken up with the kind of people who snickered at Sunny
in the airport.

"Aunt Sunny," I said, "can I ask you something?"

"What, hon?"

"When's the last time you saw my grandparents?"

"Years and years," she said. "How come?"

"What did you think of them?"

Sunny put her plastic fork down.

"I didn't know them too well," she said. "Your granddaddy
went to college in Charleston, which is where he met your
grandmother. My daddy said when he went off to college he
was Chuck and when he came back he was Charles. Know
what I mean?"

I nodded.

"After that, they weren't too close. My daddy was bass fishing and squirrel hunting. Your granddaddy was golf and cards.
Plus our side of the family was Baptists. Your granddaddy's
was Presbyterian. Daddy said Presbyterians were just Baptists
with airs, you know."

She sipped her tea.

"We didn't see much of your mama's family outside of the
holidays and at the big reunion in the spring. Your great-aunt
Norma was the one who kept it going. They'd rent some place

out and get the whole clan together for a big fish fry every year. That's how I got to know your mama. She was cute as pie. You know the way you get attached to people.

"Those reunions were a hoot. Most of our family was tee-totalers, so nobody drank anything stronger than lemonade. But there was a mountain of fried catfish and hush puppies and coleslaw. A bunch of the cousins would bring their guitars and banjos, and after supper we'd all gather 'round together and sing old-time music. Believe it or not, your granddaddy was a heckuva singer. That song I did back in the church was one of his favorites. He used to get up and sing 'Wayfaring Stranger' like to put Glen Campbell to shame."

"You were amazing," I said.

"Well, thank you. It's a sad song, isn't it?" Sunny said. "You can sing it country or gospel. I like it both ways, myself. Chuck done it real different from how I done it today. Why are you asking, hon?"

She picked at her chicken.

"I wish I knew them."

"You might one day."

"They didn't want to know me," I said. "They wanted to get rid of me."

"Honey, seventeen years ago, most any girl from a family like your mama's who got in that kind of trouble would have been treated the same way. Especially in a place like Greer. Hell, not much has changed, even here. What do you think that Haltom girl's folks would do if she got knocked up?"

"She's way too smart for that," I said.

"Thinking you're too smart's usually what gets folks in trouble. But the point ain't whether or not it could happen.

What if it did? Do you think Big Jim Moneybags would order up a ticker-tape parade? Would the Swan Ball queen call up the *Tennessean* to make sure the news got into the society pages?"

"No," I said.

"Then you shouldn't be so quick to judge."

"I'm not," I said. "Just trying to understand."

She stared off toward the windows on the other side of the hall.

"There weren't gonna be no happy ending for your mama back there," she said. "If she'd stayed, you'd have been someone else's kid. Maybe you'd have been better off. But that ain't how it went. Anyway, things aren't turning out so bad for you now, are they? Either one of you, for that matter."

She looked back at me. I found myself unable to hold her gaze. I shook my head, my eyes still lowered, studying the pattern of the yellow-and-brown linoleum floor.

"Guess I better get going," I said. "Arch will be here soon."

"You didn't say hey to Terrence yet."

She nodded toward the other side of the room. I'd been so caught up in her story that I hadn't noticed Terrence and his family enter the fellowship hall. He was seated at a table with his friends who had carried the casket.

"He might not want to talk to me," I said.

"Don't be silly," she said. "You're his oldest friend."

"Was," I said.

"Still are. And always will be."

She slid her chair back and stood. "I've got to go to the little girls' room, then I'm stepping out for a cig. You give me a hug and kiss and then get your butt over there and pay your respects."

"Yes, ma'am," I said.

I kissed her cheek and hugged her. She smelled good, familiar, like menthol cigarettes and hairspray.

"I'll see you soon," I said.

I looked back toward where Terrence was sitting. Our eyes met. I waved; he replied with a curt nod.

"Go on now," Sunny said. "He ain't gonna let those boys do nothing to you at his grandmama's funeral."

Sunny gave me a light push on the shoulder and disappeared through the door into the hallway.

I didn't have to worry about Terrence's friends. He was halfway toward me already. It was as if he knew I was afraid—of his friends; of him, even.

"Whassup, Charlie?" he said.

"Hey," I said.

"Thanks for coming," he said.

"I'm really sorry," I said, and meant it, both about Louella and about the two of us, though I didn't imagine Terrence missed me much. He had never needed me as much as I'd needed him.

"It's okay," he said. "She's with Jesus now. No pain no more."

Terrence smiled. I looked at my watch.

"You got somewhere to be?" he said.

"Sorry," I said. "Somebody's picking me up in like five minutes."

He put his arm on my shoulder.

"I'll walk you out."

We stood outside on the sidewalk together. I asked him

about football, and school, and when and how he'd become a fiery lay preacher.

"That was something else," I said.

He grinned.

"When did you learn how to do that?"

"I felt the call a few years ago. Made Gran-Lou happy, so I just listened to the spirit, you know?"

"I never made you for a preacher," I said.

"Why? 'Cause I'm a sinner?" he asked. "We all sinners. Look at Rev Joseph. He's God's messenger to the Lighthouse. But every Sunday after church, he's out front with the women, on the make."

Terrence pointed through the windows of the fellowship hall. Sure enough, the reverend was surrounded by women, none of whom looked old enough to be his wife.

"Shoot," Terrence said, "for all I know, I got the spirit because he's my daddy."

"You really think so?"

"Naw," he said. "Could be though, right?"

When we were boys, Terrence and I would make up stories about the fathers we had never known. The only difference between us was that I knew my father's name. Terrence's mother refused to say. She later told Louella that it was one of three, that she couldn't be sure which; she was only certain none of them were worth holding to account. But in our games, Terrence's father was a soldier like mine. They had met in Vietnam, just as Terrence and I had met in Montague Village. They were POWs on the run, or ex-Green Berets, sent back to save their captive brothers.

"How's your mom doing?" I asked.

"Hell if I know," he said. "She just showed up today. They heard she was flopping with some fool out in Bordeaux. My uncle drove out and found her. She's already gone. Probably smoking rocks as we speak."

"I'm sorry," I said.

"Ain't nothing to me," he said. "I just buried my real mama."

"What are you going to do?" I asked. "I mean, are you still living at Montague?"

"Was. I been living with Rev since Gran-Lou went in the hospital."

"How long has that been?"

"'Bout a year."

"Jesus," I said. "I wish I'd known. Sunny didn't say anything."

"She came to the hospital every day."

"You can always count on Sunny," I said.

"Yeah, she cool."

Terrence offered me his hand.

"Thanks for coming," he said. "I mean it, you feel me?"

A deep sadness came over me. I longed for the closeness I'd once felt with Terrence—the sense that we were more than friends, almost brothers. He'd protected and defended me and stood by me for years when he could easily have moved on and left me to be the outcast I'd most certainly have been without him, and it had taken little more than the allure of wealth and the illusion of a better life for me to forget him almost completely, so much that I had not even known his grandmother was dying—sweet, noble Louella, who had looked after me when I was a child, who had made sure I was fed and cared for when I was a solitary latchkey kid in Montague Village, who had never judged me or my mother, who had prayed for us to find our way in the world. I had not even known that Terrence, my first best friend, had essentially been orphaned a second time. And even if I had, I'd likely have done little or nothing for him. And now, here we were, and he was thanking me.

"I'm so sorry," I said.

I could see in his expression that he knew I wasn't talking about Louella.

"It's all good," he said. "We all got to keep living, right?"

Arch's truck rolled into the parking lot and turned toward us.

"There's my ride," I said.

Arch pulled to a stop at the curb. The passenger-side window rolled down.

"Hey there," Arch said.

"Arch, Terrence," I said.

"Pleased to meet you, Terrence," Arch said. "I'm real sorry about your grandmother."

Terrence nodded.

"See you soon," I said.

"Yeah," Terrence said, both of us knowing it wasn't true.

AN HOUR LATER, Arch and I pulled into the parking area at the Harpeth Trace Racing Park, out Highway 100, in Bellevue, where the Tennessee Breeders' Cup was already underway. Every spring, people descended on the race park, dressed in Sunday morning finery, to get drunk while a horse race was going on somewhere out of sight. This was my second T-Cup, and I'd been looking forward to it almost since the last. Booze, horses, and money—what wasn't to love? The girls

milling around the tailgate parties were a feast of shapely color
and shining long hair. Everyone wore Wayfarers. I never saw
a horse.

All around the parking lot, frat boys and sorority girls
unloaded large coolers from SUVs. Black men ranging from
elderly down to about the same age as the college kids milled
around, ready to carry the coolers from the parking lot to the
tailgate area for a fee. Arch and I had no cooler—we were still
underage, and anyway, Arch never drank anywhere he thought
he might get caught. He admonished me to abstain as well, in
order to avoid being on the annual docket of careless Yeatman
boys to end up with citations and a trip before the disciplinary
committee. Dean Varnadoe had lobbied for years to make the
T-Cup off-limits for Yeatman boys, but every time he brought
up the idea, he was shot down by Dr. Dodd, who argued that
banning the T-Cup sent the wrong message, both to the community and to the boys themselves. How could Yeatman claim
to be succeeding in its mission to cultivate gentlemen with good
manners and judgment if we couldn't be trusted to behave well
at a popular social gathering?

I followed Arch across the parking lot toward the gate,
walking past a tall, burly frat boy in a green shirt, madras
bow tie, and Nantucket Red pants. An old black man with a
thin white mustache followed him, carrying an enormous red
cooler with a Confederate flag painted across its top.

"Jesus," I muttered.

"It's just a flag, Charlie," Arch said.

"Not to some people," I said.

"Yeah," Arch said. "Well, that guy will probably make more

today hauling coolers than he makes in a month. Assuming he even has a job."

"Is that supposed to make me feel better?"

"Lighten up, will you?" Arch said. "We're supposed to be having fun."

By the time we reached the infield, I'd spotted at least twenty Confederate flags—stickers on the backs of trucks, flying off bamboo poles beneath fraternity flags, hanging from portable cabanas next to the state flags of Tennessee, Mississippi, and Alabama. We spotted Jamie on the roof of a Jeep Wagoneer with two fraternity boys. The three of them took turns waving a large battle flag and attempting, with limited success, to engage the surrounding crowd in a sing-along of "Friends in Low Places." After they repeated the chorus for the last time, Jamie threw his head back and held his arms up to the sky.

"*This . . . is . . . heaven!*" he bellowed.

Beneath him, a group of black children scooped up discarded beer cans and stuffed them into plastic garbage bags.

A pang of shame seized me. I knew that I was a coward. An hour earlier, I was in a black church, where I'd watched my best childhood friend deliver a fire-breathing sermon over the casket of his grandmother—grieving her loss and, moreover, the loss of my first real friendship. Now I was surrounded by Confederate flags in a field of drunken white college students. Soon, I would be with Arch and Vanessa and my mother in the Haltoms' box, enjoying the buffet. Later that night, I would attend a party in a fine house in Belle Meade. I would think a bit here and there about Terrence walking back toward the

Lighthouse fellowship hall alone and maybe even lie awake in bed for a while, remembering how that must have felt. But I knew even before it happened that the guilt and regret I might feel on behalf of my first best friend would not persuade me to renounce my new one.

TEN

Arch started at Vanderbilt in the fall. He pledged SAE and threw himself into whatever campus activities Mr. Haltom advised him to pursue, but he was never far from me. We got out to the hunting camp when we could, to shoot birds and to fish and talk about what lay ahead of us. As far as Arch was concerned, Vanderbilt was the only choice for me. Mr. Haltom would get me in and pay my tuition. Beyond college, Arch and I would soon be paving our road forward into the future together.

This is not to say I did not savor my last year at Yeatman. Even at the outset of our final year, we newly minted seniors could already see ourselves wreathed in celebratory cigar smoke in the blue gloaming of June. Most of us would soon be accepted into Vanderbilt, Washington and Lee, Sewanee, Davidson, Furman, or Rhodes. A few would be off to the Ivy League or Stanford, Duke, or UVA. The rest would happily head off to SEC schools, to major in fraternity and minor in football. The faculty gave us a wide berth in the final months, doling out "gentleman's Bs" with abandon. The last year was meant to be remembered as a honeymoon, seducing us into enduring affection for the school, which would eventually translate into generous contributions to the annual fund. Even before the first day, we were feted at a barbecue in the backyard of the headmaster's residence. There were father-and-son dinners, mother-and-son breakfasts, and special meals for both the two hundredth and one hundredth days until graduation.

We were perched on the precipice of manhood, drunk on our own importance, our futures promising, the present full of opportunity for seemingly endless firsts and lasts— first drink, first kiss, first love, first lay; last dance, last test, last performance, last season, last game. There were many dances and parties to attend: homecoming at both Steptoe and Yeatman, Steptoe's winter formal, holiday celebrations, and, in the spring, proms and the Tennessee Breeders' Cup. At times, it seemed our education was getting in the way of the events surrounding it. But Arch claimed that this *was* the education: learning how to mingle, how to hold one's liquor in public, how to know what to wear, whom to flatter or shun, when to show up, and when to leave. Calculus mattered, Arch explained, but more in the figurative than the literal sense.

In December, Vanessa got her letter from Princeton. Mrs. Haltom had my mother order a cake, which went largely untouched ("Sugar is your enemy," Mrs. Haltom liked to tell Vanessa) and a dozen orange and black balloons. Arch came over with his mother. Even Jamie seemed happy.

After the holiday, Arch began to come around more often with his new friends: young men of a similar mold, who dressed and carried themselves not just with the air of privilege but with a sense of ambition and seriousness of purpose, which made it easy to foresee their ascent in law firms and brokerages and private medical practices all around the South and beyond. I wondered if all of these boys had a father or a mentor like Mr. Haltom whispering in their ears, advising them how best to position themselves for the swiftest possible rise.

As the weather got warmer, Mr. Haltom began to host Arch's friends for barbecues with his own circle of friends and business acquaintances. The Haltoms' backyard became a veritable feeding trough for the recruitment of future captains of industry. Jamie and I often lurked around the periphery of these events, a bit stung by how invisible we were in such company. Vanessa fared better with the college boys. They all knew she was Arch's girl, but regardless, anyone who planned to make a go of it in Nashville could benefit from knowing a girl like her.

But really, how could anyone know a girl like Vanessa?

I thought I did. Living nearby, studying with her every night at the breakfast table in the great house—or, rather, pretending to study just to be close to her—I thought I understood her, that, as it was with Arch, there were no secrets between us.

Vanessa had the rare ability to carry on a conversation while doing her homework for AP Calculus; I was taking College Math and cruising toward graduation, confident that, thanks to Mr. Haltom's influence, the letter offering me admission to Vanderbilt would arrive any day. I was far more worried about getting a prom date.

"Who should I ask?" I said.

"'Whom,'" Vanessa said.

"Huh?"

"It's 'whom,' Charlie. A personal pronoun as direct object must be in the objective case."

I rolled my eyes.

"Okay," I said. "Whom should I ask to the prom, Miss Priss?"

"Whomever you like."

"Maybe I should ask you."

"Maybe you shouldn't."

"Arch wouldn't mind," I said. "Don't you want to go?"

She put her pencil down.

"I don't know, Charlie."

"It wouldn't be a date," I said.

"I know," she said. "I just think maybe you should ask someone else."

"*Whom?*" I said.

"I don't know."

I had been only half serious; it wasn't something I'd really considered. And yet her reaction had wounded me. If I'd thought about it before I opened my mouth, I wouldn't have risked the rejection. But once it had occurred, my pride drove my mind to see deeper implications.

"What's the matter?" I asked. "Am I too far down the social ladder to be seen with?"

"I don't care about that."

"But I am," I said.

"What?"

"Socially inferior," I said.

"That's not what I meant," she said.

"Think of it as an act of charity," I said. "Won't everyone admire you for stooping to go to the prom with the son of your mother's servant? Wouldn't that look good? If you weren't in Princeton already, you could probably put it on your application."

"Now you're just being cruel," she said.

"Then why not?" I asked. "Is it Arch? Did he tell you not to go?"

"Don't talk about Arch," she said.

"Maybe I should ask him," I said. "For permission."

"Shut up, Charlie."

I pressed on, oblivious. I mimed picking up the phone and dialing it. "'Hello there, bud. It's me, Charlie, your poor relation,'" I said. 'Would you mind letting Vanessa off the leash for a night? I'll have her home before bedtime.'"

"*Just shut up, Charlie!*" she hissed.

A sob broke in her throat.

"I'm sorry," I said.

Tears streamed down Vanessa's face. She pushed back from the table and stood.

"Don't leave," I said.

"I just need to go," she said. "Come with me."

"Where are we going?"

"For a drive."

We took Vanessa's Saab. She drove out Highway 100, toward the Natchez Trace Parkway. It was already dark; once we passed over the bridge in Bellevue, the only lights we saw were the high beams on the road.

"There's something I have to tell you," she said. "I can't keep it to myself anymore. It's eating me alive. But it has to be a secret. That's the only reason I'm telling you—because I know you can keep a promise. Do you promise?"

"I promise," I said.

What she had to tell me should come as no great surprise. Such things happen to so many young women—even girls like Vanessa, who, as I had once suggested, should be too smart for such a thing to happen. I remembered what Aunt Sunny had said to me at the reception in the Lighthouse Church fellowship hall after Louella's funeral. "What do you think that Haltom girl's folks would do if she got knocked up?" she'd said. "Do you think Big Jim Moneybags would order up a ticker-tape parade? Would the Swan Ball queen call up the *Tennessean* to make sure the news got into the society pages?"

Vanessa told me how she'd found out, what she'd done. How she'd kept it a secret from everyone, even Arch; even Alice. There was a clinic in Nashville, but she couldn't risk being seen there. So she'd gone to Memphis, alone. The procedure had taken only a few hours. The hardest part, she said, was getting in and out of the building, past the protesters. On her way in, they begged her to reconsider. On the way out, someone had spit on her.

By the time she finished, we were up on the parkway. I felt weightless, as if the car were floating above the road.

"I'm sorry," I said. "I don't know what's the right thing to say."

"Just don't judge me," she said.

"Never," I said.

I reached for her hand and squeezed it.

"What about Arch?" I asked.

Her head snapped up.

"Arch can *never* know anything about this."

"I didn't mean anything. I just thought—"

"You promised," she said.

Her grip became so tight that I winced. She glanced over and saw my pained expression and relaxed her hand.

"I'm sorry," she said.

"It's okay."

"I know how this must seem to you, of all people. I should have been like your mother. It would have been the right thing to do. It was my fault, after all. But I can't do that to my parents. Can you imagine how my mother would react? With everything my father's been preparing for the past year, with all of those late-night meetings."

"Huh?"

"I guess that's what you have to do," she continued, "if you're running for governor."

"Your dad's running for governor?" I asked.

"How could you not know?" she said. "Arch has known for months. He didn't tell you?"

"No," I said.

"Well, he is."

"Wow," I said.

We were on our way back now. In the foreground, the lights of Bellevue became visible, shining in the rippled surface of the Harpeth River like quivering fireflies.

"What about Arch?" I asked.

"What about him?"

"I thought you two were . . . I don't know . . ."

"What?" she asked. "In love? Arch doesn't love anyone as much as he loves being loved."

I didn't consider what I said next; it just came out.

"I love you," I said.

"I know," she said. "I'm sorry."

A car whipped by us. We came over the hill and down into Belle Meade.

"Is that why you won't go to the prom with me?"

It was a stupid question. But I had to ask.

She dabbed at her eyes with the heel of her palm.

"I guess so," she said.

"Because I love you?"

"Because I'm not what you thought I was," she said. "Now you know."

"It doesn't change anything," I said.

"It does for me."

We reached the Boulevard. Before long, we were up the driveway, back at the great house. Vanessa put the car in park and cut the engine. She rested her head on her forearms, draped across the steering wheel.

"I'm so tired," she said.

"I know," I said.

She lifted her head.

"I'm trusting you, Charlie," she said.

"I promise," I said.

"Not even Arch."

"Not even Arch."

THE NEXT DAY, I began sketching out a new painting. I didn't need a photograph or a plein air study; the image was with me all the time, floating at the edge of my consciousness. A group of black children in white T-shirts, gathering empty cans on a green field, dropping them into white garbage bags beneath a sky turning orange and purple in the sunset. Behind them, an oblivious crowd of partygoers in sunglasses, the men in pastel chinos and dress shirts and bow ties, the women in flowery dresses. In the distance, a Confederate flag flying atop a bamboo pole reaching just above the tree line, framed against the yellowing sky. The connotation—the symbolism, you might say—was blatant. But I hadn't thought at all about its implications; I was painting what I remembered, what moved me. I wanted it to express a feeling, an emotion I considered to be complex—the juxtaposition of allure and revulsion, guilt and desire, remorse and indifference.

"Wow," Miss Whitten said. "I'm genuinely impressed."

We were alone in the art room after eighth period. Through the open window, I could hear the sounds of the baseball and lacrosse and track teams heading out from the locker rooms to the fields. The fragrance of the spring air challenged the sour scent of drying oil paint.

"This one might push a few people's fur back," she said.

"I don't know what you mean."

"I think you do."

She looked off, out the window, as if searching for someone.

"There's something I should probably tell you," she said.

"What is it?"

"I'm leaving."

"You quit?"

"I've been let go, actually. Dodd didn't renew my contract."

"Why not?"

"I can't say."

"You mean you don't know, or you won't tell me?"

She didn't answer.

"God," I said. "I'm sorry. What are you going to do?"

"I'm going to live in Mexico for a while," she said. "In a little town in the mountains, San Miguel de Allende, a few hours' drive north of the capital. A friend of mine teaches at the Instituto Allende. He got me a gig teaching summer classes to retirees. I'm hoping I can turn it into something full-time. San Miguel is a good place to sell paintings. Lots of rich tourists, you know?"

"Do you speak Spanish?"

"A little. You don't need much. All of the students are gringos anyway."

"When are you leaving?"

"My lease is up at the end of May."

"You're not staying for graduation?"

"Don't take it personally, Charlie, but I'm not exactly keen on hanging around for all the pomp and circumstance."

I thought I saw the beginnings of tears forming in Miss Whitten's eyes. I looked back at my canvas.

"Maybe I shouldn't finish this."

"Once you're done, I think you should hang it in the main lobby," she said. "Right outside the door of Dodd's office."

"I don't want to get in trouble."

"What are they going to do?" she said. "They're not going to withhold your diploma over a painting."

"If they do, maybe I'll join you in Mexico."

"You'd be very welcome," she said.

"We could set up shop," I said. "Sell paintings to the tourists."

"We'd make a killing," she said. "Just don't forget me."

"I could never forget you."

"You'd be surprised, Charlie, how easy it can be to forget."

VANESSA SKIPPED YEATMAN prom, but she took Arch to Steptoe's. I went with Alice Hudson. Jamie was asked by Melissa McDaniel, at Alice's behest. We all rode together in the Haltoms' Suburban, usually driven by Scott. There was a dinner at Payne Curry's house and an overnight after-party out at Christine Brennan's farm in Franklin. The house had a hot tub and a pool, though it was still a bit cool for swimming at night. At some point, I ended up in a basement room with Jamie and a bunch of juniors I didn't know very well, taking something they called bandanna shots, with vodka and Coke. Jamie and I had lost track of our dates. Couples disappeared to the bedrooms. Everyone else kept drinking.

As the sun came up, people began to emerge and trickle outside, stripping down to their underwear and leaping into the pool. Two couples initiated a spirited chicken fight. I walked out onto the deck just in time to see Arch executing a perfect flip off the diving board, surfacing a few feet away from where he went in, right into Vanessa's outstretched arms, whereupon they started necking with abandon. This seemed to set off some sort of chain reaction; within moments, all of the couples were making out in the pool. The sadness I felt watching Arch and Vanessa there, both of them so beautiful, felt beyond reckoning. I was drunk, of course, which didn't help. But I was alone, and very lonely, and they had each other, and I knew then that they were a unit, a circle that was closed to me.

I went back inside and returned to Jamie and the juniors

with the vodka. We sat at that table taking shot after shot. Jamie smoked cigarettes and told dirty jokes. A stereo was blaring a Van Halen album, but no one seemed to be listening. Upstairs, a caterer was laying out breakfast. We kept drinking until Alice and Melissa came down to tell us it was time to leave.

Arch and Vanessa were waiting for us in the Suburban. Arch sat behind the wheel. Jamie and I climbed in after our dates and took the two middle seats.

"You two reek," Vanessa said.

I couldn't help myself. "Don't judge me," I said.

We had to stop twice for Jamie to get sick. Finally, we reached Belle Meade. Arch dropped off Melissa and Alice. Both seemed relieved that neither Jamie nor I was capable of walking them to the door.

Back at the Haltoms', Vanessa guided Jamie along the pathway toward the kitchen. Arch grasped my hand over his shoulder and led me into the carriage house. We found my mother in the middle of the floor, her eyes puffy and red, stuffing clothes into suitcases.

"What are you doing?" I asked.

"Get your things," she said. "We're leaving."

"What do you mean, we're leaving?" I said.

"Bonnie?" Mr. Haltom said. He was standing in the doorway behind us. He looked from my mother to Arch to me and back at my mother.

"I'm not afraid of her," my mother said. "Not anymore."

"I know you're not," he said.

"Mom?" I said.

"Archer, you and Charlie go back to the car," Mr. Haltom said.

"Mom?" I said again.

Arch dragged me outside. He opened the car door and pushed me up onto the second seat. I had yet to gather the strength to sit up when I heard Mrs. Haltom shouting.

"Where do you think *you're* going, Archer?"

"Hi, Aunt Cici," Arch said.

"Don't you 'Aunt Cici' me," she said, moving toward us fast enough that the tails of her robe and sash flared up on the air behind her. "Get that piece of shit off of my property."

"Calm down, Aunt Cici," Arch said.

"Shut your smug little mouth."

Arch held his hands up as if she were robbing him at gunpoint. Her eyes narrowed.

"You knew, didn't you?" she said.

Arch looked at me.

Mr. Haltom came out of the carriage house, his face a grimace of fury. "Nancy!"

"Is your whore still in there?" Mrs. Haltom said.

That was the last I heard. As we turned sharply onto the Boulevard, my head began to spin as if the Earth were tilting off its axis.

"Pull over," I said.

I had just enough time to get the door open before I retched. When I caught my breath, I sat up, leaned back, and rolled my head toward Arch.

"I'm sorry," I said.

"No worries, bud," he said. "I've got you."

ARCH DROVE US out to the hunting camp. When we arrived, I went straight into one of the guest bedrooms and fell into a deep, troubled sleep. When I awoke, I had a terrible headache. My mouth tasted of bile. I walked to the kitchen and drank a glass of water in one long gulp. The water spread across my gut like ink on blotter paper.

The sun was bright but on the wane. The clock on the stove read 2:06. I called through the house for Arch but heard no answer.

I walked into the clearing and found him lying down, stretched out on top of his father's grave. It was a soft spot, thick with pine needles. Arch's hands were tucked into his armpits, his feet crossed at the ankles, his eyes closed. A shotgun leaned up against the tree behind the headstone. I sat down on the bench. His eyes opened slowly. He tilted his head toward me but did not lift it from the ground.

"Hey, bud," he said.

"What's the gun for?" I asked.

"Snakes," he said. "It's that time of year. How long have you been up?"

"Not long."

"You were pretty hammered," he said.

Arch lifted himself onto his elbow and rolled into a sitting position, wrapping his arms around his knees.

"Did you know?" I asked.

"You didn't?"

"No."

Arch looked up as the wind rushed through the high branches of the poplars, scattering the rays of light through the canopy.

"I talked to Uncle Jim while you were sleeping," he said. "He and your mom are going to live at the farm in Leiper's Fork for now. Maybe for good."

He stood up and brushed the pine needles off the back of his T-shirt and the seat of his pants, and sat down beside me on the bench. The breeze picked up. A shiver passed over me. I rubbed my arms. Arch walked around the edge of the circle and then sat down again, casting a furtive glance toward the woods behind us, as if he thought someone might be eavesdropping.

"Why didn't you tell me?"

"I don't know. I should have. Every time I thought about it, I told myself you probably already knew."

"I didn't," I said. "I should have, though. I saw things."

"Most of the time, we see what we want to see," he said. "I'm really sorry. I just didn't know how you'd take it, that's all."

"I feel like an idiot."

"I do too."

"What about Vanessa?" I asked. "Does she know?"

"She knew a long time ago," Arch said.

"Did you tell her?"

"She figured it out on her own."

"So you talked about it?" I asked. "That's just great. I mean, terrific. Really."

"She said she thought you knew. And if you didn't, it wouldn't be right for us to tell you," he said.

"Bullshit."

"It's not bullshit. I mean, yeah, we were scared of what might happen. Uncle Jim was going to run for governor, for fuck's sake. You think I wanted to be the one to blow that up?"

"You think I would have told?"

"I don't know," he said. "It was just easier not to say anything."

"And what about Jamie?"

"He would have told you."

"Yeah," I said. "Jamie couldn't keep a secret like that to save his own life."

"Fucking A," Arch said.

I shook my head.

"All that crap Mr. Haltom's always preaching to us about," I said. "Honor, loyalty, integrity. It's just a bunch of bullshit to him, isn't it? He's just another creep."

"That's not fair," Arch said. "Uncle Jim loves your mom—can't you see that? And from what I can see, she loves him too. I think it just happened. Things like this happen, you know."

"Like your dad and Mrs. Potter?"

"That was different."

"What makes you think so?"

I stood and turned my back to Arch so he wouldn't see the tears forming in my eyes.

"Shit," he said. "I thought Aunt Cici knew anyway. I love her, but you know Aunt Cici. She's nuts. I mean, hiring your mom as her assistant, moving y'all into the house—I figured it was one of those 'keep your enemies closer' things. Or maybe she was okay with it so long as no one else knew, and having your mom around all the time would make it easier to hide. Or maybe it was an arranged thing. I don't know. I didn't want to know. You know?"

All at once, the last four years came flooding back to me, cast in a different tone and hue. I saw my mother in her former life at Café Cabernet, leaning over a bar table to serve drinks to Mr. Haltom and a couple of business associates. I saw him come back alone, again and again. I saw her slide into the booth next to him when the floor was slow, heard him ask her about herself. I imagined her describing her lonely, introverted son and his troubles at his rough public school in East Nashville, musing about moving to the west side when she could save the money. I saw his eyes brighten, saw the wheels spinning in his head, heard him say, "I've got just the solution for your problem." Then I pictured Mr. Haltom calling Arch into his study, sitting him down, confiding in him, man-to-man. "I'm going to need a favor from you," he would've said.

I looked over at Arch.

"Is this why we're friends?" I said. "Why I'm at Yeatman?"

"Uncle Jim has helped a lot of guys over the years," Arch said.

"Was he poking their moms too?"

"Come on, Charlie."

Would I have turned down everything I'd been given by the Creighs and the Haltoms if I'd known it was all because of my mother? Of course not. Still, it felt cheapened and tainted. For so long, I'd believed that Mr. Haltom had seen something in me—that Arch had too. What a fool I'd been.

"When I first met you, I was doing a favor for Uncle Jim," he said. "But once I got to know you, you were my bud, for real. My brother. I'm sorry I didn't say anything before. I didn't really know how to bring it up. But here we are."

Arch looked down at his father's headstone.

"My father was weak," he said. "Truth be told, he was a fucking joke. I can work for the rest of my life to live down his mistakes, and it won't be enough. He had everything handed to him, and he couldn't do shit with it. About the only thing he had going for him was Uncle Jim. And if he hadn't died, he would have stayed a joke for life, and I'd be a joke too."

"You don't know that."

"You're missing the point," he said. "Uncle Jim is a self-made man. He's a winner. You could do a hell of a lot worse for a stepdad."

Arch's words rang hollow. I didn't want a stepdad. I wanted to remain in teenage oblivion, where none of us had to know or care what the adults in our lives were doing when we weren't watching. I wanted to keep pretending I was special, that I belonged at Yeatman—and with the Haltoms. Above all, I wanted to feel again as I had felt ever since that first day, when Arch appeared before me and extended his hand and lifted me up, out of a drab, colorless, meaningless life and into the bright and beautiful world over which he seemed destined to preside.

ELEVEN

A little after five, Arch delivered me to the Haltoms' farmhouse in Leiper's Fork. I waited until his truck was gone before I knocked. Mr. Haltom met me at the door.

"Come on in, son," he said.

He had been calling me "son" for as long as I could remember. The term had never seemed unwelcome before. I resisted the urge to say something childish and followed him into the living room. My mother didn't get up when she saw me, nor did I go to her.

"Sit down, Charlie," he said.

I sank into the couch across from my mother. Mr. Haltom stood in front of the fireplace.

"Your mother and I have been discussing how to break this news to you and to the twins for quite a while," he said. "We didn't want you to find out the way that you did."

My mother snatched a tissue from a box on the coffee table and dabbed at her eyes.

"I love your mother very much," he said. "Neither of us wanted this to happen, but it did."

My mother cast a wistful glance over her shoulder at Mr. Haltom. Or perhaps that was a performance. How was I to know? She'd fooled me for months—perhaps years.

"There's no delicate way to tell you this," he said. "You're going to have a sister, Charlie."

My mother reddened. Mr. Haltom paced in front of the fireplace, hands in his pockets.

I looked around the room. Boxes and suitcases were stacked in the corner. On the table in the adjoining dining room: stacks of books and papers and a rotary phone with a cord stretching out of the kitchen.

"Do you have anything to say, Charlie?" my mother asked.

"I don't know," I said. "Congratulations?"

My mother began to cry. I felt a twinge of shame. I had not meant to be kind, but neither did I intend for the remark to sound as ugly as it did. My stepfather-to-be took it in stride. He was not one to tolerate insolence, but he was coolheaded enough to know when venting his spleen wouldn't serve his purpose.

"So you're going to live out here now?" I asked.

"Yes," he said. "I've already asked your mother to marry me, and she's accepted. I mean to make the divorce happen as quickly as possible. I'd like to do it sooner, but the divorce will take some time—probably a year or more."

I understood. Mrs. Haltom would fight over every penny, every stock, every property, every stick of furniture—not out of need, but out of pure (and perhaps justified) spite.

"What about Vanessa and Jamie?"

"They're legally adults now. I assume they'll want to stay with their mother for the sake of convenience. I hope they'll give me equal time."

I wondered what he meant by "equal time." Even compared to other ultrarich Belle Meaders, who depended on a bevy of nannies and maids and golf and tennis pros to do most of the child-rearing for them, the Haltoms were pretty hands-off parents. What would equal time consist of in their minds—an hour a week between cocktail hour and dinner?

I looked at my mother.

"Why is he doing all the talking?" I said.

"What do you want me to say?" she asked. "You're so angry."

"How should I feel, Mom?" I asked. "Proud?"

"Oh, Charlie," she said.

"It's all right, Bonnie," Mr. Haltom said. "He has a right to be upset."

I hated myself for agreeing with him.

He sat down next to her and grasped her hand.

"You need to know this doesn't change anything," he said. "I've come to love you like a son. And I'm going to continue to take care of you."

Like a son? I thought. He had a son. If the way he treated Jamie was what he called love, I wasn't much interested. Did he love me as he loved Arch? I couldn't imagine he ever would. But what did I know of love? I loved Arch in the needy way of a disciple following a guru, feasting on his attention. I loved and needed him in a way he could never requite, even if he tried. I loved Vanessa just as much, albeit in a more complicated manner. I felt loyal to Jamie, but I didn't love him or even particularly like him. I loved Sunny, but not enough to visit her or even call her between Christmas and her birthday.

And I loved my mother, though I can see now with the gift of hindsight that my love for her was very selfish and self-absorbed. This is true for most children, but I think it was worse with me. I had become so consumed by my own wishes and desires that I had never entertained the possibility that she might have wishes and desires too. The discovery that she'd had a life of her own, of which I had been ignorant, filled me with jealousy and resentment—of her, more even than of Mr. Haltom. For so long, I had taken her love for granted, and had even felt superior to her, as if all the good fortune that had befallen her was the result of her connection to me. I now knew the opposite was the case—that everything had come to us because she had finally found the perfect man to lift her out of the gutter into which my arrival had cast her.

"Can I use your phone?" I asked.

I called Arch first, but he didn't answer. I dialed the number for the Haltoms and held my breath. To my great relief, the voice on the other end of the line was Shirley's.

"This is Charlie," I said. "Is Vanessa around?"

I heard Shirley call for her and hand her the receiver.

"Hello?" she said.

"Do you hate me?" I asked.

"No," she said. "God, no. Of course not."

"Then please," I said, "please come."

"I'm on the way," she said.

WE DROVE ALONG the Natchez Trace Parkway in silence—the same road we'd traveled just a few weeks before, though it looked much different in daylight.

"It's very French, don't you think?" she said.

"What are you talking about?"

"Men have mistresses in France all the time. Separate families. Their wives often know about the mistresses. They don't care. It's just an accepted part of the culture."

"This isn't France," I said. "And your mother cares."

She pulled the car into an overlook.

"Do you hate me?" I said.

"You already asked me that."

"But do you?"

"You're one of my dearest friends," she said. "You know things about me that no one else knows. Nothing could ever make me hate you."

"What are we going to do?" I asked.

"I don't know," she said. "Move on, I guess."

"You're much better at moving on than I am, I think."

"Don't be mean."

"I'm not," I said. "I mean it. I'm not good at getting over things."

She pushed her sunglasses onto her forehead so I could see her eyes.

"Who says I've gotten over anything?" she said.

"You don't show it."

"It isn't easy."

"How do you do it?"

"I just think of something to look forward to. I think to myself, 'If I can just make it to that next thing, I'll be all right.'"

She reached for my hand and held it. "In two weeks, we're graduating. Then there's summer, and then we'll be in college."

"I won't be as far away as you are."

"You don't ever have to come home if you don't want to," she said. "You won't ever have to even see any of them."

"What about Arch?"

"Forget about him for now."

She squeezed my hand. I looked over at her. Without thinking, I leaned across the console and kissed her. She pushed me away, fleetingly wincing.

"Oh God," I said. "I'm sorry."

She calmed herself. The flash of horror that had come over her face melted into pity.

I hid my face in my hands.

"It's okay," she said. "You're upset. People do crazy things when they're upset."

I couldn't bear to look at her.

"I wish I could just die right now," I said.

"You don't mean that."

If we hadn't been so far from home, I'd have jumped out of the car and run away.

"Let me take you to the carriage house," she said. "Mother's sleeping. You won't have to see her. I'll help you pack your things. Jamie will help too. You can drive the Jeep out to the farm after that."

"I don't think I can go back there."

"Most of life is doing things we don't really want to do, Charlie," she said. "Once you accept that, life gets a lot easier."

She put her sunglasses back on.

"It's only a couple of weeks."

I nodded. She started the car and drove back down the Parkway toward Highway 100. When we got to the house, Jamie was waiting for us in the driveway.

"Welcome to the family, brother," he said.

TWELVE

I spent a torturous two weeks living at the farm, rising early in the morning so I could begin the commute from Leiper's Fork before Mr. Haltom and my mother woke, going straight to my room when I came home, emerging only for meals, during which I said as little as possible and left the table as soon as I was finished eating. At Yeatman, I overheard remarks muttered behind Jamie's and my backs in hallways and classrooms. None of this seemed to bother Jamie. Still, I felt ashamed around him and tried to avoid him without seeming to be aloof. It wasn't hard; the long drive back and forth made it easy for me to disappear.

Arch showed up unannounced at the farm the day before graduation. His magnanimity in the face of my sulking made me feel like a huge brat. Maybe I was.

"Think about the fall," he said. "We'll be back together again, at Vandy. You'll be a shoo-in for SAE. First ballot, I guarantee it. You can be my little brother. Focus on that. The rest of this stuff will all settle out."

I thought of the lame pass I'd made at Vanessa. I pictured her telling Arch, the two of them having a laugh at my expense. I wondered if Arch would feel so superior if he knew what I'd promised Vanessa—that she had trusted me with her secret. I imagined the look on his face if I were to tell him. I thought about doing the same to Mr. Haltom, just to prove to him that he couldn't control and manipulate everything—that there were choices and consequences beyond his power. Then again, he'd already learned this lesson from my mother.

MR. HALTOM WAS to give the commencement address at Yeatman that year. It was unusual for a board chair to do this; usually, the school invited some local eminence or a distinguished alumnus. An exception had been made for him; his "invitation" to speak had been calculated as a platform from which he could announce his run for governor. He'd abandoned his presumed candidacy too late for a replacement speaker. So he went on with the address, most everyone in the crowd well aware of his looming divorce.

That week, I was told that my painting of the children gathering cans at the tailgate—the one I'd thought might get me kicked out of school—had, to my astonishment, won the school's Art Purchase Prize. It would sit on an easel behind the dais for the duration of the graduation ceremony and then be hung in a place of honor somewhere in the library. Before the ceremony, I went to the art room to collect the painting and deliver it to the podium. There, I found Dean Varnadoe, dressed in a seersucker suit, white panama in one hand, brass-handled cane in the other, appraising my work.

"You have some talent, Mr. Boykin," he said. "So your time here hasn't been a complete waste."

"Thank you," I said.

Varnadoe's eyes wandered over to Miss Whitten's bare desk.

"I don't blame her for leaving," I said.

"No, I don't either," he said. "Still, it's sad, isn't it? To come in here and see the place stripped of every trace of her. Every trace, that is, but her influence on this fine painting you've produced."

"You like it?" I asked.

"I do," he said. "It's a bit heavy-handed, mind you. But it's quite powerful, and technically quite accomplished. And you may be aware of my low opinion of the Tennessee Breeders' Cup."

"Why'd they fire her?" I asked.

"I can't say."

"Can't, or won't?"

Varnadoe ignored the question. He took off his glasses and set them on the table.

"I'm very much looking forward to your benefactor's speech this evening," he said.

"Are you being sarcastic?" I asked.

"Not at all."

"I might also have heard something about your low opinion of Jim Haltom, you know."

Varnadoe smiled.

"I've sat through more than twenty-five commencements," he said. "They can be a bit tedious. Mr. Haltom's decision to appear in spite of recent events should make this one a bit more—memorable."

"You hate him, don't you?"

Varnadoe took a moment to consider his words.

"It seems these days more and more that people assume that because a man is wealthy, he should be trusted to lead, or to govern," he said. "They overlook the fact that wealth is often acquired without discipline or principle. Plato believed that wisdom led to virtue. But one needn't be wise to become wealthy. One certainly needn't be virtuous. Of course, all men are flawed, aren't they, Charlie?"

He had never called me Charlie before.

"*Latet enim veritas*," he said, "*sed nihil pretiosius veritate.* Do you remember it?"

I'd memorized the aphorism my first year in Dean Varnadoe's class. It was printed on yellowed paper and taped to the wall above his blackboard: a line from El Brocense—Francisco Sánchez de las Brozas, a sixteenth-century Spanish philologist who three times faced the Inquisition for daring to criticize the Gospels as literature.

"Truth is hidden," Varnadoe said, "but nothing is more beautiful than the truth."

I nodded.

"Goodbye, Mr. Boykin," he said. "You have all my best wishes."

He picked up his glasses, slipped them into his breast pocket, and disappeared through the open door.

SINCE DIPLOMAS WERE distributed alphabetically, I was separated from Jamie during the ceremony and so was spared his sneering at his father's remarks about the value of loyalty and integrity. It was a good speech and would have

gone over well, I thought, if not for the embarrassing circumstances. I was too troubled by Dean Varnadoe's words to care
one way or the other. My distraction was so complete that I
didn't notice when Dr. Dodd announced me as the winner of
the Art Purchase Prize. Hugh Bowling, who was sitting next to
me, had to punch me in the shoulder.

"Go get your money, dumbass," he said.

Vanessa sat off to the left, with Mrs. Haltom and her parents, who had flown in from their assisted living facility in
Florida for the twins' graduation ceremonies. My mother sat
on the far right, near the faculty, with Arch and his mother. I
had insisted that we invite Sunny, but she called to tell me she
just couldn't get out of work that evening. Instead, she sent me
a card with a fifty-dollar bill inside.

The headmaster shook each graduate's hand as we crossed
the stage, after which the board chair handed each of us a
diploma and posed for a photograph. As my future stepfather
and I stood holding the green leather-bound cover between us,
I spotted smirks on the faces of my classmates.

Afterward, as the graduating class gathered under the red
oak trees on the quad to smoke our celebratory cigars, Arch
and Jamie and Vanessa found me.

"We're going to Chris Presnell's party," Arch said. "Why
don't you ride with me?"

"I drove the Jeep," I said.

"I'll bring you back to get it later."

"I think I'd rather drive."

A flicker of irritation flashed across his face.

"All right," he said. "Suit yourself."

"I'll meet you over there," I said.

Instead, I drove out to Percy Priest Lake with a bottle of Jack Daniel's and got drunk on the dock by myself. I fell asleep in the back seat of the Jeep, repeating El Brocense's proverb in my head, over and over. *Latet enim veritas, sed nihil pretiosius veritate.* Truth is hidden, but nothing is more beautiful than the truth.

THE NEXT MORNING, I awoke with a dry mouth, a splitting headache, and an overwhelming sense of despair. I pictured my mother in bed with Jim Haltom at that very moment; Mrs. Haltom in her bedroom at the great house on the Boulevard, face stained with mascara, her indignation temporarily numbed by chardonnay and Seconal; Jamie flopped on the couch in the pool house, preparing to wake up from a hangover worse than my own; Arch and Vanessa, up early, plotting their illustrious future together over coffee and eggs Benedict on the patio at the country club. I couldn't bear the thought of facing any of them anytime soon—perhaps ever again.

Driving back from the lake, I looked up and saw the signs for I-40. Call it the curse of my blood, inherited from my mother, perhaps my father as well: when in doubt, run away and begin again. The highway stretching off toward the horizon is always an answer and a possibility. I had a few hundred dollars' cash, thanks to graduation gifts and the prize money. I didn't think about whether anyone would come looking for me. I just drove. The tank in the Jeep was near full, so I was able to make it all the way across the North Carolina border before stopping for gas. I bought a cup of coffee and kept going.

Outside Spartanburg, South Carolina, I stopped again to fuel up and piss. I bought a road atlas containing a map of Greenville, which included the town of Greer. In a phone booth, I thumbed through the worn pages of a phone book to look up the address for Charles Boykin. There was only one. I found the street on the map. I had to stop three more times for directions before I found it—a large white house with a red front door and a wraparound porch lined with blooming azaleas.

I'd imagined that my mother's childhood home had been something more than our walk-up apartment in Montague Village, but I'd never gone so far as to picture exactly what it looked like. I sat in the car for a long time, trying to summon the courage to walk up to that porch and knock on the door.

An old Cadillac pulled into the driveway. A man and a woman climbed out. The woman was petite, a bit stooped, in a flowery dress and carrying a large wicker bag on her shoulder. The man glanced down toward the Jeep but did not appear to notice me watching him. They walked up the steps and into the house. A light came on in the front window. The woman appeared there to part the curtains.

All at once, a great weariness overcame me. I felt as if I lacked the strength even to drive around the corner, much less to go home or find a hotel or a rest stop. I eased the seat back and closed my eyes.

I awoke with a start. The light of the day had faded to dusk. I glanced toward the window. There stood my grandfather with his arms crossed, peering down at me through the open window.

"Can I help you?"

"No, sir," I murmured.

"You've been napping here for a while," he said.

"I . . . I got tired," I said.

My grandfather leaned over. My voice felt trapped in my throat.

"I'm sorry," I croaked.

I turned the ignition and put the Jeep into gear and lurched away from the curb. I caught a last glimpse of my grandfather in the rearview mirror, staring at the car. Was I imagining a hint of recognition on his face?

I drove until I saw a sign for I-85 South. *Why not?* I thought.

The first night, I pulled into a rest stop outside Columbus, Georgia, and slept in the Jeep. On the second, I stopped in New Orleans at a cheap motel on the shore of Lake Pontchartrain, where I rented a room with pale-pink walls and a bathroom that smelled of mildew, brine, and cigarette smoke. The day afterward, I made it all the way to San Antonio and sold the Jeep at a used-car lot for a thousand dollars cash. *There,* I thought. I had stolen a car. No turning back now.

I thumbed my way to the bus station. You didn't need a passport to cross the border in those days, and I was eighteen, old enough to travel abroad alone.

By midafternoon on the sixth day, I was standing in the courtyard of the Instituto Allende in San Miguel de Allende, Guanajuato, Mexico, asking people if they knew Teddy Whitten.

She seemed less surprised than amused to see me.

"Charlie Boykin," she said. "Did they really kick you out over a silly painting?"

"No," I said.

"Then what on God's green earth are you doing here?"

"I don't know," I said.

"You look hungry," she said. "Are you hungry?"

I nodded.

"Come on," she said. "Let's get you something to eat."

Teddy Whitten understood better than most people that sometimes, one has no choice but to follow reckless urges.

PART TWO

||||||||||||||

Vaulting Ambition

ONE

More than ten years passed before the morning when, while sitting on a bench in the Parque Juarez, drinking coffee, I heard a familiar voice and looked up from my newspaper to find Arch Creigh standing in front of me.

"Hey, bud," he said.

For the first few years of our estrangement, whenever I thought of Arch, I felt dizzy with the wounded resentment of a jilted lover. Later, my feelings softened into longing. I wished something would occur to give me an excuse to contact him, something that would feel less humiliating or risky than the facts. Eventually, a gauzy film of nostalgia settled over that time in my life, such that I stopped hoping as I once had that I'd look up one day and he'd be there, as he now was.

"Arch," I said.

"That's some beard," he said.

Arch looked different too—hairline rising a bit on his forehead; crow's feet at the corners of his eyes when he smiled—but still young, still beautiful.

"I've missed you," he said.

"I've missed you too," I said.

WHEN I'D FIRST found Teddy Whitten in San Miguel de Allende, she took me home and fed me tamales. She had a small place, the corner of an old building a few blocks from the Instituto—a tiled kitchenette; a living room with a futon couch, a bookshelf, and a woven rug spread out on the floor; a single bedroom with a twin bed strewn with clothes. It seemed just the sort of place someone like Teddy would have.

I told her what had happened, what had led me to follow her.

"Does anyone know where you are?" she asked.

I shook my head.

"You should call your mother," she said.

I shook my head.

"They'll find you, you know," she said.

"They can't make me go back."

"I'm not sure about that."

"Let them try."

Teddy lit a cigarette.

"Can I have one of those?" I asked.

She hesitated for a moment before offering me the pack. Thus began but one of the regrettable habits I've been incapable of breaking.

"What are you going to do now?" she asked. "Do you have a plan?"

"No."

She glanced around. She seemed anxious, as if she were

expecting someone and wanted to get me out before anyone saw me there.

"You can stay here for a while," she said. "As long as you need, I mean. I don't have much room, but you're welcome to the futon."

"I have money," I said. "I can get a hotel room."

"Save your money," she said. "Are you tired?"

I nodded.

"You should sleep," she said. "I have to go out for a while. Just try to rest. We'll figure something out in the morning."

The next day, Teddy walked me down to the historic city center, showed me the great Gothic Parroquia and the other old churches, pointed out the color and the light and the space. The wrought iron window frames dripping with blooming bougainvillea set into aqua and crimson and yellow stucco walls. The narrow cobblestone streets. The statue of Ignacio Allende on horseback, saber extended, covered by pigeons, under an endless blue sky.

We stopped at a small tienda, with a window in a wall facing the street. Teddy ordered tortas and bottles of water. We walked a few blocks, and she took me to her classroom, where she collected an easel and a few small canvases and a satchel. She stuffed brushes and paints into the satchel, handed it to me, and led me outside to an ATV. She got on and patted the seat behind her.

We sped out of the city, up to the rim of the valley, through narrow dirt paths until we reached the edge of a steep canyon surrounding a lake. Teddy led me toward the edge of the cliff.

"They call this La Cañada del Charco," she said.

Teddy reached into her bag and handed me a torta and a water bottle.

"Eat up," she said. "Then get to work. And make it good."

"What for?"

"Your audition."

She set down the bag with the art supplies.

"See you in a few hours," she said.

When she returned at dusk, I had a decent study. Over the next few days, I worked on a full-scale version of a barrel cactus against a crumbling stone wall. The giant green bulb reached the edges of the canvas. The golden needles jutted out and slashed across the edges of the frame. I mixed paint again and again, layering it for a rough texture that I hoped would convey the urgency of the strokes and the feeling I had when I painted it, which was like I was trying to speak but had gone mute.

With that painting and a little persuasion from Teddy, I was accepted into the Instituto and given a scholarship, which, combined with the strength of the dollar against the peso, would get me through a semester before I ran out of money. Teddy had a plan for that problem too.

Her friends Pancho and Murray lived in Barrio San Antonio, close to the Instituto. San Antonio was just then beginning to be revived by the droves of wealthy gringos who were moving to San Miguel, buying up crumbling houses far from the city center, gutting and demolishing what was left of the villas, and replacing them with homes better suited to their extravagant tastes.

We arrived at an ornate door behind a barred entry gate. Teddy rang the bell, and a few moments later, Pancho appeared in a lemon-colored guayabera and cream-colored muslin slacks. He had pale-blue eyes and a shock of curly red hair that swirled wildly around his forehead and ears. He looked me up and down and smiled.

"Hello, my dear," he said. "And hello, Charlie. Please, come in. Murray's on the terrace."

We followed Pancho into a courtyard lined with columns and arches. An architect in his former life back in the States, Pancho had designed the house himself. A narrow spiral staircase led up to the second floor; balconies overlooked the fountain and the palms between the master bedroom wing and the guest rooms and an art studio on the opposite side. We passed through a great room with a giant fireplace and high vaulted ceilings out to the patio, where Murray sat at a wrought iron table smoking a fragrant Cuban cigarillo. He was barefoot, in jeans and a white T-shirt.

"Welcome, Charlie," he said.

Murray was around seventy, lean and compact, with a shiny bald pate. He had a familiar air of authority, softened by the languor of retirement. They were a handsome couple, clever and gentle and funny.

Pancho and Murray wanted someone to look after the house, especially when they were traveling. Pancho had brought a decent nest egg to the relationship—he'd inherited a bundle from his father, who had owned a shoe company in eastern Pennsylvania (his real name was Eugene; he'd taken on the Spanish sobriquet to signify the shedding of his closeted life back home)—but Murray had been lead business counsel for Exxon in South America for nearly thirty years.

They offered me the room at the front of the house and use of the kitchen. I was to maintain the gardens, look after repairs when needed, run errands, be their driver.

"How's your Spanish?" Pancho asked.

"*No hablo*," I said.

"We can fix that," Murray said.

Murray knew a great teacher, Mariela Suarez, who met with me at the house three hours a day; by the end of the summer, I was fluent in both the language and the rhythms of life in what I thought then would be the last place I called home.

I CAME OUT of a portraiture class a few days after I started at the Instituto that fall to find Jim Haltom waiting for me.

"Hello, Mr. Haltom," I said.

He smiled—a little sheepishly, I thought.

"Seems a little formal, don't you think, Charlie?"

"What would you prefer?" I asked. "I don't think I'd feel comfortable calling you Dad."

"How about Jim?"

"All right," I said. "Hello, Jim."

I wasn't entirely unhappy to see him. We all get a little charge out of being pursued.

"How's my mother?"

"Well," he said. "The baby will be coming soon. Everything seems to be going fine."

"Glad to hear it."

"Is there someplace we can talk?"

I let him buy me lunch and answered all of his questions about school and life and money before he made his pitch with the old "your mother's worried sick" line and a lot of crap about throwing my future away. I told him I wasn't going back.

"If you'll come home," he said, "I promise you'll have all the support you need to do this art thing for as long as you like, here or anywhere else. New York, Paris. Wherever you want to go."

I lit a cigarette.

"You're breaking your mother's heart, son," he said.

"With all due respect, *Jim*," I said, "go fuck yourself."

I stood up from the table and walked off, with the fierce pride of a child who has just announced his plan to run away from home until he realizes no one will come after him.

I spent the rest of the afternoon desultory. I came very close to caving in and calling to beg for forgiveness. But that stubbornness I'd inherited from my mother kicked in and screwed my courage to the sticking place. I might have been more likely to give in if I'd been living in a hovel instead of the guest room of a swank villa in which I could sit and paint the Parroquia over and over again against a dozen brilliant sunsets.

SEVEN YEARS AFTER I'd last seen Arch and Vanessa on the lawn at Yeatman, I stumbled upon their wedding announcement while reading Murray's *New York Times*. Beneath the photograph was a short paragraph describing their illustrious accomplishments. (I also learned from the announcement that Jim and my mother had finally married.) They were living in the city; Arch managed something called a hedge fund. Vanessa was an associate at a law firm with a string of officious-sounding names. The wedding had been in Nashville, at Saint John's. They were honeymooning in Bali. Opening the paper to find the two of them gazing back at me, Arch's arm draped around Vanessa's shoulder, he grinning, she close-mouthed and demure—even a little wistful, I thought, but that was probably just a projection—left me feeling as cold as if I had drifted off to the edge of space, far removed from their bright center but close enough to remember what it felt like to be warmed by it.

This was the last I knew of them until that afternoon when I looked up and found Arch in front of me. And yet I felt as if I'd been waiting for him there—as if the two of us were merely keeping an appointment.

ARCH HADN'T HAD breakfast. I suggested a place in the Jardin, which was what the locals called the central square.

"You should have let me know you were coming," I said.

"I wanted to surprise you."

"I'm glad I was in town. I was in Guanajuato all of last week. And I'm leaving Thursday for Mexico City."

"I know. We've been keeping tabs on you."

"Really?" I asked. "What, do you have someone following me?"

"No, no. What I meant to say was that we've been watching your career. Vanessa says you've developed some serious fans among the bridge ladies of the South. She called your agent, or manager, or whatever he is."

"He's just Pancho to me."

"Well, Van called your Pancho to see where you'd be and when."

"I wonder why he didn't say anything."

"She didn't mention that the two of you were old friends,"

Arch said. "I've seen some of your work. It's good. You're a real artist, Charlie."

A real artist? Was I? No. I understood the unadventurous taste of my target audience: churches and landscapes, blue skies and sunsets, women in traditional dress manning vegetable stalls at the open-air market. Pictures that complemented a piece of furniture or a fabric pattern, vaguely exotic but still soft and quiet—and, hence, tasteful. So I did well enough. But I was less an artist than a purveyor of high-end souvenirs.

"I found my niche," I said.

The Jardin was filling up with vendors. Children chased one another around the feet of *viejos* and *abuelitas* sitting on the wrought iron benches beneath the ficus trees. We took a table in the portal outside the café and ordered coffee and huevos rancheros. The coffee was hot and fresh and strong.

"I saw your wedding announcement in the *Times* a few years ago," I said. "How's life in New York?"

"We've been reclaimed."

"Reclaimed?"

"Do you remember Alice Hudson?"

"Sure," I said. "We went to senior prom together, remember?"

"That's right. Well, Alice finally found herself a nice fellow to marry," Arch said. "Van was in the wedding. At the reception, I was swarmed by a bunch of Belle Meade blue-hairs. 'Archer,' they said, 'when are you going to bring poor Vanessa back to the South?'"

Arch sipped his coffee.

"We were ready," he said, "New York is great, but I don't want my kids to be Yankees."

It was sort of a track for Yeatman alpha males: Ivy or Vandy or W&L, a few years on Wall Street or the junior executive track, an MBA, then a few more years in the city before migrating back home, marrying a Steptoe girl, and going to work for a firm full of partners who still wore their high school rings. Thereafter, a lot of hunting and fishing and playing golf. The Steptoe wife would get into tennis or golf or whatever happened to be the trendy workout of the day, get the occasional nip-and-tuck and plumping injection, work part-time or volunteer at the private schools. Together, they would raise a slew of beautiful children destined one day to do the same.

"How is Vanessa?" I asked.

"Busy," he said. "Since we moved back to Nashville, she's been an associate at Wilton, Mosby, and Cobbs. Contract law."

"Sounds thrilling."

"Well, it isn't sexy, but it pays," he said. "Besides, she won't be doing it much longer."

"Why wouldn't she?"

"Vanessa wants to be a stay-at-home mom."

"I don't believe it," I said.

"She doesn't want our kids to grow up the way she did."

"In what sense?"

"Raised by the help. She's scared to death they'll end up like Jamie."

"I can understand that," I said. "How is Jamie, by the way?"

"Remember Café Divorcée? He bought it," Arch said. "The old owner got into a little trouble with the IRS. Jamie was looking for something to do with his trust fund. He hired a consultant from Dallas to come in and rebrand the place. They reopened last year. He calls the place Harpeth Junction. It's actually a pretty nice place. Good food. Jamie gives away too many free drinks, but he doesn't really need it to be profitable."

I laughed. "I can't see Jamie running a restaurant."

"He pays someone to do that for him. Jamie just shows up whenever he likes and holds court."

"I guess he's still boozing pretty hard, then."

"He's cooled out a little since his son was born."

"Jamie has a son?"

"Yep. Name's Isaac. Three years old. Real sweet kid. The mom's a little rough around the edges. Crystal was a cocktail waitress at the restaurant. I warned Jamie it was a bad idea to sleep with the waitresses. 'Don't shit where you eat,' I said. But when did Jamie ever take advice? Anyway, when the girl told him she was pregnant, he insisted on a paternity test. Once he was sure it was his, he accused her of getting pregnant on purpose. So they didn't exactly get off on the right foot."

"Your mother-in-law must be thrilled to have another cocktail waitress in the family. Especially one named Crystal."

"Don't be a snob."

"I'm not," I said. "But the former Mrs. Haltom is."

"Fair enough."

"How happy is Aunt Cici to be a grandmother?"

"I think she's seen Isaac maybe twice. Won't even be in the same room with Crystal. Aunt Cici and Jamie don't cross paths much anyway. She spends most of the year down in Florida now. Found herself this French Canadian guy. Kind of her 'kept man.' When she's home, she stays in this little town house she bought out near Cheekwood."

"Who bought the house?"

Arch scratched the back of his neck.

"Actually," he said, "we live there now. Vanessa and I. Aunt Cici offered it to us. Made a big pitch about not giving up the family home and so forth. Signed over the deed and everything."

"What about Jamie?" I said. "Isn't he entitled to half of it?"

"Aunt Cici wrote him out of her will after Crystal," he said. "Don't worry about Jamie. His tastes are too unimaginative to run through his trust fund for at least another ten years."

The food arrived. The bells from the Parroquia pealed. Nine o'clock. It felt earlier.

We talked about Nashville, and painting, and the Yeatman people Arch kept up with. He'd joined the Young Alumni Board. Kip Dodd had retired. They'd had a bust made of him to be displayed in a glass case in the library. Walker Varnadoe had died, of pancreatic cancer.

"Varnadoe gone," I said.

I thought of the last time I saw him, reciting El Brocense in the art room. For a moment, sadness overcame me, as if all the truths in Varnadoe's Latin aphorisms had died with him.

"He'd been sick for a long time," Arch said. "He was already dying when you were still in school."

"Is that another thing you knew but thought better of telling me?"

"No," Arch said. "No one knew. Not even Dodd."

"I haven't seen the man in ten years," I said. "I never expected to see him again. So why do I feel so sad?"

"Because you're a good person."

"Am I?"

"Indeed you are."

I couldn't fight it; my heart swelled. This was part of Arch's great gift: he could not only make anyone believe in him, but he could also make anyone believe in themselves.

"What about you?" Arch said. "Are you married? Kids?"

"No," I said.

"Girlfriend?"

"Not at the moment."

"So you're alone?"

"Not exactly," I said. "I have a roommate."

"I thought you lived with your manager."

"I did, for a few years, until the work picked up and I could afford my own place," I said. "Say, what's with the interrogation?"

"Just curious, that's all," Arch said.

An awkward silence fell over us. I can't speak for Arch, but the feelings stirred in me by the sight of him after what seemed then to me a very long time made the small talk feel hollow. Yet I couldn't find my way beyond it to what I really felt or wanted to say.

"Would you like to see where I work?" I said. "It's not far from here. About five minutes in a cab."

"I'm ready when you are."

My work space was a barren room in a repurposed textile mill. There were a few easels, a cheap clock radio on a shelf in the corner, a desk with a phone, a lone lightbulb hanging from a wire in an iron safety cage, and a single picture window in an unpainted cinder-block wall, delivering a dusty shaft of light to the paint-strewn floor.

"So you're making a living at this?" he asked.

"I do all right."

A voice called to me from outside. Teddy stepped through

the door gingerly, but prattling in rapid Spanish. She was wearing a pair of old jeans and a paint-spattered hooded sweatshirt with the sleeves pushed up, her hair pulled back in a messy ponytail.

"I'm sorry," she said. "I didn't know anyone else was here."

"Teddy, you remember Arch," I said.

She frowned for a moment before smiling.

"Hello there, Arch Creigh," she said.

"Miss Whitten," Arch said. "You look well."

"And you also," she said. "You haven't changed a bit."

It was an odd moment.

"Where are you staying?" Teddy asked.

"The Sierra Nevada," Arch said.

"That's a great hotel," she said. "And how long are you planning to stay?"

"Did you need something?" I interrupted.

"Mariela called this morning," Teddy said. "Lupita fell last night. They think she broke her hip."

"That's terrible news," I said.

"Mariela called me because Lupita was supposed to clean the Aldama house today. So we're going over there to do it for her."

She glanced at her watch.

"I should go," she said. "I have the car. I might be a little late."

"Okay. I left the keys on the kitchen counter."

"Pancho and Murray are coming over for dinner tonight, remember?" she said.

"Oh shit. I forgot."

"Charlie can't remember what day of the week it is half the time," Teddy said.

"He was never much for details," Arch said.

"Will you come for dinner tonight, Arch?" she asked.

"I'd be delighted," he said.

I followed Teddy to the door. "See you at home."

"What's going on?" she said.

"I don't know," I said. "He just showed up."

"You don't think that's strange?"

"Do you?"

"Charlie," she said.

"You can ask him at dinner."

"Don't worry," she said. "I will."

I waited until I heard the door to the studio outside slowly close and latch. When I went back inside, Arch was appraising the work leaning against the walls to dry.

"You're living with Teddy Whitten?" he asked.

I shrugged.

"That must be a dream come true for you."

"We're just roommates, Arch."

"Sure you are."

"Really," I said. "I'm not her type."

"You're joking, right?"

"The person she was talking about, Mariela?" I said.

"Yeah, what about her?"

"Mariela is Teddy's type."

"I see."

"Mariela manages the kind of places you and Vanessa are accustomed to," I said. "Teddy helps her out. They're pretty serious. I'll probably be needing another roommate before long."

"Well, good for Teddy," Arch said. "We all deserve to be happy."

He glanced around the room. "Is there some place we can sit down?"

I led him out the back door. We sat on the stairs leading to the parking lot. A car door slammed shut, followed by the distant laughter of small children and the sound of a radio through an open window.

"You haven't asked me about your mother," he said.

"I was waiting for the right moment."

He looked at me, and then he looked away. "She's sick," he said. "Stage four breast cancer. She's dying."

All at once, the colors of the world seemed too bright. I could smell everything—flowers and herbs in the beds around the factory, woodsmoke and tamales over hot coals in the open-air market across the highway.

"Uncle Jim asked me to come down and bring you home," Arch said. "He told me exactly where I could find you, down to the bench you like to sit on in that park."

"He had me followed?"

"He'd do anything for your mother. He wanted to come for you himself, by the way, but he doesn't dare leave her side. He's a complete mess. You wouldn't believe it. He can barely talk without bursting into tears."

Arch went on, but I wasn't listening. Instead, I was thinking of my mother—young and carefree in jeans and a T-shirt with cutoff sleeves, laughing with the women of Montague Village; in that blue dress she wore on the day she took me to see Yeatman for the first time; the two of us on the couch at the carriage house, eating popcorn and watching *Gone with the Wind.*

"I don't know how quickly I can get a flight," I said.

"I came on Uncle Jim's plane. We can leave as soon as noon tomorrow. I assume you have a valid passport."

I nodded.

All at once, a little childish bitterness, nursed into a ten-year grudge held firm by mutual stubbornness, was obliterated. In a matter of seconds, I'd gone from hating Jim Haltom to accepting a ride on his private jet.

"We should probably call Jim, though," Arch said. "So your mom will know to expect you."

We went back inside. I pointed to the phone on the desk at the far end of the room and explained the procedure for placing international calls. Arch picked up the handset, dialed, and waited. A muffled voice came through the receiver.

"Hi, this is Arch Creigh," he said. "Is Jim there?"

He nodded at me.

"I have Bonnie's son with me," he said. "Can you put me through to him, please?"

For years, I'd played out the moment I spoke to Jim again for the first time. In those rehearsals, I always had the upper hand. Fate had flipped the tables.

"Uncle Jim?" Arch said. "Yes. He's right here . . . All right . . . Yes, sir, tomorrow afternoon. Probably between six and seven . . . All right. Here he is."

He handed me the receiver and gave my shoulder a squeeze.

"Jim?" I said.

"Hello, son."

I tried to keep my voice steady.

"Can I talk to my mom?"

"She's sleeping. I can try to wake her."

"No, don't do that. Just tell her I'm on the way. Would you like to speak to Arch again?"

"If he's available."

I handed Arch the receiver. He turned toward the desk. I walked back out onto the stairs. Beyond the parking lot, the land opened up to raw desert. In the foreground below the purple shadows of the mountains, the landscape was dotted with scattered cacti and flowering Judas trees. I closed my eyes and remembered the farm in April and the endless green meadow in the cool, misty damp of early morning. I thought of my mother there, the way she had looked to me, in love, but also afraid. And I wondered, as she must have then, and perhaps for many years after, why I had found it so hard just to be happy for her.

TWO

I found Teddy in the kitchen, still dressed in her cleaning clothes, her face a bit begrimed. A pot of mole bubbled on the stove. I could smell chiles rellenos in the oven.

"How did it go?" I asked.

"I've cleaned a few bathrooms in my life." She turned her back to me and chopped the vegetables on the cutting board with cold precision.

"He didn't tell me he was coming."

"He just popped in," she said.

"That's right."

"Why?"

"My mother is dying," I said.

Teddy placed the knife on the counter and turned around. "Your mother?"

"Yes. She hasn't got long to live."

"Oh, Charlie."

Teddy came to me, arms outstretched.

"I haven't spoken to her for ten years," I said.

"I know."

Her arms tightened around me, and I clung to her, but I was thinking about Arch. What would he think of our house? Would he like the food? How would he behave toward Pancho and Murray and Mariela?

Outside, the sun was dipping toward the horizon, turning the patch of sky through the window orange and pink.

"Arch wants me to leave with him tomorrow," I said.

"Can you get a flight that fast?"

"He came down here on my stepfather's jet."

"Right," Teddy said. "Of course. And how long will you be gone?"

"As long as it takes, I guess."

The words gripped me with their cold finality. I was going home, I thought, to watch my mother die.

Teddy turned the gas down and covered the pot.

"I don't know what to say, Charlie."

"I don't either."

"I'm sorry."

"I know," I said. "I am too."

Teddy left the pot to simmer and went to her bedroom to get dressed. I went up to the roof and took out a cigarette and watched the sky purple as the last sliver of sun slid beneath the distant mountains and the lights began to come on along the church spires. Bells pealed from the Parroquia and the Iglesia de San Francisco, marking vespers.

It was almost dark when I heard a knock at the door below. I hurried down the stairs and opened the door for Arch. He was dressed in pressed slacks, alligator loafers, a polo shirt, and a navy blazer with gold buttons.

"Am I overdressed?" he asked.

I looked down. I was still in the same paint-stained clothes I'd been wearing when Arch found me in the park.

"Sorry," I said. "I lost track of time. Teddy should be ready by now. Mariela and Pancho and Murray should be here in a few. Come on in. You can have a drink while I throw something decent on."

I led Arch through the living room and into the kitchen and offered him a drink. I had bought a bottle of twelve-year-old scotch the day before for Murray. Arch helped himself to a tumbler and poured a few fingers over ice.

"Nice place," he said.

"It's Teddy's," I said. "Mariela's, actually. She owns it. I pay a little rent."

"You've always had a knack for getting the discount upgrade."

Teddy came out of the bedroom in a black cotton dress, large silver earrings, and a turquoise pendant she'd bought in Chiapas. I went to the bedroom to wash my face and change. When I came back out to the courtyard, Teddy was flushed, giggling at something Arch had said. It reminded me of that time I'd found them together outside the great house on the Boulevard. I smiled, recalling how I'd thought I'd walked up on something inappropriate.

Pancho and Murray arrived, followed shortly by Mariela. Introductions were made. I served drinks in the courtyard, then left to help Teddy and Mariela with dinner. Arch and

Murray seemed to have a lot to talk about. Pancho joined us in the kitchen.

"Archer knows quite a bit about the oil trade in the Southern Hemisphere," Pancho said.

"Pancho," I said, "I have to go back with Arch to the States. My mother's very sick. She hasn't got long to live."

"Your mother?" Mariela said. "Oh, Carlitos, *lo siento*. Teddy, why didn't you tell me?"

"I just found out myself," she said.

"Do you need money?" Pancho asked.

"No," I said.

"When are you leaving?" Mariela asked.

"In the morning," I said.

"How'd you get a flight on such short notice?" Pancho asked.

"Arch has a private jet," Teddy said.

Pancho's eyes widened.

"It's not his," I said. "It's my stepdad's."

Mariela let out a low whistle.

"You said they were rich," she said. "You didn't say how rich."

"My stepfather prefers the term 'affluent.'"

"My, my, Carlitos," Pancho said. "Maybe you should be loaning money to *me*."

He leaned out the kitchen door.

"Murray," he shouted, "did Archer tell you about Charlie's mother?"

"Charlie has a mother?" Murray called.

"I know," Pancho said. "Can you believe it? After all these years."

"What's happened?" Murray asked.

"Cancer," Arch said.

"How long has she been sick?"

"A little over three years," Arch said.

"Three years?" Pancho said. "Shame on you, Charlie."

"Go easy on Charlie, Pancho," Arch said. "She kept it very quiet. I didn't even know myself until very recently, and Charlie's stepdad is my father-in-law. But we were great friends before all of that."

"So the two of you are stepbrothers-in-law, but you were friends before," Pancho said. "There must be a story."

"It's a long one," I said.

"Do tell," Pancho said.

"I'd rather not."

"If you won't tell, I'll just ask Archer," Pancho said. "You'll tell us all about it, won't you, Archer?"

"I'm an open book," Arch said.

"Save it for the table," Teddy said from the kitchen. "Dinner is served."

Looking back, I wish I'd savored the taste of Mariela's family mole, a recipe handed down for hundreds of years. Instead, I ate little and gulped the fine wine Pancho and Murray had brought as if it were cheap sangria.

"So, Arch," Pancho said, "tell us about Nashville."

"Well, it isn't all honky-tonks and ten-gallon hats," he said. "But you must know that from Charlie and Teddy."

"I almost forgot," Pancho said. "You lived there as well, didn't you, Teddy? But not long."

"Less than a year," Teddy said. "I barely remember it."

"You wouldn't recognize it if you did," Arch said.

He regaled the table with tales of Nashville old and new. I was too drunk to remember anything but the way they looked at him, the way they hung on his words, the way his beauty and his charm captivated them all. It was enormously confusing to sit there knowing that my mother was across the border in Tennessee dying—perhaps already dead, for all I knew—and there I was being overtaken again by Arch—the sound of his laughter, his easy manner, the flash of mischief in his eyes, the way he could simultaneously enthrall both two gay men and two lesbians who usually regarded wealthy gringos like Arch with a suspicion bordering on hostility.

When Murray began to fade, Arch and I helped Pancho get him out to the car.

"Will I see you in the morning?" Pancho asked me.

"I don't think so," I said. "I'll call when I get there."

"*Lo siento, mi hijo,*" he said. "*Te amamos.*"

"*Y tu tambien.*"

When I came back in, Arch and Teddy and Mariela had moved into the living room. Mariela spread out across the length of one couch, the hem of her dress pulled up over her knees, Teddy curled up next to her. Arch sat in a club chair admiring the two of them with a faint leer, which, against all reason, engendered a pang of jealousy in me.

"Well, bud," I said, "we have an early morning."

Arch glanced at his watch.

"Indeed we do," he said.

I led him to the door, then stepped out onto the curb and hailed a cab. Arch buttoned his blazer.

"Don't forget your passport."

"I'll be ready," I said.

Teddy and Mariela had disappeared, so I went into my bedroom and spread out on the bed the nicest clothes I had, folded them neatly, and stacked them into a suitcase. Afterward, I went into the bathroom and turned on the hot water to fill the sink. With a pair of scissors, I trimmed away the dense clumps of wiry hair from my face. Soon, all that was left was uneven stubble. I dipped a towel in the hot water and dampened my face, covered my cheeks with shaving soap lather, and began to shave, something I hadn't done in months.

My cheeks were leaner than they had been before the beard. The flesh was pink, compared to the tanned nose and forehead. It felt as if Carlitos were a pile of hair in the wastebasket and a scattering of whiskers in the sink. The person getting on that plane the next morning would be Charlie.

I felt a deep sadness. It wasn't for my mother—that was not yet real to me. It was something else. I felt as if everything about my life since I got off the bus in San Miguel ten years before had been one long, listless dream, that the life I'd thought I'd been building was always temporary, an illusion, something I'd invented to cover up that ceaseless longing, and I'd just been waiting for Arch to wake me up so I could go on living.

THREE

After we boarded, Arch sent me back to the bedroom. It's quite a feeling, taking your shoes off and crawling under the covers of a queen bed at cruising altitude. One could get used to it.

When I woke, I came out to find Arch in a reclining chair, scratching notes on a legal pad. He motioned for me to sit down across from him.

"Good nap?"

"Yes," I said.

He pointed at my face and stroked his own cheek.

"It's nice to see your face again, by the way," he said. "I mean, all of it."

"I wanted my mother to recognize me," I said.

"I thought of that," he said. "I was afraid you might take it the wrong way."

"Glad I figured it out on my own, I guess."

Arch straightened the papers in front of him and slid them into a calfskin briefcase.

"We'll drive straight out to the farm," he said. "Your sister will be there. She goes by Dolly. She's in the fifth grade at Ensworth. I thought you might want to bring her a get-to-know-you gift. I had my girl pick something up."

My girl, I thought. I remembered hearing Nancy Haltom refer to my mother with the same words, and I thought of how to people like the Haltoms and the Creighs, servants and assistants were possessions, no different from houses or cars or private jets.

"I should have brought her a painting," I said.

"Maybe you can paint something for her while you're in town."

"So what am I giving her?"

"A silver heart necklace from Tiffany's."

"My mother used to love those blue boxes," I said. "What kind of kid is she?"

"She's beautiful," he said, as if that were all that mattered.

"I don't doubt it," I said. "How is she handling everything?"

"All right, all things considered. Her mom's been sick for so long she barely remembers her being different, so it's sort of normal for her. I don't think she understands what's coming. I'm not sure any of us are ready for that."

I gazed out the window. The plane floated above a blanket of clouds.

"So what else do I need to know?" I asked.

"I expect you've already thought about this, but your mom—well, she doesn't look the way she did when you left. She's very thin. She's lost all her hair. She wears a turban most of the time, but you might see her without it, which is pretty hard. She looks much older than her age."

I nodded. I knew I wasn't prepared for any of this, that nothing Arch could say to me would make it easier. I was just going to have to go through it.

"Anything else?" I asked.

"Just your arrangements. You can stay out at the farm if you like, but I thought it would be better for everyone if you stayed over at our house. It might make things smoother."

"Is that what my mother wants?"

"She isn't lucid very often. She has a few decent hours in the daytime. And Dolly's at our house too—she's using Vanessa's old room. It's too hard for her to be at the farm with your mother being so sick and Uncle Jim being so helpless and pitiful. Van thought that would be better for everyone, and Uncle Jim agreed. So you'll see a lot more of Dolly if you stay with us. What do you say?"

"Whatever you think is best."

Before long, we plunged through the canopy of clouds, and the green hills and blue lakes of Middle Tennessee came into view. When we'd landed, Scott, the Haltoms' old caretaker, was waiting for us. Arch seemed to have inherited him along with the house. His hair had turned from dark brown to salt and pepper, but otherwise, he seemed unchanged.

"It's good to see you, Scott," I said.

"You too, you little turd."

As Scott drove us out to Leiper's Fork, I asked him about his wife and boys—they were in the seventh and eighth grade now, attending Yeatman at Jim's expense.

"That's one hell of a perk," I said.

"I call it the golden handcuffs," Scott replied. "He's got me for six more years at least."

"Next thing you know, he'll be offering to pay their way through Vanderbilt."

"I won't say no if he does," Scott said. "You, my friend, are about the only fool in history to turn down that deal."

I had forgotten the humidity of Tennessee in spring. Every lungful felt like a drink of water. There had been several days of rain before we arrived, followed by clear skies, such that the sun lit up the verdant pastures in greens so bright and vivid they all but begged to be painted.

"You won't recognize Nashville," Scott said. "Especially since the tornadoes."

"Tornadoes?" I said.

"You didn't know? Just last April, two megatwisters ripped right through the middle of the city. They jumped the Cumberland and made mincemeat of your old neighborhood. Leveled thirty-five buildings downtown and three hundred homes in East Nashville."

"Your old home at Montague Village?" Arch said. "Gone. Completely demolished."

"Jesus," I said.

"Don't worry, everybody there got out before the tornado hit. And your aunt wasn't living there anymore anyway. She moved out to Donelson a few years ago."

"You've kept tabs on her?"

"She comes around every now and then."

"When can I see her?"

"Whenever you like."

"Maybe I'll wait," I said. "Until I get the lay of the land."

"Understood," Arch said.

"The developers have descended like vultures to snap up

all those federally funded building projects," Scott said. "You haven't seen so many carpetbaggers on the streets of Nashville since Reconstruction. But Arch here will save us from the Yankee invaders."

I looked over at Arch.

"How're you going to do that, exactly?" I asked.

"Later," he said as we turned into the long driveway out to the farm.

The car came to a stop in front of the house, and the front door opened, and a little girl—*My sister,* I thought, as if such a thing were as rare as a white elephant—came bounding out, the dark ringlets of her hair bouncing as she descended the porch steps and stopped to stare at me. Behind her was Vanessa, her hair a whiter blond than it used to be, her body longer, perhaps a bit heavier, but only in the way girls become women. Her eyes were as they had always been, and so my own were drawn to them, and to her serene expression, which moored me, for a moment at least.

I looked down at little Dolly.

"Hello," I said. "I'm Charlie."

"I know," she said.

"You do, do you?"

"Yep," she said. "Who's that for?"

She pointed at the Tiffany bag dangling from my fingers.

"I think you know," I said.

A gap-toothed grin spread out across her face.

"Can I open it?"

I handed the bag to my half sister. Vanessa descended the stairs and embraced me. I held her—not too tightly, I hoped. The moment I touched her, to my great shame, but not my surprise, all the feelings I'd thought I'd outgrown came flooding

back. The passage of time, her remoteness from me, her marriage, my life in San Miguel—none of these had dimmed my
infatuation in the least; it had lain dormant in me like a seed
stirred to life by the coming of spring.

As I let her go, she let her arms slide down mine and grasped
my hands. On her left ring finger she wore a platinum band
and a large diamond engagement ring.

"Congratulations," I said.

"You don't say 'Congratulations' to the bride, Charlie,"
Vanessa said. "You say 'Best wishes.'"

"I missed that day in cotillion class," I said.

"I'm just teasing," she said. "I don't think very many people remember those little rules. Only people like my mother
care about that stuff. Isn't it funny how someone so rude could
make such a fuss about manners?"

Dolly tugged on Vanessa's elbow.

"Look," she said.

She held up her hand, dangling the little heart necklace from
the ends of her fingers.

"Would you like me to put it on for you?" I asked.

Dolly nodded. I knelt and unfastened the clasp and lifted
the silver chain over her head. She turned around, beaming.

"Do you like it?"

She nodded.

"What do you say, Dolly?" Arch asked.

"Thank you."

Dolly broke away and ran to Arch. He scooped her up into
his arms and held her, kissing her on the cheek.

Envy: it seems sometimes to be the greatest and deadliest of
my sins.

Arch set Dolly back on the ground. She grasped his hand and looked at me.

"Want to see the ponies?" she said.

I caught Vanessa's eye.

"Charlie needs to see Mommy first," Vanessa said.

"Will you come with me?" I asked Dolly.

"Are you afraid?" she asked.

"A little," I said. "But I won't be if you're there."

I glanced at Vanessa. Her eyes were wet.

"Is it okay if Dolly comes in with me?" I said.

Vanessa wiped her eyes and nodded.

"I'll show you the way," Dolly said.

She took my hand and led me into the house, past the Audubon bird prints in the hallway and through the warm den with its great stone hearth, up the two flights of stairs and past my old bedroom. The door was shut; I imagined its walls painted a pale pink. The door at the end of the hall stood open. My sister pulled me along, straight into the room, so that it came to me all at once: my mother, curled up in the bed, and Jim, seated in a straight back chair pulled close to her so that he could hold her hand.

The lids of my mother's eyes lifted. Her lips formed a weak smile.

"Hey, baby," she murmured.

Jim did not stand to greet me; instead, he began to sob.

"Daddy's crying again," Dolly said. "It's all he ever does anymore."

My mother stayed conscious for only a few moments and then closed her eyes, drifting off to the sound of her husband's whimpering.

I thought of all of the things I had wanted to tell her over the years, and the things I wanted to say now. That I had missed her. That I was sorry. That I had wanted *her* to be sorry, but I had also wanted her to be happy. That I loved her.

But I couldn't say any of that in front of these people.

FOUR

Dolly was waiting for me when I came down the stairs, Vanessa beside her. I offered one hand to my sister, and Vanessa took the other, and together the three of us walked down the porch steps and off toward the pasture.

On the other side of a white rail fence, the horses were grazing in the center of the field. Dolly explained to me which one was which and what they were like.

"So you like to ride?" I said.

"Oh, yes."

"My father was good with horses."

"Daddy?" Dolly said.

"No. We don't have the same daddy, remember?"

"But we have the same mommy."

"That's right."

"Dolly," Vanessa said. "Would you like to go down to the barn and feed the chickens?"

"Sure," she said.

"Charlie and I will catch up."

Dolly broke away from us and ran down to the barn.

"Arch says you're trying for children," I said.

The color rose in her cheeks.

"I'm sorry. I didn't mean to embarrass you. I just thought—I was just going to say, I can tell that you're going to be a wonderful mother."

"I'm getting a lot of practice these days."

"Along with the lawyering."

"Actually, I'm leaving the firm. Daddy can't seem to manage at the moment, so I've started to take over his responsibilities. But I can do most of that from home."

"Arch told me you were thinking about taking a break," I said. "Mind if I smoke?"

"Go right ahead," she said. Then as I lit up, she said, "Can I have a drag?"

I handed her my cigarette. She took a long pull and exhaled a luxurious plume of smoke.

"Have your own," I said, offering her the pack.

"Arch would kill me," she said. She winked.

"I hear your mother has a new companion," I said.

"Not new to us. But yes. She's better with him than without."

"I'm glad she has someone to keep her company."

"We don't see her much."

"That must be a relief."

"She's still my mother, Charlie," Vanessa said.

"I'm sorry. I didn't mean anything."

I flicked the ash off the end of my cigarette, pinched the butt, and tucked it into the front pocket of my jeans.

"So you like the new man?" I said.

"He's a bit of a sponge, but he keeps her occupied. I do worry that she might be fool enough to marry him, but I doubt her accountant would let her do it without a prenup," she said. "And what about you?"

"I'm between things right now."

"Arch says you're living with your old art teacher," she said. "I remember thinking you had such a crush on her."

"If I had, I'm not her type, so nothing would have come of it," I said. "I expect Arch told you that too."

"He did," she said. "I never would have guessed. We were so sheltered, weren't we?"

"I guess we were."

"We'll have to come down to see you in San Miguel," she said. "A friend of Daddy's owns a hotel there."

"Which one?"

"Where Arch stayed, I assume."

"I didn't know that."

Dolly emerged from the barn, waving her hands over her head. A scattering of clouds moved across the sky, sending swift-moving shadows across the meadow.

"Why did it take this to bring you back to us?" Vanessa asked.

"I don't know. Pride, I guess. Habit. You get used to living a certain way in a certain place, and you just keep doing it."

"What about your family? Your home?"

"This was never home to me. I was always living in someone else's house."

"We missed you," she said. "Very much."

My throat ached. Why did it matter to me that she had said "We" and not "I"?

Dolly waved at us.

"Come on," she said.

We walked down the hill toward where my sister stood waiting for us.

FIVE

The roads leading into Nashville, pure farmland and hill country the last time I'd seen them, were now lined with strip malls and apartment complexes, and residential developments full of starter homes and condominiums with identical facades and floor plans.

"You told me I wouldn't recognize it," I said.

"You're either growing or you're dying," Arch replied.

On Belle Meade Boulevard, however, things were as they had always been. When I saw those houses for the first time as a boy from the wrong side of the river, they had dazzled me. Now, they filled me with a sense of the familiar, albeit tinged with melancholy.

They put me in the carriage house, in my mother's old bedroom. Mine had been turned into an office, which I found filled with a dozen blank canvases, along with an additional rolled canvas, an easel erected in the corner, and another portable one on a desk next to a few hundred dollars' worth of new acrylic and oil paints.

"I called the art department over at Vanderbilt and asked them what a painter like you would need," Vanessa said. "I had Scott pick everything up. I hope he got the right things."

"This is about a year's worth of stuff," I said.

"We didn't know how much to get," Arch said. "Better too much than not enough."

"Will you teach me how to paint?" Dolly asked.

"I would love to," I said.

After dinner, I took Dolly back out to the carriage house. I set up three small canvases on the floor over butcher paper. With a piece of charcoal, I drew the head of a bull on one panel, a can of tomato soup on the next, and a bouquet of flowers on the third. Dolly filled the lines with random colors.

When we were finished, I took her back over to the house to be bathed and put to bed.

"Are you tired?" Arch asked.

"Not really," I said.

"Then what do you say we go to Jamie's place? He's dying to see you. Might be good to get that out of the way so he doesn't show up at the farm half-drunk or hungover."

The sign that once read CAFÉ CABERNET had been replaced by another, which read HARPETH JUNCTION. The old white plaster exterior had been replaced by reclaimed wood, no doubt from one of those collapsing barns I'd seen along the road out to Leiper's Fork. A pair of wrought iron gaslights framed the door beneath an antique-looking neon sign. Steely Dan and Supertramp had been usurped by Kenny Chesney and the Dave Matthews Band. The restaurant floor was mostly empty—it was nearly ten on a Tuesday—but the bar was full, with the same sort of people I remembered from when my mother worked there, different only in the change of hairstyles and clothing. Cigar smoking seemed to be experiencing a renaissance of popularity. The whole place reeked like a riverboat casino.

I spotted Jamie behind the bar, dressed in a garish plaid blazer and a white shirt that stretched at the collar despite being open to the third button. His hair was thinning on top but boyishly long on the sides.

"Charlie Boykin!" he bellowed. "I'll be goddamned!"

He barreled around past the cocktail waitresses' pickup station, knocking over an empty wineglass with his elbow. The glass fell to the floor and shattered. Jamie didn't break stride. Before I could speak, he'd embraced me, pulling me tight against his girth.

"I know," he said. "I'm a big lard-ass now."

"No," I said. "You look good."

"You were always a shitty liar. Want a drink?"

"Scotch," I said.

"Excellent, excellent. I've got a fleet of single malts. You ever tried Oban? I love Oban."

"Johnnie Red is fine," I said.

"Oh, don't be such a cheapskate. I'm putting it all on Arch's tab."

Arch was already on the other side of the bar, at a table with a group of two men who looked to be about Jim's age and a guy about our age, a louche preppy with a deep tan that brought the sun out in the shock of blond hair that fell across his forehead. I looked back at Jamie. A flash of disappointment flickered across his face, and he was again familiar to me.

It was an expression I recognized from the very first day I had known him, drinking beer after beer by his pool. Now, Arch was the master of Jamie's old house, and Jamie was still the same boy—only nursing his loneliness with top-shelf scotches instead of beer and a host of "friends" with tabs that most likely went forever unpaid.

"I love what you've done to the place," I said.

"It's great, isn't it? I brought the chef in from Charleston. He's an award winner. Write-ups in *Gourmet* and *Southern Living*. We've been open for almost two years now. Packed every night. You wouldn't believe how much has changed around here. We're bringing Midtown back."

"That's great," I said. "I'm proud of you."

"Thanks," he said.

"I hear you've had some other changes in your life."

Jamie rolled his eyes. "Let me put it to you this way: Marriage and kids are the best things that will ever happen to you. Put them off for as long as possible."

He pulled out his wallet to show me pictures of his son.

"He's beautiful," I said.

"It changes you, you know," he said.

"Absolutely," I said, though I had yet to see evidence of much change beyond his having lost hair and gained weight.

He slipped his wallet back into his pocket and wrapped his arm around my neck.

"Man," he said. "I didn't realize how much I missed you 'til I saw that sweet face of yours walking through the door."

"I missed you too," I said.

"How long are you home? For good, I hope."

The sweetness in my face must have gone sour; Jamie went a bit pale.

"Oh shit," he said. "I mean, I know you're not home just for a visit, but I was just hoping maybe you'd be around for a while. I always loved your mom, you know. She's been so good to the old man, whether he deserves it or not."

"It seems that way."

"So you've been out to the farm?"

"This afternoon."

Jamie shook his head. "Goddamn," he said. "Ten years. Has it really been that long?"

"It seems strange, doesn't it?"

"It sure does," he said. "Look at old Archer over there. How long has it been since he was sitting in the back of a pickup truck in some field, drinking beer and dipping snuff on a school night? Now he's about to run for fucking mayor."

"You're joking," I said.

"Shit," Jamie said. "He didn't tell you? I don't think it's a big secret. He hasn't made his official announcement, but everyone knows. This is sort of his campaign headquarters, if you know what I mean. See those guys over there? The bald one is Randy McArthur. He runs the Metro Tourism and Convention Commission. The one with the glasses is Buck Mangold. He's head of the transit authority. Arch has had all kinds of guys like that in here. Marshaling his columns to charge the foe."

"Who's the foe?"

"Well, there will be at least three to start with, but the only serious contender is Clem Cardwell."

"I feel like I know that name. Is he a Yeatman guy?"

"No, those guys are all lining up behind Arch. Cardwell's boys went to Montgomery Bell, but he grew up in Donelson himself. Self-made man. Put himself through UT and made his millions in real estate. Big-money guy for the Democrats. More of a backroom wheeler-dealer than a politician. But he's got a lot of people around the city in his pocket, and the hicks love him, 'cause he's one of theirs. Plus he's built about three-fourths of their houses and just about every apartment from Nashville to Lebanon and Murfreesboro. He's also built a lot of the new public housing, and the apartment complexes in North Nashville, and he's held the rent down, so he's got most of the black preachers too. Arch has his work cut out for him."

"He's a little young to be running for mayor, don't you think?"

"Kennedy was twenty-nine when he ran for Congress."

"Yeah, but his dad pretty much bought his seat for him, didn't he?"

"Exactly."

That familiar sadness flared up again in Jamie's eyes. I remembered how Jim had been grooming Arch almost since birth, how Jim himself had intended to run for governor before my mother and Dolly sidetracked him. Arch had plenty of advantages—the largest of which was Jim Haltom, the fortune and influence he brought to bear—and no liabilities. At least none anyone knew about.

"Who's the guy next to Arch?" I asked.

Jamie sighed.

"That's Nick Averett. He's a consultant Arch brought in from Texas. Some Ivy League hotshot who made his bones working for the Bushes. He's all right, I guess, but he's got his nose so far up Arch's ass you can see the tip of it every time Arch opens his mouth."

Arch whispered something to Averett that brought a smile to his lips. He reminded me of myself at fourteen, my whole sense of self immersed in my association with a superior specimen of manhood. I wondered if anyone had ever viewed me with the same envy and contempt I now felt for Nick Averett.

Jamie signaled the bartender, a rangy man with a goatee and longish black hair slicked back into a small ponytail.

"Roger, this is my oldest friend," Jamie said. "His money's no good here, capisce?"

"Sure, Jamie," Roger said.

Jamie pulled out a cigarette and placed it in his mouth. Roger produced a lighter from his breast pocket and lit it and then lit one of his own.

This is the way the world ends, I thought.

"I gotta take a piss," Jamie said. "You need to go?"

"No," I said.

"I mean, do you need to *go*?" Jamie tapped his nose with his index finger.

"I'm good," I said. "But thanks."

"Suit yourself."

Jamie slid off the stool and ambled over toward the restrooms. Roger was drying cocktail glasses with a bar towel and hanging them upside down in the narrow brass racks above our heads.

"My mother worked here," I said. "Years ago."

"What was her name?"

"You wouldn't know her," I said. "It was a long time ago."

"Try me."

"Bonnie Boykin," I said.

Roger dried another glass and slid it into the rack. "She's your mom?"

"Yeah," I said.

"Shit, man, me and Bonnie go way back."

"No kidding."

"Yeah," he said. "I'm real sorry, man."

I didn't know what to say. "Thank you"? Was there a code, like saying "Congratulations" to the groom and "Best wishes" to the bride? I could have used Vanessa to give me cues.

Arch took the stool next to me, where Jamie had been sitting.

"You might have told me about your new career plans," I said.

He signaled the bartender.

"Club soda, Rodge," he said. "And the tab."

Roger nodded. A moment later, he returned with the drink and a slip of white paper. Arch pulled two one-hundred-dollar bills from his wallet.

"Give Teri the change, will you, Rodge?" he said. "And call a cab for me."

He sipped his soda.

"I was going to tell you," he said. "I was waiting for the right moment."

A twinge of resentment seized me as I recalled Arch's past history of keeping secrets from me until the arrival, in his judgment, of the right moment.

I lifted my glass, shook an ice cube into my mouth, and sucked on it.

"Too much club soda to drive?" I asked.

"The cab's for you," he said. "I've got a meeting."

"This late?"

He nodded.

"I might be a while. I could leave you here, but Jamie would probably try to stuff an eight ball up your nose."

"He already offered," I said. I signaled Roger for another drink.

"Jim used to have a lot of late-night meetings," I said. "I think most of them were with my mother."

"This is how it gets done, Charlie."

"Politics."

"Yep."

Jamie returned from the restroom, his mood considerably elevated. He stood between me and Arch, and slung his arms around our shoulders.

"Here we are, together again," he said. "The three amigos. God, weren't those days the best?"

Jamie lurched forward, reached for the string hanging beneath a large brass bell fastened to one of the pillars that held up the glass racks, and rang it three times.

"Roger," he cried, "a round for everyone, on the house. I want to make a toast."

Roger had skill behind the speed rack. He filled every order in under five minutes. The last drink went to Jamie. He rang the bell again and held his drink aloft.

"A toast," he said. "To Charlie Boykin, my dearest and oldest friend, home from the wilderness!"

The drunken lot cheered in unison. Jamie raised his hand.

"And to my brother-in-law, Archer Creigh," he said, "the next mayor of Nashville. To Arch!"

His name echoed off the exposed brick and reclaimed lumber on the walls, and another round of cheers went up. But Arch had already left.

SIX

I lay awake in my mother's old room for what felt like hours that night, scrolling through the gauzy, imperfect catalogue of my remembrance, sorting through emotions long repressed, things I'd wanted to forget, because it had seemed easier to push them down and behind me than to make peace with them. This was why I'd left in the first place: I couldn't reconcile the love and need I had for my mother, for Arch and Vanessa—even for Jim Haltom—with the indignation I'd felt when I discovered that all of our lives had been governed by a grand deception of which only I was unaware. It was easier to cut them out of my life, to behave as if I'd never known them, than to make sense of how I could so desperately love people who thought nothing of lying about things of such great consequence. Had they never considered how it would feel to discover that my very identity, my entire sense of self, was built on a delusion?

But memory doesn't let go of us. We can no more choose to put away the past than we can cease to breathe and go on living. And yet we try. We persuade ourselves that a new city or a new country, a new job, a new life, a new religion, a new love, will remake us and liberate us from the prisons of our old errors and the wrongs dealt to us, real or perceived. But the old sins and scars always come to reclaim us, whether borne along by memory alone or in the form of a private jet.

When sleep finally came, it swallowed me with such force that not even the full sun pouring through the open windows could wake me. When I lifted my head and looked over at the clock on the nightstand, I saw that it was after eleven. I dressed and went over to the main house. I hesitated at the kitchen door—*Should I knock?* I thought—before entering. There was coffee, still hot. I knew where to find a cup, as well as where the sugar bowl was kept. I dropped a cube in the brew, stirred it, and went back outside—to the rose garden. I was still there twenty minutes later when Arch arrived, toting a blue plastic bag from an electronics store.

"Good morning," he said. "It is still morning, by the way. Just barely."

"I'm sorry," I said. "I'm usually an early riser."

"Travel takes it out of you."

"What's that?"

He handed me the bag. Inside, I found a box containing a new BlackBerry, identical to the one Arch was always fiddling with.

"Now you can reach me, or anyone else, whenever you like," he said. "It's all ready to go. I got you the international calling plan. And I had the guy at the store load my address book into it. Vanessa, Jim, Jamie, Scott—all of their numbers are in there. Probably a few other folks you might want to catch up with too. And me."

"I don't know how to use one of these things," I said.

"In another year or two, you won't be able to get along without one. These little fuckers are going to make some people very, very rich."

"They haven't already?"

"They're just getting started. Here, let me show you."

Arch explained how to summon numbers from the address book, how to place calls and send text messages.

"Text messages?" I asked. "Why wouldn't you just call?"

"I know, it's weird, but that's how people do it now. There," he said. "It's easy. There's a manual in there if you want to learn how to use the calendar and so forth. But you've got the basics. So you can get in touch with any of us anytime."

He handed me a set of car keys.

"Use my Range Rover while you're in town. Consider it yours. Just promise me you won't drive to Texas and sell it to a chop shop on the border."

I blushed. Arch gave me a playful punch on the shoulder.

"Is Jim still sore about that?" I asked.

"I think he's ready to call it even. Just promise me, okay? That you'll stick around. See this through."

I winced at the thought that Arch might think me capable of deserting my mother on her deathbed. Then again, I'd yet to give him reason to believe otherwise.

"I promise," I said.

"I talked to Uncle Jim," he said. "Your mom's a little better today. I'll take you out to the farm. But take a shower first. You reek."

ONLY AFTER I went inside did I remember that I hadn't spoken to anyone back in San Miguel since I'd left. I set the sleek little phone on the dressing table and stared at it for a solid minute before picking it up, punching in the numbers, and pressing the CALL button. I listened to the crackle of static and the beeping of the international tone. At last, the answering machine picked up, and I heard Teddy's voice on the recording. I left a message: The journey had been uneventful. I'd seen my mother. I didn't know how much longer she had—maybe a few days, maybe a week, maybe more, but not much. I did not say how strange it felt to be back in the carriage house, to see Arch and Vanessa, to slip right back into my old life—different for sure, but similar enough to make everything since feel like a lost weekend.

I showered and shaved. I was still unsettled, even alarmed, by the sight of myself in the mirror. I dressed and ran a comb through my damp hair, stuffed the little phone and the keys into my pockets, and hastened down to meet Arch. He insisted that I drive. We stopped at a diner on the way out to the farm, for coffee and eggs.

"I always thought if you got into politics that you'd set your sights higher," I said.

"It's not about my sights. It's about the city."

"Arch," I said. "It's me."

"I'm serious. A lot has changed since you lived here. People are moving to Nashville in droves. The economy is booming. Estimates suggest that the population of Middle Tennessee is going to grow by a million people over the next twenty years. A million. The traffic's already a nightmare. Can you imagine what it will be like with a million more people here? And where are they all going to live?"

"In whatever all those cranes are building?"

"Sure, some of them. A lot of them are moving into neighborhoods like the one you came from. East Nashville is filling up with artsy types and yuppies migrating from out of town. They've already broken ground on a new condo development right where Montague Village used to be. You better believe those units won't be occupied by your old neighbors. People from New York and Chicago come down here, decide they like the weather, and see a slick new condo or an old Craftsman they can buy with cash or for a note that's a third what they used to pay for half the space. They can't believe their luck. They aren't turned off by discount cigarette shops and check-cashing businesses. Some of them lived in rougher places back where they came from."

"What's so bad about that?"

"Nothing," he said, "if you forget about the people who lived there before. What's going to happen to them? Terrence and his grandmother couldn't live in East Nashville today unless they went into public housing in some shithole like Cayce Place. So they get pushed over to Bordeaux, where half the blocks look like fucking Sarajevo, or they move out to Madison or Donelson or Antioch and have to spend three or four hours a day sitting on a bus. That's no way to live. And where are all of these new people going to send their kids to school? How are we going to move them around the city? Who will pay for all of this shit Metro's buying on credit? It's a real problem. And if you want to make a difference, you need to be at the top of the chain. There's a way to fix these issues, but it needs to be top-down. We don't want to end up like Atlanta."

I thought of all the old talk of tradition back at Yeatman—the notion that we were obliged to uphold our way of doing things, to push back against the tide of mediocrity and vulgarity. And I remembered what Yeatman had taught me about Tennessee history—how the gallant knights of the South had fought and died for the Southern Way of Life; how they had resisted the so-called tyranny of Reconstruction, often under the cover of white hoods; how they had rebuilt their fortunes and the order of things and somehow managed through the civil rights era to avoid being cast as scoundrels or losing control of their city, the way it had happened in Memphis and New Orleans and Jackson and Birmingham. I doubted that Arch's desire to prevent Nashville from ending up like Atlanta had as much to do with keeping down housing costs, fixing the schools, and keeping the traffic under control as it did with preserving an order in which people like him continued to decide what was best for the rest of us.

"Well," I said, "best of luck. I think you'd make a fine mayor."

"Thanks for saying so."

"And after that?"

"Let's win first."

That word—"let's"—gave me a jolt, not unlike the one I'd felt the first time Arch shook my hand; the first time he said "Hey, bud"; the first time he called me "brother."

I TOOK A walk around the farm that afternoon with Jim. He had lost a dramatic amount of weight. The old fullback's neck was thin, his shoulders were sloped, and the shock of cropped black hair was silvery and longish. He moved slower, took shorter strides.

"I want to thank you for coming," he said.

"I should have come a long time ago," I said.

"You didn't know."

"I don't blame you for not telling me until now," I said. "I was a terrible brat the last time we spoke. I'm sorry."

"You were a boy," he said. "You had a right to be hurt. I didn't think enough about how *you* would take it. I was too much in love. I didn't try as hard as I should have. I only wanted your mother to be happy."

"She seems to have been pretty happy."

"Yes," he said. "But she missed you every day."

"You'll understand if I find that hard to believe."

"Let me show you something."

We rounded the barn and made our way back toward the house through the vegetable gardens—a project of my mother's, Jim said. As we neared the house, I mentioned Arch's mayoral candidacy.

"I'm not sure it's the best thing," Jim said.

"I assumed he had your support."

"Clem Cardwell's an old friend," Jim said.

"Do you mean to say you're not backing him?" I said. "Arch, I mean."

"He's my godson, and my son-in-law. Blood comes first. But I advised him to wait, or look at another opportunity. It's Clem's turn. He has more of a centrist appeal anyway. It's hard for a Republican to win anything in Davidson County. Regardless, I'm giving Arch my full support. But he doesn't have all of Clem's advantages."

"You think he's going to lose."

"I didn't say that."

We reached the house, on the end where they'd added a new sunporch and a corner with a wet bar built into the wall. Jim led me back through a large door, into a drawing room with a steep vaulted ceiling, the walls adorned with dozens of framed paintings.

Scanning the walls, I became overwhelmed with emotion. Every one of them—I counted twenty-four—was mine.

"Did you get these from Pancho?"

"Pancho?" he asked.

"Eugene Craddock," I said. "He represents me. His friends call him Pancho."

"I see. No, we didn't get them directly. I have a buyer."

I walked around the room, taking in the career retrospective hanging on the walls before me. At the center of one wall hung the painting I'd done in high school, the infamous scene at the T-Cup.

"How'd you get that one?"

"When I stepped down from the board at Yeatman, Kip Dodd wanted to give me a gift. So I asked for the painting. Your mother loves them all, but that's her favorite. She used to sit in here for hours. She'd take a book and say she was going in to read, but whenever I found her, she was looking at the paintings."

"I don't remember Mom being much of a reader," I said.

"You never knew her very well then, did you?"

"No, sir, I did not."

"As children, we only see our mothers in relation to ourselves. It's only when we're older that we get a chance to know them."

"I guess I missed out on that."

"You did indeed."

"I wish I hadn't."

Jim walked around me and gazed out the window.

"I have a proposition for you," he said. "Would you paint your mother for me? Not as she is now, but as she was before."

As she was before.

"I don't do very many portraits," I said.

This wasn't true. I painted faces almost as often as land-scapes. But to reproduce my mother as she had been before the cancer ravaged her—did I dare attempt such a thing?

"I'll have everything set up for you in her room," he said. "You'll work there, by your mother's bedside. She wants you near her. I have some pictures for you to use. There's one in particular that I like."

He paused to catch his breath.

"For the completed portrait, I'll pay you ten thousand," he said. "And I'll see that you're taken care of, in every respect."

"I don't want your money," I said.

Jim sighed. "I've only ever shown you kindness," he said.

"I know."

I almost wanted to hug him.

I began that afternoon, sketching studies from a photograph of my mother taken at their wedding. She looked so beautiful. The complexity of Jim's divorce had forced them to wait until well after Dolly's birth to marry; in the photograph, my mother had lost her pregnancy weight, though she still seemed to have the famed prenatal radiance.

I raised all the windows to let in fresh air when I set up my easel. The bedroom was large; I had plenty of room to work without interfering with my mother's care. Years of painting in far more inhospitable conditions had inured me to distractions.

It occurred to me that I was now almost twice as old as my mother had been when she left home. I thought of how I would have felt had I been in her place, knowing as little as I did about the ways of the world. Would I have understood how beauty made one both powerful and vulnerable? Would I have been more wary? How jealously did she guard her virtue before she met my father? How wily and persuasive had he been? Or was it just the time and the place?

Not even Sunny could have said for certain what was going through my mother's mind in those days. All I had to hold on to were memories of her: softly singing to me at bedtime when I was small, or the nights she came home stumble-drunk and snuggled up next to me, clinging to me like I was the only thing in the world that mattered to her.

My mother spent most of the hours I sat in that room sleeping, peaceful but too weary, I hoped, to think of what would soon come. I had little time alone with her: nurses came and went; Jim sat on the other side of the bed, holding my mother's hand or slouching in the corner chair, staring off toward the window, falling into fitful sleep here and there and then waking with a start to ensure that my mother did not go while he was unconscious.

Every day, Dolly was impatient for me to finish the painting. She felt somehow that my work was time taken from her. I told her I'd promised her father.

"I thought he wasn't your daddy," she said.

"He's paying me a lot of money," I said.

"For painting a picture?"

One afternoon, when I was nearly finished with the portrait, my mother sent the nurse out of the room.

"Let me see," she said.

I lifted the canvas and turned it around. I had worked my way from the eyes outward, so that the canvas surrounding her head and shoulders was still blank.

"Look at me," she said. "Inside a cloud."

I smiled. "Do you like it?" I asked.

She nodded. "Come sit with me."

I put the painting back on the easel and walked over to the bed. She reached up with a frail hand to my shoulder and pulled me down to lie beside her.

"You'll always be my baby," she said. "You know that, don't you?"

She was barely conscious when she said it. Perhaps she was dreaming, or hallucinating. It made no difference. And because I knew she could not possibly hear or feel or remember, I let go, and I wept.

The next Saturday, my mother died in her sleep.

I took the painting back to the carriage house and finished it there in time for Arch to have it framed and hung in the sunroom at the farm, facing out toward the garden and the meadow, where we would gather after we buried her.

SEVEN

Jim sent the jet back down to bring Pancho and Murray and Teddy up for the funeral. I vacated the carriage house for the three of them and took the guest room at the end of the hall opposite the master suite.

The funeral was held in Saint Matthew's Church in Leiper's Fork, a little Anglican parish, to which my mother and Jim had retreated, both out of convenience and for the comfort of being around a congregation consisting of good country people rather than the social-club atmosphere of Saint John's in Belle Meade. The priest spoke of my mother with sincere familiarity. In my absence, both she and Jim seemed to have become devout.

Here's one reason to go to church: people will show up for your funeral. Little Saint Matthew's could not contain the crowd that assembled on my mother's behalf; the members of the congregation were pressed in by my mother's many other friends and acquaintances. Initially, I assumed the Belle

Meaders were there for Jim, or for Arch and Vanessa, but as it turned out, many of them had come to regard my mother as a friend. One after another, they cornered me at the visitation, to pass on some surprising anecdote or to assure me that my mother would be remembered always for her graciousness and generosity. Who was this woman they described to me?

I saw so many old faces—Kip Dodd and his wife, now retired themselves and living nearby in a farmhouse of their own; Ellen Creigh; a slew of old classmates and their parents. Just after we sat down, I felt a tap on my shoulder and turned to find Sunny and Terrence in the second row of pews. Up to then, I had mostly kept my composure, even at the final moment in the carriage house, when Jim had sat up from his chair and grasped my mother's hand and knew it was over. But when I saw Sunny and Terrence, my own sorrow poured out of me in streaming tears. Terrence embraced me across the pews. The years had changed everyone, but the bonds of childhood felt, at least, as if they were still binding.

Later, at the reception, Terrence and I stole away together for a few minutes. We had so much to say to each other, and so little. I learned that Terrence's life had taken a path even more circuitous than my own. He had gone to Tennessee State on a football scholarship, but a knee injury had cut short his great promise as an athlete. Even before that, he'd had a divided soul, split between the gratification and rhapsodies of lay preaching and the money he could make on the corners of our old neighborhood. He'd done two short stretches in state prison for it.

Recently, however, Terrence had returned to the church and

given up dealing, working as a trainer at the Y and a mentor and football coach in a program for "at-risk youth." He was back living with Rev Joseph and had begun to preach again. His story of reform gave him enormous credibility with young people. And he hadn't done anything that wasn't being done by a dozen Jamie Haltoms in prep school dorm rooms and fraternity houses. Rich kids go to rehab; black kids go to prison.

"I'll have to come to church sometime," I said. "See you preach. You have the gift."

"It's just the spirit talking," he said. "You saved, Charlie?"

"No," I admitted. "Not yet."

"When you're ready, he'll be waiting."

I nodded. Terrence shook his head.

"What is it?" I asked.

"Where the hell you been, boy?" he said.

"I took a wrong turn," I said. "But I found my way home."

"You call this 'home'?" he asked.

Later, back home—back at the Creighs', I should say—I went out with Teddy to smoke in the breezeway beside the carriage house.

"I liked your friend Terrence," she said.

"We go way back." I unknotted the tie I'd borrowed from Arch.

"When are you planning to go to his church?" she asked.

"I don't know. I probably won't," I said. "Thank you for coming, by the way. I know you hate it here."

"How could I not?" she said. "But, yes, I do hate it here. I can't stand the humidity. Or the good ole boys. I wish we could go home this afternoon."

"I think I'm going to stick around for a while longer," I said.

"How long?" she asked.

"I've got some work lined up," I said. "Houses, portraits. Enough to keep me busy for a while."

"You have work in San Miguel too."

"Yes, but these are commissions. Guaranteed money. *Good* money. It might be pity, but all of a sudden, everyone in Belle Meade wants me to do a painting for them."

Teddy gave me a long look. "You're staying," she said.

"That's right."

"I mean for good," she said. "You won't come back."

I didn't know how to answer. I wanted to say "Of course I will. It will be only a month or two, and I'll come back flush with cash, and life will go on as it was before." Or that I just needed a little time to make peace with the past, to make sense of what I was feeling. To hang around long enough to remember that Arch and Vanessa hadn't needed me before and didn't need me now. To realize that the life I had in Mexico was enough—more than enough; better than I deserved. That San Miguel was home; that I knew what was gripping me was just nostalgia, but I needed to feel it and see it through to the end so I could go back without regrets. But I knew if I said those things, they would just be what I wanted to be true, and not what was. So I said nothing, which was the same, it seems, as saying yes.

"I need to take a shower," she said. "I've been sweating like a pig all day."

The next day, Teddy, Pancho, and Murray went back to Mexico.

After two months, I received a box containing some clothes and a few other things I'd left behind, along with a single black-and-white photograph Teddy had taken of me in sunglasses and a wide-brimmed straw hat. On the back, she'd written: *Carlitos, como lo recordaré.* Charlie, as I'll remember him.

EIGHT

The last week of May, Arch gave the commencement address at Yeatman—an eerie echo of my own graduation. Arch knew what a powerful platform the lectern at a Yeatman commencement could be: a captive audience, which included many of the city's most affluent and influential citizens. He was not naïve to the length of his odds.

Arch's sole experience in politics had been a term on the school board, where his most memorable accomplishment had been a concerted effort to blow the whole thing up. Citing "irreconcilable dysfunction" and "well-intentioned but incompetent" members, Arch had sent a letter to the mayor's office and the news media, calling for a resolution to disband the elected school board and return to a system where the mayor appointed representatives of his own choosing.

"Speaking as one myself, I believe our school board representatives want what's best for our young people," Arch had written in the letter. "But as a whole, we lack the experience, expertise, and available time to accomplish our aims."

Off the record, he'd been blunt: "It was an idiot circus," he told me, "run by some of the stubbornest jackasses who ever stumbled out of the barn."

The initiative died, but its failure turned out to be a boon for Arch. The newspapers painted him as a truth-telling idea man. He didn't have the support of the mayor's office or the city council. But he had the papers, especially the *Herald*, owned by Engage South, a media company belonging to a Yeatman alum. And the television stations could never resist a pretty face. Arch looked like a savior to the white working class, just as disgust with politicians was peaking.

How did a guy like Arch Creigh—born into wealth, educated privately from pre-K through graduate school, married to the daughter of a billionaire, as handsome as a film star, with family ties going back almost to Jamestown—become a Man of the People? After all, the People were the ones who shopped at Wal-Mart, who spent their lives traveling back and forth between backbreaking jobs and weary inertia at home, who ended up being forced to live off disability and Medicaid benefits. How on earth could the People see a guy who lived on Belle Meade Boulevard as their champion?

There is nothing in this world to which people connect more willingly in uncertain times than the appearance of genuine certainty. If there was one true thing that could be said about Arch, it was this: he seemed so sure of himself that people couldn't help but believe in him.

All of which led up to that moment on the quad at Yeatman.

"Just a little more than a decade ago," he said, "I sat where you boys are sitting now, at the end of six years of the hardest work I've ever done. Trust me, Wall Street is a piece of cake after AP Physics and Latin during football season. So when I was asked to speak to you today, I was a little intimidated. I know from experience that you hear a lot of speeches. You might get a little numb to so much good advice."

Laughter rippled across the assembly. They were all primed to love him before he even opened his mouth.

"I had to spend a lot of time thinking about what I would say to you," Arch continued. "Then just last week, I came across an article in the newspaper that really got my attention. The title of the piece was 'Why Men Fail.' According to this piece, nationwide, over the last ten years, we've seen a sharp decline in male academic performance at every level. Statistically, fewer men are graduating from college than women, and even fewer are going on to complete graduate programs. There are a lot of single moms in America, but they are staying single by choice, because the fathers of their children aren't providers. So the women are taking care of themselves. When I first started working in finance, my mentor told me that his best employees were single moms, not guys like me. I got the message. This message really got me thinking about the importance of what you've experienced here at Yeatman. It's trained you to hold on to something most people have lost."

Arch let that note linger. A dramatic hush fell over the assembly.

"While we must meet the challenges of a changing world with fresh ideas and perspectives, there's a sense here in Nashville, and especially at Yeatman, that some of the old stuff is worth holding on to. It's this stuff—these ideals—that are the foundation your life will be built upon."

He went on like that for a while, paying homage to Yeatman,

celebrating the graduating class as exceptions to the trends he'd just described. He then shifted into his own narrative: the privilege in which he'd grown up, followed by the wrenching ordeal of his father's illness and deterioration and the devastating blow of his death. The courage he'd learned both from the way his father had faced sickness and death and from his mother's stoic determination to nurture and shelter her children while nursing her husband and, after his death, her stoic resolve to shepherd the family through their collective grief. The strength of character and generosity he'd learned from his uncle Jim, and the parallels between the path Arch's mother had walked and the one Jim now followed himself as a widower and father of a young daughter. The grace and wisdom Arch had learned with Vanessa by his side, brilliant and driven and more accomplished than most of her male peers.

All of it was crafted to signal the formation of his own ambitions, his will to power, as it were, couched in the impression of a labor of love—as an exhibition of noblesse oblige.

"You are coming of age in a world that wants you to believe it's okay to be mediocre," Arch said. "There are no really great men left, the world tells you, so why bother trying to be one? I believe there are bigger things—harder things; things that must be done by the people who are capable of doing them. Our city needs the right kind of leadership to carry us into the new century, so that we can build a better future without giving up the best parts of the culture and traditions that define what I like to call 'the spirit of Nashville.' So I'm making it official, right here and now. As of this morning, I've resigned my position at Chadderton Dobbs. I want to be your next mayor."

Before he could say another word, the whole assembly was

on its feet, cheering. You would have thought someone had paid them. Maybe someone did.

I was on my feet as well, my eyes damp with tears of awe and admiration. No one had to pay me. I believed it all; I still do. Some people are exceptional. And without a doubt, Arch was the most exceptional person I ever knew. But no one, however exceptional, transcends the bitter fact of his humanity. Like the man says in that old book they made us read back in senior year: "There's always something." And no great temple was ever built without a few bodies buried beneath its foundation.

NINE

Arch set up his campaign office in an old storefront at the edge of Germantown, on the north side of downtown, west of the river. The location provided easy access to the bypass and the interstates, and put some distance between Arch and Belle Meade. He went to a different church every Sunday and started sprinkling conversations with references to scripture. He visited schools and scout troops and civic organizations. There were fish fries and softball leagues, potlucks and neighborhood block parties. There were also private donor dinners and gatherings at country clubs and the lavish homes of Arch and Vanessa's neighbors.

Arch had the right side of the spectrum locked up. The only other conservative candidate in the race was Justin Jeffs, a certifiable kook whose campaign promises included a plan to require all Tennessee state flags be shorn of gold fringe "so they'll fly right" and a proposal to refurbish the infamous statue of Confederate hero and Klansman Nathan Bedford Forrest on I-65 between Nashville and Brentwood.

By tradition, mayoral elections were not partisan, but tribalism had long since infiltrated every aspect of American life, and the gulf between Arch, with his GOP ties and conservative rhetoric, and Democrat operators like Clem Cardwell and the outspokenly liberal upstart councilwoman Marylou Greene could not be ignored. Davidson County tilted to the left, but not so far that a conservative couldn't win over the more independent-minded voters. All Arch had to do was sit back, let Clement and Greene rip each other apart fighting over the Democratic base, wait for the smoke to clear, and step forward as the voice of reason and moderation, free of ties to the Clintons. His charm would offset his inexperience. People were sick of politicians anyway. They were ready to get behind a charismatic businessman with a smart, beautiful wife and a fortune in the bank, to prove he knew what he was doing—never mind that he'd been born with money and married even more of it.

Fair bet, I thought. What did I know anyway? I was too busy painting to pay much attention. Ironically, the portrait I'd made of my mother, borne of the deepest pain I'd ever experienced, had turned my work into just another thing people with means felt compelled to acquire; in short order, a Charles Boykin of the wife or the kids became another status symbol, like Spode china or a BMW or a Yeatman class ring.

I hadn't spent much time with children until I'd started painting them for a living. I was struck by how much more complex they could be than they seemed from a distance. The girl who compulsively scratched at scabs on her knees and arms. The restless boy with the hovering mother who corrected his every gesture. Nary a father was to be seen; in this milieu, even the working mothers appeared to be responsible for all of their children's appointments and obligations.

Most of the children I saw were not obviously troubled; they were sweet and generous, well-mannered and mature. Groomed. They would follow the same path as Arch and Vanessa: private elementary; Yeatman or Steptoe or one of the other pricey day schools in Nashville, or maybe a boarding school in Virginia or New England; respectable university; graduate school in business or law or medicine. They would play golf and tennis, become skilled swimmers, go to summer camp in the Carolinas, spend a semester abroad in Europe, and maybe work for a while on a dude ranch in Wyoming, learning to love the arts and the wonders of history and the great out-doors. They would go on church mission trips to poor coun-tries and come home swollen with pride for having touched the lives of the less fortunate. They would volunteer at soup kitch-ens and homeless shelters, tutor at public elementary schools, make a black friend and form a genuine respect for the chal-lenges he faced. They would "give back," as the saying goes, in the form of generous contributions of both money and time to church and charity.

And they would marry others of their ilk, with the occa-sional interloper—a Yankee or an Italian or a Jew. Their for-tunes would grow. They would build homes of their own or move into the ones in which they were raised. Their lives would not be untouched by hardship; there would be the same spillage of infidelity and divorce, disease leading to prolonged illness and sometimes death, business failures and other reversals of fortune, struggles with addiction and mental illness. But most of them would land on their feet, as would their children, who would be just as beautiful and charming as *they* had once been, and who might one day sit for an hour or so with me while I sketched and took photos as studies for their portraits.

I did most of the portraits outside, and I generally finished them ahead of schedule. I never lost my love of art, nor my obsession with getting every detail right. But I'd been at it for so long and with such steadiness of practice that I could blow through a house-and-garden painting in a few weeks. There were commissions enough to keep me working for two more years.

"If only we'd known," Pancho said. "You might have tapped this well a long time ago."

With a steady income, I had enough in the bank to make a down payment on a place of my own: a two-bedroom bungalow in East Nashville, only a few blocks from the condo complex where the Montague Village Apartments once stood. These were the early days of gentrification. There was color and light, and grass in the yards, some respectable landscaping, wooden privacy fences replacing chain-link, people walking dogs and strollers down the trash-strewn sidewalks, waving as they passed while I sat on the porch smoking and drinking coffee in the mornings. We did not see that we weren't integrating the neighborhood so much as we were colonizing it.

One morning, I answered a knock at the front door and found a woman in a slim black skirt and a white blouse, looking fresh despite the sweltering heat of early August.

"Hi there," she said. "I'm Marylou Greene, and I'm running for mayor."

"Oh yeah," I said. "I'm sorry I didn't recognize you. You look different in person."

"That's what people tell me."

She pointed at the sign in my yard.

"I see you're supporting Archer Creigh," she said.

"That's right," I said.

"I'd like to see if I can change your mind."

I gave her a cup of coffee and sat with her at my kitchen table and listened as she outlined her vision for the city. She had plans. A new convention center and a baseball stadium downtown. Parks rehabilitation, bike and walking paths, sidewalks in the neighborhoods. Footbridges across the Cumberland. High-speed rail. She had figures, graphs, statistics. Numbers of hotel rooms and apartments. Projected tourism dollars. Tax revenues. If Arch weren't my best friend in the world, I think I would have gone to work for her.

"Arch Creigh is a friend," said Marylou Greene. "But we have a fundamentally different view of where the city is heading. Arch calls it 'the spirit of Nashville.' I call it 'holding on to the past.'"

"He just doesn't want the city to buy a bunch of stuff it can't pay for," I said. "What if something bad happens, like a flood, or a bunch of tornadoes ripping through downtown, like a few years ago? Or what if the stock market crashes, or people stop traveling, because of an oil shortage or something? The city's still stuck with the bill for all this stuff, right?"

"You sound just like Arch," she said.

She looked down at my paint-spattered shoes and jeans and the stains on my fingertips.

"Oh!" she said. "You're the painter!"

"You've heard of me?"

"I've known Jim for years. What a coincidence. Your mother was a lovely woman."

"Now you're starting to sound like a politician."

Her phone pinged. She picked it up out of her purse, looked at the screen, and tapped out a reply with the same practiced skill I'd seen Arch deploy on dozens of occasions.

"I hate those things," I said.

"Me too," she said. "It's a necessary evil." She stood up.

"I hope you don't feel like you've wasted your time," I said.

"Not at all," she said.

"I'd vote for you if I could," I said.

She winked. "It's a secret ballot, you know," she said.

That very afternoon, I went to his campaign office and told Arch and his staff all about my visit with Marylou Greene.

"She's knocking on doors in East Nashville?" said Nick Averett. "Oh, please."

Averett had a surly mouth and an air of entitlement I recognized from my past encounters with a certain class of Texans from the suburbs of Dallas and Houston. I preferred his deputy, Bart Walsh, a Belle Meader like Arch, who projected an air of calmness and Tennessee gentility. He waited for Averett to finish before he lifted his hand.

"I think Marylou deserves a little more attention," Walsh said.

"It's a moot point," Averett said. "We're playing for the runoff. She'll be out of money long before then."

"She doesn't need money to knock on doors and talk to people," I said.

"Charlie—it's Charlie, right?" Averett said. "No offense, but I've done this a few times."

"You're the expert," I said. "I'm just telling you about a conversation. She was very persuasive."

"He has a point," Walsh said. "We could spend a little more time canvassing. Just personally talking to people, especially in North and East Nashville."

"We're already doing that," Averett said.

"I mean Arch," Walsh said. "Not just the volunteers."

"Do we have time for that?" Averett asked.

"We'll make time," Arch said. "Hey, guys, can I talk to Charlie for a minute?"

Walsh and Averett excused themselves.

"I've got something important to tell you," he said.

"What is it?"

"Vanessa's pregnant."

"When's the due date?"

"Late December, right around Christmas," he said.

"After the election."

"Thank Christ."

"I don't know what to say."

"What do you mean?"

"I'm just—I'm really happy for you, Arch. Truly."

"Thanks, bud."

It all seemed too much. But this was the way of things for Arch. The plate could never be too full. Even when covered by clouds, the sun never ceased to shine.

TEN

Vanessa played the role of dutiful wife at Arch's campaign events but spent most of her time preparing for the arrival of the baby: remaking her old bedroom into a lavish nursery, attending birthing classes (Arch never missed one; Nick Averett always sent a photographer), learning to prepare homemade organic baby food, reading book after book about natural childbirth and baby's first year. Arch thought it was silly, but he tolerated Vanessa's obsessions. Averett tried to exploit "the whole organic thing" to soften Arch's image for educated, health-minded women. Vanessa knew she could do whatever she liked so long as she showed up and smiled.

I never got the sense that Arch thought of the baby as a distraction. He read the birthing books and rearranged his schedule to join her at the doctor's office for checkups. Every time I saw him greet Vanessa, he placed his ear against her belly so he could listen to the sound of life floating around in its little amniotic sea.

"Do you know the sex yet?" I asked.

"We could find out," Arch said, "but Vanessa wants it to be a surprise. I told her we should just find out so people will know what sort of things to buy. She says it doesn't matter. She's painting everything gender-neutral. But I'd love to have a girl. Then again, if it's a girl, she can't go to Yeatman."

You would be surprised how many Yeatman alums make this observation about their future children.

AS PREDICTED, THE media identified Clem Cardwell as the front-runner. He had the deepest pockets, the widest connections. But everyone who voted along party lines or hated tax-rate hikes to pay for public services or considered the annual increase in population a sign of imminent apocalypse had no dog in the hunt but Arch. Three times during the first debate, he made sure to mention that we didn't want to end up like Atlanta, which was dog-whistle code for "too much traffic and too many queers, Yankees, and brown people."

"What happens when there's a shift in the economy?" Arch would say. "The market always corrects. It's a matter of when, not if. Banks don't feel pity or make allowances. When the bill comes due, they expect you to pay it or else. I lost my father when I was young, but I remember a few things he taught me. One of them was this: Live within your means. That's a value we should still hold dear in this town, however much we grow. It's a big part of the spirit of Nashville."

Marylou Greene had a long list of talking points to beat back at Arch's assertions, and a fluency with economic data and statistics. Furthermore, she was unflappable and unwaveringly cheerful. You could never catch her scowling or raising her voice in such a way that she might be construed as being bitchy or shrill by the sort of people who weren't yet used to the idea of a woman in charge.

One choice was made much clearer from the debates, however: Clem Cardwell was shit on the stump. He sweated a lot and was as red-faced as a drunk on a bender. He fumbled questions and seemed to forget what he was talking about at times.

"He's a disaster," Averett said.

"Does anyone really pay attention to mayoral debates?" I asked.

"Donors," Averett said. "They're all that matters."

"Cardwell doesn't need donors," I said.

"Marylou Greene does," Arch said. "Clem's perspiration problem is helping her immensely."

"How's that good for you?" I asked.

"Who do you think we have a better chance against in the runoff?" Averett said. "A good ole boy from a rural town with a classic bootstraps story and a ton of friends in both Belle Meade and Browntown, or a carpetbagger married to a commie professor?"

"Her husband's a communist?" I asked.

"He's an academic," Averett said. "Nothing rubs Southern voters the wrong way more than overeducated Jews telling them what to do."

"He's Jewish?"

"For fuck's sake, Boykin," Averett said. "Are you even paying attention?"

On the morning of Election Day, I walked down to the polling station at the elementary school around the corner from my house. Coffee and cookies were served in the cafeteria. Outside, kids were running around on the playground. People

were smiling, chatting with one another in line and around cafeteria tables. I had never voted before; I walked home swollen
with pride for having done my civic duty.

Later, I drove downtown to the Sheraton, where Arch was
holding his election night party in one of the ballrooms. Bart
Walsh met me downstairs and led me up to the room where
Arch waited with Vanessa and the rest of his inner circle. A
few bottles of good wine were breathing on the kitchen island.
Averett opened a bottle of good scotch. Someone was out on
the balcony smoking.

"Charlie!"

Dolly darted through the adults gathered in front of the
television and embraced me. I spotted Jim in an armchair by a
window that faced out toward the Capitol. Dolly led me over
to him.

"You made it," Jim said.

"This is so boring," Dolly said. "Can we go home, Daddy?"

"Not yet, honey," he said. "It's a big night for Arch,
remember?"

"Can I go watch TV in the bedroom?"

"As soon as Arch and Vanessa come out."

Finally, they emerged. Arch wore a navy-blue suit and a
tie the color of the decanted Bordeaux on the table. Vanessa,
great with child, wore a cream-colored dress with black borders around the sleeves and neck, and a strand of pearls and
matching earrings. They looked exactly as they should have:
the golden couple, handsome, brilliant, peerless, invincible,
primed for the commencement of their predestined ascent. And
I, looking on from afar, their erstwhile friend and confidant,
admired them with both ardor and spite.

By nine thirty, the returns were in. Marylou Greene had finished first, with 35 percent. Arch followed with 30, two percentage points ahead of Clem Cardwell, forcing a run-off between Arch and Greene. The remaining 7 percent was split among the other three.

The campaign staff had a celebratory champagne toast before heading down with Arch to greet his supporters. I went out onto the balcony to smoke. I heard the door open behind me and turned to see Vanessa, a champagne flute filled with sparkling water in her hand. I tossed the cigarette off the balcony.

"I hope that doesn't hit anyone," she said.

"I'd rather burn an unwitting citizen than poison your unborn child."

"And I suppose you'd throw your cloak across a puddle for me to walk on too."

"Without hesitation."

"But I'm no Virgin Queen," she said. "As you know."

"Shouldn't you be downstairs?" I asked.

"Shouldn't you?"

"I'm on the way. I just thought you'd be with Arch."

"I had to go to the restroom," she said. "He's waiting for me."

"Are you ready for this?" I asked.

"I don't have much choice," she said. "This is what I signed on for."

"Do you still want it?"

"Shouldn't I?"

"I wouldn't."

"This is just the campaign," she said. "What comes after is different."

"Until the next one."

"True," she said. "But what happens between matters more. It's where we can make a difference."

The only thing I envied more than Arch and Vanessa's marriage was their conviction that what they wanted was what was best for everyone.

"All the same," I said. "You look great, by the way. Did I tell you how beautiful you look tonight?"

"No, you didn't," she said. "Thank you."

Vanessa was never one to behave as if she didn't know that it was true. Pregnancy had only enhanced her loveliness. On the balcony in the darkness, she did, in fact, seem to glow.

ELEVEN

Nashville has always been proud of its reputation for good manners. You really notice it when you've been away. You stop for gas driving into town; the lady behind the counter calls you "hon" and wishes you a "blessed day." Drivers slow down to let you in when you're pulling onto the freeway. Strangers wave and nod when you make eye contact. The general kindness of the place works on you like a balm. You get the sense that things just go a little smoother, a little easier, a little less nastily here. This is what Arch meant by "the spirit of Nashville."

But there's a fine line between politeness and fraudulence. This became obvious during the brief runoff campaign, when the public air of mutual respect between Archer Creigh and Marylou Greene dissolved into a morass of ugliness.

I'd like to lay all the blame on Nick Averett—this was his specialty, after all. He didn't normally run city election campaigns; he was a GOP operator who'd come to Nashville because he had seen the future and wanted to jump on Arch's wagon to ensure that he'd be sitting up front when said wagon pulled into Washington, DC. His tactics were meant for bigger battles.

The night after the election, the television on behind me while I put the finishing touches on a portrait, I was surprised by the sound of Vanessa's voice. I turned around to find her on the screen describing Marylou Greene as a "liberal Trojan horse." She added a few remarks about health care and feminism, likening Greene to Hillary Clinton. Vanessa's Southern charm—her soft accent thickened to a drawl, her hair a bit bigger and blonder, her dress a little more back-porch than boardroom—obscured the fact that she herself had much more in common with Hillary Clinton—or, for that matter, Marylou Greene—than with Laura or Barbara Bush.

The next day, listening to the radio as I drove across the river from East Nashville to Belle Meade, I heard a campaign spot with the voice of a woman speaking in exaggerated black dialect, questioning whether Marylou Greene was a Christian. The next morning, an article ran on the front page of the *Tennessean* with a photo of Marylou Greene surrounded by black preachers from North Nashville laying on hands.

When I met Arch for coffee in his office, he slid the paper across the table and let out a long sigh as I peered down at the photograph.

"Pitiful, right?" he said.

I could offer nothing more than a weary shrug.

"What's the matter?" he said. "You don't like the action?"

"I don't mind the action," I said. "I just don't like the advertising."

"Nick says it's necessary. I can't do any good for people if I don't win."

I glanced across the room at Averett, who was always on the phone or in some huddle with one or more shadowy-looking operators presumably tasked with unearthing some bombshell to blow up Marylou Greene's campaign.

"He's an asshole, Arch," I said.

"Maybe," Arch said. "But sometimes you need someone to shovel the shit so you can keep your own shirt clean."

Later that afternoon, between appointments, I dropped in on Vanessa at the house on the Boulevard. She knew what was on my mind.

"Don't say it," she said.

I couldn't help myself. "'Liberal Trojan horse'?"

"He's my husband," she said. "Would you have said no if you were me? Would you have said no if he'd asked *you*?"

"Here's a better question," I said. "Would *you* have asked *him*?"

"We've put a lot into this," she said. "And it's not just for Arch. It's for all of us. You too."

"I just didn't think—I mean, is this the spirit of Nashville?"

"Maybe it's not the same Nashville you knew before you left," she said.

"Or maybe it is," I said. "Maybe it always was."

"Thanks for the lecture. Don't you have something to paint?"

Rather than feeling affronted, I felt chastened. Who was I to question her? She was guilty of nothing but loyalty. I'd made more than my share of compromises for love, after all.

Two weeks before the runoff, Arch called me into his office.

"I want you to reach out to your buddy Terrence," he said.

"Why?"

"I have a proposition for him."

The way he said it sounded wrong to me. "What'd you have in mind?"

"I need a little help in North Nashville," he said.

I reached for my cigarettes but remembered Arch didn't allow smoking in the office.

"I don't know, Arch," I said. "That would feel a little weird."

"I'm just asking you to make a phone call," he said. "I'll take it from there."

"All right," I said.

Terrence picked up on the third ring. "Charlie," he said.

"How'd you know it was me?" I asked.

"Caller ID," he said. "Got you in my contacts."

"I just got one of these things," I said. "I'm still learning my way around it. So what are you up to?"

"Gettin' swole," he said.

"Huh?"

"Working out."

"Oh," I said. "Right. Look, is this a bad time?"

"No, I'm good," he said. "You got me between sets."

"Okay."

Arch signaled to me to get on with it.

"Listen," I said. "I'm calling you for a favor. You know who Arch Creigh is, right?"

"Seen him on the TV. Spirit of Nashville."

"Yeah," I said. "Well, he's an old friend of mine, remember?"

"I remember," he said. "What do you need?"

"Arch wants to meet you."

I heard muffled voices in the background. It sounded like Terrence had placed his hand over the receiver.

"Terrence?" I said.

"Yeah, I'm here," he replied. "He with you now?"

"He is," I said.

"Let me talk to him."

I handed Arch the phone.

"Terrence," he said. "Arch Creigh."

Arch motioned for me to leave the room.

I walked out of the office and sat down next to Nick Averett.

"What's going on?" I asked.

Averett shrugged.

A few minutes later, Arch emerged, slipping his suit jacket over his shoulders. He handed me my BlackBerry.

"Let's go," he said.

"Where are we going?" Averett asked.

"Bordeaux."

We met Terrence at his gym, an old warehouse filled with aging workout equipment, in front of a lot with a miniature football field chalk-lined into the grass, where every weekday afternoon and for a few hours a day during summers and holidays Terrence ran skills drills and calisthenics and organized touch games for some three to four dozen boys from the neighborhood. At the end of each practice, they took a knee and listened to Terrence give motivational speeches on the importance of hard work, staying clean, paying attention in school, going to church, and giving their lives up to God, etc. He called the program Forward Progress.

We found Terrence inside, finishing up a set of shoulder

shrugs, two enormous men in workout clothes spotting, a fourth in a white shirt and tie leaning up against the wall behind him. Terrence had the bar so loaded with forty-five-pound plates on both sides that it bent and rocked with each repetition. His trapezius muscles had become enormous, sinewy ridges of flesh. I felt certain he'd timed the set for the moment we came through the door.

"Damn, son," Arch said, putting on the homespun-everyman act he pulled off so well at American Legion halls and church socials. "What's that you got on there, five fifty?"

"Six seventy-five," said one of the two men beside Terrence, sliding the weights off the ends of the bar.

Terrence rounded the rack and opened his arms to embrace me. "Good to see you, Charlie," he said.

"You too."

"Terrence," Arch said, "thanks for letting us come over."

"Thank you for coming all the way out here," Terrence said. "Haven't seen much sign of you or your people in Bordeaux."

"I've been around a few times," Arch said.

"Guess I missed you," Terrence said.

Arch feigned interest in Forward Progress. Terrence humored him, walking us around the warehouse, pointing out its modest features, lamenting the lack of a suitable indoor facility, praising the kids he worked with and the good he felt the program was doing, both for them and himself.

"When you've been down and you get back up," he said, "you want to keep as many of those kids like you from following that dark path too, you feel me?"

"I sure do," Arch said. "You're doing good work here,

Terrence. This is exactly what this city needs more of. We could use something like Forward Progress in your old neighborhood too. And in Madison, and Edgehill, and Antioch."

"That's where we're heading," Terrence said. "God willing."

"I'd like to help you along."

The door opened. A group of men in suits and ties entered. I recognized the one in front; it was Rev Joseph, the preacher from Louella's funeral.

Terrence smiled. "Right on time, Rev," he said.

"God willing," Rev Joseph said.

"Reverend," Arch said. "Thank you for coming over."

"Glad to meet you," Rev said. "So what can we do you for, Mr. Arch?"

"Is there someplace we can talk alone?" Arch said.

Terrence tilted his head toward an open door that led to a windowless box of a room.

"Step into my office," he said.

Arch and Averett went in first, followed by Terrence and Rev Joseph. Once they were all in that small, cramped space, they shut the door behind them, leaving me and Rev Joseph's entourage with Terrence's enormous companions. One wore a red bandanna as a headband and a cutoff Tennessee Oilers sweatshirt. The other wore a T-shirt with a giant Warner Brothers WB emblem on the front, surrounded by the words IF YOU SEE THE POLICE . . . WARN A BROTHER!" Both had on those hideous baggy patterned bodybuilding pants worn by the sort of people who sell steroids in the locker room at Gold's Gym.

"You guys work out a lot?" I asked.

"Yeah," said the one in the bandanna.

"Cool," I said. "I think I'll have a smoke. Should I step outside?"

"The body is a temple, cuz," said the Warn a Brother guy.

"Right," I said.

By the time I went back in, the four who'd been meeting privately were coming out of the office. Arch and Terrence grinned and laughed as if it were Arch and not I whom Terrence had known almost all of his life. Rev Joseph was laughing as well. Nick Averett had the look of a man who had picked up the wrong suitcase at the airport by accident and arrived home to open it up and find it full of stacks of cash.

"Pleasure doing business with you, Mr. Mayor," Terrence said.

"Let's win first," Arch said. "But thank you, Terrence. We'll see you Sunday."

Arch and Averett started toward the car. Rev Joseph and Arch's workout companions headed back inside. For a moment, Terrence and I were alone.

"What the hell happened in there?" I asked.

"Politics," Terrence said.

He laughed.

"What is it?" I asked.

"Nothing," he said. "You be careful, you hear me?"

"Careful of what?"

"Nothing," he repeated.

The same sadness I'd felt at Louella's funeral crept up again.

"I gotta go," I said.

Terrence nodded.

"I'll pray for you," he said.

The next Sunday, at last, I made good on my promise to

return to the Lighthouse Church. I came in behind Arch, alongside Averett and Walsh and Lonnie, Arch's assistant. We were led up to a reserved pew right in front of the pulpit. The church was packed; people stood in the rear and along the side aisles. My shirt was already stained with sweat before Rev Joseph and Terrence entered from behind the altar.

The service began with a series of hymns and a raucous performance by the choir, backed both by the organ and a full band, with drums, bass, electric guitar, and a horn section. The dislocation I'd felt years before at Louella's funeral came flooding back to me.

Terrence spoke first. His skills had matured over the years. In terms of charisma, he was every bit Arch's equal. The words seemed almost irrelevant. I was keenly aware even then of the irony: how, if you stripped away race and economics, style and culture, Arch and Terrence could easily have traded places.

"Jesus tells us," Terrence said, "render unto Caesar what is Caesar's. We know what matters in the kingdom of heaven, don't we?"

Amens cascaded from all around.

"But sometimes, we got to do God's work in the voting booth, you feel me?"

There were nods and murmurs of assent. Everyone there knew where Terrence was going.

"We got a choice to make, and we got to pray about it," he said. "We got two folks who can lead us. I've only seen one of them up in Bordeaux. He's right here today. Him and me, we go way back. I know his heart. Y'all listen to what he has to say, hear me?"

The crowd grew still and quiet. Arch stood, and Terrence

embraced him as if they were the best of friends. Arch took the microphone.

"Thank you, Terrence," he said, "for allowing me to be here today and share a few words with you all about my vision for the future of our city."

He paid appropriate homage to the history of the civil rights movement in Nashville, from the early years of Fisk, the legacy of W. E. B. DuBois and James Weldon Johnson and Aaron Douglas. If anyone took offense or even felt cynical about the blatant pandering, they didn't let on. It was a dance with which all present were familiar.

"But let me get to what really matters to all of us here," Arch said. "There's been so much talk in recent years about how Nashville is booming, and how that's good for us all. I want you to ask yourself: Has it been good for you? There has been so much growth. How have you felt that growth? Are your kids' schools better than they were five years ago? Are your opportunities increasing as quickly as your taxes? Do you recognize your neighborhoods? Do you feel like we're moving in the right direction?"

The crowd was restless. No one seemed to disagree. There was the usual talking-point bullshit. Then Arch did something Terrence and Rev Joseph were expecting, but which came to me as a complete surprise.

"I don't think many of you know this," he said, "but I've been to the Lighthouse before, many years ago. The occasion was the funeral of Mrs. Louella Robie, Terrence's grandmother, one of the most loyal and faithful members of this congregation, for many years."

I felt the pulse of the room quicken. I watched the faces of the parishioners, so as to avoid making eye contact with Arch. I could not help but look at Terrence, who met my gaze but did not break character. Perhaps he thought I knew this was coming.

"I think of Miss Louella often," Arch said. "She worked hard all her life, took care of the people she loved, raised her kids alongside her husband, Carl, and then raised Terrence on her own after Carl passed. And she might as well have been a mother to the children of the families she served, and they loved her."

Everything he said was true. Arch had been to the Lighthouse on the occasion of Lou's funeral—to pick me up in the parking lot. He had, in fact, met Terrence then, and so neither of them could be accused of outright falsehood. Arch never knew Louella, but his description of her life was accurate, down to the name of her deceased husband and the basic narrative of Terrence's childhood and the families for whom Lou had worked as a maid. If anyone remembered that funeral, they might recall seeing a white boy there who was a friend of Terrence's, but would anyone remember that the white boy they saw was me and not Arch?

If they did, they weren't going to say anything about it.

I tried not to glare as Arch finished up his little charade with a pitch about preserving neighborhoods and holding down the cost of housing and the usual talking points about the spirit of Nashville. When he was finished, he handed the microphone to Rev Joseph and sat back down. I leaned up from my seat behind him and whispered in his ear.

"You might have told me you were going to do that," I said.

Arch glanced over his shoulder, bemused.

"Do what?" he said.

Rev Joseph finished off the act by offering a prayer for Arch's candidacy and informing the congregation that the church bus would be making the rounds on Election Day to make sure anyone who wished to cast a vote would be able to get to the polls.

Arch spent the better part of an hour on the sidewalk outside the church, flanked by Terrence and Rev Joseph. Two local television news crews were on hand. Arch, Terrence, and the reverend gave interviews both together and individually. I stood off to the side with Nick Averett.

"Your idea, I presume?" I said.

"That's why I get paid the big bucks, Charlie-boy," he said.

I could only shake my head.

"If you don't like the way the sausage gets made," he said, "stay out of the fucking kitchen."

ARCH HOSTED A viewing party for the five o'clock news in his campaign office. The act looked even better on television than in person. Terrence played his part perfectly. Arch came off looking like a white savior, sent down from heaven to save black Nashville.

"Fucking brilliant," Averett crowed. "Just perfect."

Arch opened a bottle of good bourbon, splashed a healthy shot into a half dozen Styrofoam coffee cups, and passed them out. We emptied the cups, and Arch poured another round. I tried to act happier than I felt. The only answer at the moment seemed to be another shot of bourbon—and another, and another. I wanted to drink the whole bottle, and might well have done so if not for the news that came when there was a knock at the door. When I opened it, I found Lonnie standing there, her face ashen.

"What's wrong, Lonnie?" Arch asked.

"Your wife," she said.

TWELVE

Arch reached the hospital in time to see the baby born. They had planned to name her Hope, after Arch's grandmother. Vanessa held her and kissed her tiny head and touched her little fingers and toes before the life went out of her. Afterward, they took Vanessa into surgery.

I sat with Arch outside the room where his child had been born and died. There were loud voices on the other side of the door at the end of the hall—Jamie, trying to talk his way in. Arch lifted his head and rubbed his eyes.

"Stay here," I said. "I'll take care of it."

Through the windows in the door, I could see Jamie upbraiding a stone-faced nurse. I pushed through and grasped him by the shoulders and led him away.

"Hey," I said.

"Come here, brother," he said.

He pulled me into a tight embrace, burying his face in my shoulder and weeping.

"Have you seen her yet?" he asked.

"She's in surgery."

"Holy shit," he said. "What for?"

"I don't really know. Something's wrong. She was bleeding a lot."

"Is she gonna die?"

"I don't know," I said. "They won't say much. I don't think they know what's going on."

"Oh Christ," Jamie moaned.

"Calm down," I said. "I'm sure she'll be fine. It's under control."

"But the baby," Jamie said.

I couldn't summon a response.

"Come here, man," he said, and again I was in his arms, and I felt grateful for Jamie, who, for all of his flaws, had no facades.

"How's Arch?" he asked.

"Not great. And your dad's a mess."

"Dad's here?"

"Do you want to talk to him?"

"Fuck, no."

"All right," I said. "Why don't we go downstairs and get a cup of coffee? God knows, I could use one."

This was how Arch had first made use of me all those years ago, after all: serving as a distraction for Jamie.

We sat at a small table near a window facing out onto a parking lot a few floors below. I watched the small bodies passing in and out of the light from the lampposts as people came and went, some coming to work, going home, some carrying flowers or balloons. Beyond the reflection: darkness. Inside it:

tepid coffee, dirty windows, the loneliness of scattered cars, the shadows of distant trees.

We went back upstairs. Vanessa was still in surgery. Jim stood by the window, perhaps looking out at the same view I'd had in the cafeteria—the same darkness from a different angle. Jamie went to Arch and wrapped his arms around him. Jim left his post, gently pried Jamie away, and led him down the hallway. Arch leaned against the wall, his eyes fixed on the floor, hands stuffed into his pockets.

"What happened?" I said.

"Endometriosis."

"What's that?"

"It's complicated," he said. "They're taking her uterus out. She doesn't know yet. They had to cut her open before they could see what was wrong. What they found—it's bad. I can't even describe it."

His face was a mixture of grief and horror. "I had to give consent," he said. "She would have died otherwise."

"I know," I said. "I know."

A nurse with a stubble beard, a stringy ponytail, and a pair of round wire-rimmed glasses came through the door.

"Are you ready, Mr. Creigh?" he asked.

Arch nodded.

"Where are you going?" I asked.

"To see the baby," he said.

"Let me come with you."

"All right."

We followed the nurse down the hallway to a dimly lit room. There she was, in a basinet, wrapped in a blanket so that only her tiny wrinkled head was visible. Arch peeled the blanket away so that he could see the whole body. He stroked the child's head gently and bent and kissed it. As he stepped back, his shoulders began to shake. I grasped him and held him there and waited and listened to his choked sobs, and I felt it too.

VANESSA WAS PLACED in the intensive care unit after the surgery. Arch was present when she regained consciousness. She seemed too heavily medicated to understand what had happened. And she kept asking for the baby; the drugs made her forget. Or maybe she just kept hoping the death of her daughter had been a dream.

Arch went back and forth from sitting with Vanessa to wandering up and down the hallways, his expression inscrutable. Maybe he had forgotten what it meant to feel powerless. Maybe he'd never really known.

WITH A BIT of persuasion from Averett, Arch roused himself from the darkness of his guilt and grief by deciding that the brave thing to do was to soldier on for the sake of the city. Averett spun the story with skill. The news media played along. The Greene campaign expressed sympathy. And so Arch and Vanessa's tragedy only enhanced his prospects.

Vanessa went home after two days. She could barely walk to the bathroom. Without Arch's knowledge, Averett had him photographed through the door, sitting by Vanessa's bedside, holding her hand while she slept. Averett leaked the photo and feigned righteous fury in a statement to the press at the outrageous invasion of privacy. Every outlet ran the picture.

When Arch saw the photograph in the newspaper, he shook his head.

"Vanessa's not going to like this," he told me.

"Too late now," I said.

"I had nothing to do with it, you know."

I didn't argue. I had learned by then how men in Arch's position depend on people like Averett to anticipate their less honorable wishes and needs and fulfill them without prompting.

NANCY HALTOM FLEW in from Naples. At some point, I ended up alone with her, sitting on the couch near the windows facing out to the rose garden, where Jim could be seen walking around with Dolly. Nancy leaned back and rested her head on the cushion so that her hair swept across it, her neck lengthened, and the falling light caught her face just so. In that moment of weary grief, the bitterness fell away from her expression.

"She's a pretty girl," Nancy said, gazing out the window. "Favors her mother."

"She certainly does."

"Is that hard for you? To see your mother's eyes and nose and mouth in that precious little face?"

"I don't see her as often as I'd like," I said. "The last time before today was at her birthday party. I wasn't going to go, but Arch and Vanessa insisted."

"And how did that go?"

"Fine, I guess."

In truth, it had been dreadful. Jim was still having difficulty looking at Dolly without crying. He'd never arranged a child's birthday party on his own before, and so he overdid the whole affair. The farm was transformed into a child's paradise, with mechanical rides and a petting zoo, balloon animal guys, and pony rides. He invited every kid in Dolly's grade at school and all of their parents, not a one of whom was within fifteen years of him in age. When I arrived, the young parents were getting loaded on free booze while the children ran amok.

"Jim is much more attentive to your baby sister than he ever was to either of our children," Nancy said.

"He has to be."

"Not really. He could send her to boarding school in the fall and sleepaway camp in the summer, and never have to deal with her outside of a few odd weekends and holidays. I wonder if he's more interested because he's old enough to be her grandfather. Maybe grandparents should raise all the children."

It seemed a good time to change the subject. "How long are you staying in Nashville?" I asked.

"Until tomorrow. Vanessa asked me to leave. Says she's fine. I don't think she's quite ready to accept me as a doting mother yet."

"I expect she just wants to be alone."

"But you'll be here, won't you, Charlie?"

"That's what she wants."

"It hasn't taken you very long to resume your place at the right hand, has it?"

"I hadn't thought about it."

She smiled.

"They love you, you know," she said. "Both of them."

"I know," I said.

Later on, after Vanessa had gone to bed, I sat up and had

a drink with the former Mr. and Mrs. Jim Haltom. Jim and Nancy were natural together, the way they must have been at some point long before the twins or even Arch came along. They teased each other, told stories I'd never heard about their early lives together, when they'd experienced the Belle Meade version of struggle. I could see that they had, in fact, once been in love. The thought occurred to me that, with my mother gone, the two of them might reconcile. What an ending to the story that would have been.

I DROVE OUT to the cabin with Jamie in his Suburban two days later. Scott was just putting away the riding mower when we arrived. Jim's new maid, Verneta, was inside preparing the bedrooms. We had brought sandwiches, and so the four of us sat at the table on the porch and ate. When we were finished, Jamie and I followed Scott out to the shed. We took shovels and picks and work gloves, and the three of us went out on Arch's four-man ATV to the spot in the woods across the pond where Arch's father was buried. The earth was soft and pliant for the first few feet but got denser and rockier below. Jamie threw himself into the labor, and the sweat dripped down from his shirt to stain his pants. Finally, Scott deemed the hole sufficiently deep and wide, and we sat on David Creigh's bench. Scott opened the cooler he'd brought and took out three beers, and we drank them quickly and each had another, drinking more slowly the second time.

The next morning, we were up and ready long before the helicopter landed out in the center of the field. When it arrived, we carried Vanessa from the door to a bed Scott had made for her in the back of the pickup and again from the pickup into the cabin and back to the master bedroom. Scott drove the casket out to the clearing. Is there anything more heartbreaking than an infant's casket? I know there must be, but I have never seen it.

Jim and Dolly and Nancy were there, and Arch had brought Arch's mom and Bray Hudson, the rector at Saint John's. Callie Whitaker, Nancy's favorite caterer, had driven a van out earlier in the morning and prepared a buffet lunch. There was no set schedule; when Vanessa was ready, Scott would drive her out to the clearing, and the rest of us would walk. Bray Hudson would conduct a short service. Afterward, we'd come back to the house to eat. Vanessa and Arch would stay at the cabin while everyone else who'd come out on the helicopter flew back to Nashville. I was waiting to be told what to do.

For nearly an hour, Vanessa remained alone in the bedroom. Scott drove the priest to the clearing. Arch wandered down to the dock alone. The rest of us drank coffee and talked in hushed voices. I watched Arch, standing where we used to sit casting spinner baits for bream and bass until the sun set.

"Let me see if I can help her get dressed," Nancy said.

She stood and smoothed her slacks and strode back to the bedroom, a hint of the old confidence in her gait.

"Maybe I should go check on Arch," Jamie said.

"Probably better to leave him alone," I said.

"Yeah," Jamie replied. "I'll talk to him later. Make sure he's okay."

At last, Nancy emerged from the bedroom. "She's ready," she said.

I sent Jamie down to the dock to collect Arch. From the foot of the steps, I watched them walk back toward us, arms around each other. The sight buoyed me, less for the apparent tenderness than for its value as evidence that Arch was not too far gone to tolerate a moment with Jamie.

I followed Jim on our way around the pond. Dolly walked between us, holding both of our hands. She had grown up enough for me really to start seeing my mother in her. I glanced over at Jim. I didn't think I'd ever be able to love him, but I'd certainly run out of resentment. He'd more than paid for his sins in suffering.

"If I have a baby one day," Dolly said, "I hope it doesn't die."

"I'm sure it won't."

"But Nessa's baby is with Mommy now," Dolly said. "Daddy said so."

"If Daddy says so," I said, "it must be true."

By the time we reached the burial plot, the priest had changed into his robes and set the table for Communion. A few minutes later, we heard the hum of the ATV and the sound of the wheels rolling gently through the pine needles. Scott stopped it at the edge of the clearing and Arch and Jamie helped Vanessa climb out of her seat. I don't remember what the priest said; I wasn't listening. When he was finished, he opened the Book of Common Prayer, and gave each of us the body and the blood, and we prayed again.

Vanessa stood and Arch helped her walk up to the casket. She trailed her hand across the surface of the little stainless-steel box and stood still for a moment. Then she nodded, and Arch helped her back into the ATV, and they drove back to the cabin, where Vanessa disappeared into her bedroom again.

Jamie and I were to sit down for lunch and wait for everyone to leave before going back out to cover the casket with earth, but I didn't feel like I could swallow food. So I changed out of my suit and put on an old pair of jeans and a flannel and slipped out the back door. When I arrived at the gravesite, I found Arch, alone on his father's bench, gazing toward the sky.

"I'll come back," I said.

"No," he said. "We'll do it together."

I took a shovel for myself and handed the second one to Arch. Tossing the dirt into the hole was much less taxing than digging it up.

"Vanessa's going to stay out here for a few days," Arch said. "I have to go back tonight. Will you look after her?"

"What about Jim and Nancy? They can't handle things?"

"Jim needs to get home," he said. "Dolly has school. Nancy's leaving for Florida tonight."

"Tonight?"

"Vanessa asked her to go," Arch said. "Listen, Charlie, this is all a lot to take. But I need you here. You're the only person I trust."

I stopped and set the blade of my shovel on the ground. Arch pulled this kind of shit way too often. It was as if he was tormenting me with my own loyalty.

"Maybe you should stay too, Arch," I said. "Just for a day."

"You know I can't," he said. "We're so close to the end. People are depending on me. I can't let them down."

"Maybe we shouldn't pretend you're just doing this for other people."

For a moment, I wished I hadn't spoken. Who was I to say such things to him? But his eyes softened and he nodded, and I could breathe again.

A shadow passed overhead. Above us, a large bird was circling beneath the sun.

"I have to go, you know," Arch said.

I sucked in a long breath and let it out slowly. Arch took his shovel back up again and returned to sifting dirt from the pile down into the hole. When we were finished, he went over to the bench where he'd left his clothes and put his dress shirt back on. I helped him with his jacket. He dusted off his shoes and straightened his tie.

"Ready?"

I nodded, and we began the long walk: along the path of soft pine needles through the woods, out to the field and the path along the rim of the pond, and back toward the cabin.

"You're not worried that you'll look cold, leaving your grieving wife alone for politics?"

He stopped, turned toward me, and smiled.

"I'm not leaving her alone," he said. "I'm leaving her with my best friend."

AFTER NANCY SAID goodbye the next morning, Jim and Dolly drove her to the airport. It looked like nothing so much as a happy couple taking their granddaughter off on an adventure.

I went to check on Vanessa. She was awake, propped up on pillows. Arch had left earlier.

"How are you feeling?" I asked.

"Better," she said.

"Can I fix you something? You need to eat."

"Not yet." Her eyes drifted off toward the windows. "So it's just the two of us."

"The way I've always wanted it."

"Don't tease."

"You know it's true," I said.

"Your life would be incomplete without Arch."

"I lived without him for nearly a decade."

"But he was always on your mind."

"So were you."

She sat up and pushed her hair back.

"I think I'd like to get out of bed," she said. "Maybe walk around a bit. See how it goes."

"Only if you eat some breakfast."

"I'm not hungry."

"You need something in your stomach so the medication won't make you nauseous," I said. "Toast and eggs?"

"Toast and eggs."

I brought the tray to her bed and then helped her up and held her hand as she made ginger steps down the stairs. She told me she felt stronger, that it was more in her head than anything else.

"I can't stop thinking about this void inside me. Then again," she said, smiling weakly, "I've lost a ton of weight. Maybe emergency hysterectomies will be the next big diet fad in Belle Meade."

"There's my girl."

We took a turn around the porch and went back up to the bedroom. I called Arch—no answer; I left a message. Vanessa was already asleep. I couldn't help myself; I went for my sketch-book. It was like we were seventeen again.

After an hour or so, she opened her eyes and saw me there in the corner, drawing her.

"Can I see?" she asked.

I turned the pad.

"You make me look so much better than in real life," she said.

"I draw what I see."

I went back to work. I was so intent on making the picture perfect that Vanessa startled me when she spoke.

"I knew I'd pay a price one day," she said.

I put the pad down in my lap. "Life doesn't work that way."

"Oh, yes, it does," she said. "I should have guessed that this was how God would get back at me."

"Nonsense."

"Don't you believe in karma?"

"No, I don't," I said. "Spend a few years watching people who don't have two pesos to rub together on their knees every day in front of the Blessed Virgin and getting nothing for it but the promise of salvation after death, and you'll stop believing any of us get what we deserve. And in any case, I never thought it was a mistake."

"What did you think?"

"I thought you were very afraid," I said. "And very brave."

"Your mother was brave," she said. "I was a coward."

"My mother's options were more limited."

"That doesn't make me feel better."

"I know."

She looked off, out the window.

"I don't deserve to be a mother," she said.

"Please don't say that," I said.

We left it at that. She was not open to persuasion. I would never convince her of her own innocence.

ARCH CALLED A little after noon. I spoke to him for a few minutes and then handed the phone to Vanessa. They stayed on for a very long time. I went outside on the porch to smoke. When she was finished, Vanessa hobbled out to join me. I'd lit another cigarette by then; she reached for it and took a long drag.

"Arch wanted me to take care of you," I said, "not poison you."

She eased down onto one of the rocking chairs and closed her eyes. "A little smoke can't be any worse for me than these painkillers," she said. "I feel like a zombie."

"If the doctor says to take them, it's okay, right?"

Vanessa opened her eyes and sat up. "Arch and Nick," she said.

"What about them?"

"They're . . . God, I can't even say it."

I couldn't look at her.

"You didn't know?" she asked.

The thought *had* occurred to me. The way they looked at each other, how they were often huddled together, laughing. I had assumed the suspicion I'd felt was just jealousy for the old rapport I'd never quite recovered since my return.

The silence seemed to go on forever. I lit another cigarette, took a deep drag, watched and waited for the smoke to dissipate before I spoke.

"How do you feel about that?" I asked.

"How would you feel about it?"

"I wouldn't stand for it."

"Really?" she asked. "What would you do?"

"I'd tell him to end it," I said. "Or else."

"Should I have said that to Arch when the two of you were always running off for the weekend together all those years ago?"

"I don't know what you mean," I said.

"You think I didn't notice the way you looked at him?" she said. "You were so in love with him. It would have been embarrassing if it wasn't so heartbreakingly sweet."

I didn't know how to respond. There was no point in denying it; she wouldn't have believed me anyway.

"We were kids. We didn't know what we were doing. It was a phase, like puberty," I said. "I thought maybe he'd outgrown that part of himself."

"You don't outgrow it, Charlie."

"I did."

"You're different. You aren't gay. It was just Arch for you."

"Do the two of you have some sort of arrangement?"

"No. I just look the other way, and he behaves as if he doesn't know that I know. It's not that unusual. People have lived like this for centuries."

"Only because they had to. And you don't. Neither does he."

"He does to have the things he wants."

"What about what you want?"

"Love isn't just about sex, Charlie. And marriage isn't just about love. Besides, as you well know, I have secrets of my own."

I tried to think of something else to talk about. Nothing came to mind.

Vanessa pointed at my cigarette. "Give me one," she said.

"You shouldn't."

"Please, Charlie. You're not my doctor."

I gave her a cigarette, and we sat and smoked together. When we were finished, she went back up to the bedroom.

I found her sleeping soundly when I went in. I did not allow myself to watch her for more than a moment; my heart could not bear it.

Hours passed. She did not wake. Arch did not come home or call. The sky grew dark. I fixed myself a drink and sank into the couch. The bourbon made me drowsy. I closed my eyes and drifted off into a dreamless sleep.

THIRTEEN

As expected, Arch became mayor. He named Terrence Robie the head of a new commission on racial reconciliation and the recognition of black history. More quietly, Terrence's Forward Progress after-school football program received a generous private donation to add lights, bleachers, and a turf field, and to knock down and replace the old warehouse with a new gymnasium. Marylou Greene, stung but still shrewd, accepted Arch's offer to serve as executive director of the Metropolitan Planning Commission. Nick Averett became Arch's chief of staff, Bart Walsh his deputy.

Vanessa performed admirably in the role of political spouse, showing up whenever required, smiling, saying all the right things. But at home in the great house on the Boulevard, the facade dropped. The nursery she'd prepared for Hope became a shrine to her grief, a retreat from which she rarely emerged. Arch made appropriate gestures toward helping her move on, but Vanessa refused, as if to give up her sorrow would be to accept that she was not to blame for it, and that was something she was not yet ready to do. So he gave up and went back to work. What little free time he had, he spent with Averett. No one considered this inappropriate. Averett was Arch's chief of staff, after all.

I didn't judge him. Instead, I did what I could to fill the breach. I didn't feel it at the time, but looking back, I must have sensed opportunity in Vanessa's decision to cloister herself, as it afforded me the chance to fill the role of doting husband, which Arch had at least temporarily abdicated while he busied himself serving the city. No one appeared to find this arrangement inappropriate either. Irony of ironies: everyone in the Creighs' circle thought I was gay—the homo artiste, providing safe, platonic companionship for Vanessa while Arch was preoccupied with more pressing and important matters.

But I also understood Vanessa as Arch never could, and not just because I loved her. Despite knowing better, I have never found the strength of will to stop looking backward. This is why I ran away, I think. Yet even when I found a life in a place so far removed from the leafy lanes of Belle Meade and the people there who had so entranced me, I never stopped looking toward the northern horizon.

Perhaps this willful inertia, born out of the stubborn refusal to accept that there is only today, only now, only tomorrow, is what separated me from Arch even more than the more obvious differences. When it came to the problem of regret, Arch was like a shark: if he stopped swimming, he would die. He survived by refusing to grieve or worry or look for someone to blame—least of all, himself.

IN THE THIRD year of Arch's term, the world became reordered. I was at home, alone, finishing a portrait of a tax attorney's teenage daughter, when Arch called. It was just after nine in the morning, Tuesday, September 11, 2001.

"Are you watching?" he asked.

"Watching what?"

"Stop whatever you're doing and turn on the television."

I'd been to the World Trade Center once, with Arch and the Haltoms on a fall weekend jaunt to New York. We saw the museums and a few plays and a game at Yankee Stadium. We took the elevator to the observation deck at the top of one of the towers—I'm not sure which. I remember only the magnificence of the view and that we rode back down the elevator with a group of college-aged German tourists who kept chanting *"Eins, zwei, drei, wooooh!"* all the way to the bottom floor.

In the weeks after 9/11, I heard so many stories. One person's cousin was in the first tower. Another had a brother who had missed the flight that hit the Pentagon. This person and that person, each with a story of a near miss or a tragedy. Everyone scrambling for a piece of the nightmare. Nothing else mattered anymore. It hadn't mattered before, either; we just didn't know any better.

Arch and Vanessa were often away over the next few weeks, attending funerals and memorials, in both official and personal capacities. I kept on painting. Art felt like a hollow consolation in those days. At times, it even felt like an insult.

In late January, Arch summoned me to his office.

"I assume you've heard the rumors about Thorndike," he said.

"No," I said.

I'd met Jeff Thorndike once at a fundraiser Arch hosted for his last campaign. Thorndike had started adult life as a trial lawyer. Midcareer, he'd tried a case against a company that made cigarette lighters. A three-year-old girl had taken her mother's lighter off a table and leaked fluid all over her arm and down to her torso before managing somehow to spark the flint wheel and light herself on fire. Thorndike won a massive settlement for the family and forced the company to redesign their lighters with one of those annoying safety locks. The case garnered enough attention from the media to make him a regular on nightly news broadcasts. Before long, he was showing up on the cable networks as a "legal expert." Someone in Hollywood liked the stern, serious look of his high forehead and hooded brow. He ended up with a two-decade career as an actor playing generals and admirals, district attorneys and judges.

Thorndike looked and acted the part so well that he made an easy transition into the real thing. Despite not having practiced law for twenty years nor having run for any public office whatsoever, he won election to the US Senate by twenty points. He'd done nothing remarkable as a senator; in fact, his most notable accomplishment seemed to have been having the poorest attendance record of any sitting member of Congress.

"What is it?" I asked. "Is he going to run for president?"

"He's stepping down," Arch said. "He's not even going to finish his term. There's going to be a special election."

"Is he in some kind of trouble?"

"I don't think so," Arch said. "His son's death hit him hard."

"I didn't know about that."

"Heroin," Arch said. "Can you believe it? The kid had just graduated from Georgetown Law. Apparently, he got hooked on painkillers he'd been prescribed after knee surgery. That sort of thing is getting awfully common, you know."

"What," I said. "Upper-class junkies?"

"It's no joke," Arch said. "Anyway, Thorndike said he'd been planning to retire for a while."

"So you're running," I said.

"You bet."

"Isn't that a big jump?"

"Not when you're following a guy who got elected without ever having held public office before."

"Sure," I said. "But he's older. And he played a senator on TV."

"Yeah, well, I'm gonna play one on TV too."

"Who do you have to beat?"

"The Democrats are putting up Cole Bridwell, but I'm not worried about him. The big fight will be the primary."

Coleman Bridwell had run unopposed in the last two congressional elections, but his district was Nashville, an oasis of moderation in a desert of conservatism. Nashville was split with a leftward tilt, and Memphis was still solid for the Democrats, but the rest of the state was fire-engine red.

"So who do you really have to beat, if Bridwell doesn't worry you?"

"Dan Baird."

Even I had heard of Dan Baird. He was a lot like Arch, almost a doppelgänger from a different generation. When he'd gotten his start, he was young, handsome, and charismatic, a political outsider, scion of an old Nashville dynasty. His family had owned a home on the Boulevard for nearly a century. Like Arch, his inherited wealth came from the insurance business. He'd spent fifteen years as a surgeon before running for Congress in Chattanooga. He'd then served three terms before stepping down to start a charitable foundation that sent doctors and nurses to combat AIDS in sub-Saharan Africa.

"I don't know, Arch," I said. "That guy's friends with Bono."

"Being friends with Bono won't win you too many votes outside Davidson County," Arch said.

"What does Vanessa think?" I asked.

"You're the first person I've told besides Averett," he said.

"Why me?"

"I want your opinion. What does your gut tell you?"

"My gut tells me you've already made up your mind."

"I won't get a better chance for a long, long time," he said. "What do you think?"

"Can I smoke in here?"

"Follow me," he said. "I know a good place."

Arch led me to an inconspicuous door in the corner of the hallway outside his office, which opened to a dark stairwell leading up to the roof. I lit up. Arch gazed out toward the Cumberland.

"Master of all he surveys," I said.

"You didn't answer my question."

"I'll draw up another logo, if that's what you have in mind."

"I don't need a logo," he said. "I need a body man."

"I don't follow."

"A body man. Like an assistant, only you're not typing up letters, you're just hanging with me, helping me out."

"Like your shadow."

"More like my conscience."

"I'm busy," I said.

"I need you," Arch said.

"I've got work set up for the next three months."

"Oh, come off it. Here's your chance to do something more meaningful than painting pictures."

I tossed my cigarette onto the ground and stamped it out.

"Fuck you, Arch," I said.

"That came out wrong," he said.

"No, it didn't," I said. "And let me tell you something. I don't really care about making a difference in the world. In my experience, people who try to make a difference just make things worse. I just want to paint and be left alone."

"And play house with my wife."

I glanced up at him. His expression betrayed no emotion. I wondered if this was his true self or the public one he'd cultivated over the years to the point of being able to become whoever he needed to be in the moment to get what he wanted from people.

"She's my friend too, Arch," I said. "She's been my friend almost as long as you."

"Are you in love with all of your friends?" he asked.

"Not all of them," I said.

A police siren rang out from the street below. The precinct office stood across from the building.

"I'm not angry," he said. "Vanessa needed someone. I had to work. She needed a distraction. It seemed safe. Who better than you?"

I had not thought of what I'd been doing as a distraction, for either of us. It certainly wasn't meant as a favor to Arch.

A plane passed overhead. I drew in a deep breath.

"Come work for me, Charlie," he said. "I need you."

"What about Nick?" I said.

"Nick is moving on."

"Where to?"

"Atlanta."

"To do what?"

"There's a tight governor's race down there. They offered him a lot of money."

"Your doing?"

"I helped."

"And how does Nick feel about that?"

"He'll warm up to it. Atlanta's a great place to be."

"Queer capital of the South," I said.

"I don't know what you mean."

"I just mean, maybe Atlanta's a better place than Nashville for Nick."

"Be careful, bud," he said. "I mean it."

"You too," I said. "I mean it."

"So you'll do it?"

A tense quiet set in. Arch leaned against the wall in his shirtsleeves, arms crossed, his expression calm.

"Yeah," I said. "I'll do it."

Arch smiled. "This is going to work out perfectly," he said. "You'll see."

FOURTEEN

Thus began my short, ignoble career in politics. It was really just for a few months, or so I told myself. I pushed back the delivery dates for the portraits I had been commissioned to do and bought a new wardrobe—with Arch's credit card, naturally. Brooks Brothers suits and ties and shirts, polos and chinos, loafers, and boat shoes. I cut my hair and started shaving every day. Arch rose early and went to bed late and expected me beside him almost every minute he was awake. In the morning, while he worked out in the gym at the house or whatever hotel we happened to be staying in, he took a briefing on the day's schedule from Bart Walsh, who'd taken over Nick Averett's role. Afterward, we might meet over breakfast with a donor or a local honcho of one sort or the other, followed by a photo-op visit to a school or church or community center. When we didn't have a lunch meeting, we ate in the back of a car on the way to yet another venue for handshaking and bullshitting. In the evenings, after we'd made our last pilgrimage to kiss rings and babies, and Arch had delivered his final recitation of the stump speech, we'd head back home or to the hotel and huddle up for debate prep.

Vanessa came along when Walsh thought she needed to be there. One would never suspect from watching her that she had any reservations at all about the future her husband had chosen for the both of them. At home, nothing changed. She remained consumed by her grief, so she did not seem to miss my company.

The inner circle was not much different than the one Arch had started with when he ran for mayor: Walsh, Lonnie, Jim. I'd been hanging around forever but had never been a part of things in this way. Arch brought in another experienced political operator to run his campaign: Andy Goldberg, late of Virginia, where he'd flipped the governor's office for the GOP. He had much in common with Averett, but his penchant for fast food, beer, and strip clubs made him an unlikely candidate to replace his predecessor in the more compromising capacity.

The other new addition was Marcus Hughes, a kid Arch had recruited from Terrence's after-school program for admission to Yeatman. Marcus had been given a special leave of absence from school to work as an intern. Yeatman benefited from the optics almost as much as Arch. This sort of shameless tokenism was not perceived as such by the voters of Tennessee.

Goldberg loved the idea.

"We need a little something to offset all those shots of Dan Baird hugging little Africans," he said.

Marcus didn't seem to feel used. He couldn't have been more eager. I saw a great deal of myself in him. He had been plucked up and set down in a den of opulence and power. Arch treated him as Jim had once treated me, though with even greater attention and affection. Other, more typical interns were given menial tasks, verbally abused, ignored unless needed to do something no one else wanted to do. Marcus got nothing but smiles and warm words. No one even sent him out for coffee or told him to empty the trash.

He was bright and curious, quick-witted, and self-possessed, and quickly picked up, as I had, how to dress the part: the chinos, the button-down oxfords. I knew from experience that these qualities had not endeared him to the boys he'd grown up around. To them, he was an Uncle Tom, an Oreo, a sellout. I suspect Marcus had not survived the junior school at Yeatman unscathed by the sort of ugliness that finds its most honest, unfiltered voice in the mouths of pubescent boys—but he struck me as the type of kid who cared less about fitting in with his peers than about earning the praise of adult authority figures. He so delighted in Arch's attentions that he could not possibly have recognized himself as a prop. And I liked him too much to disillusion him.

Or maybe I was the one under the illusion. Maybe Marcus knew exactly who he was dealing with and what he was doing, from the beginning. Maybe he was just wearing the mask we wanted to see. Maybe to those who possess it, ambition is an instinct as natural and unconscious as any other, the same kind of winnowing characteristic that led one ancient organism to crawl out of the water while another stayed behind, awaiting extinction. Perhaps Arch recognized in Marcus a kindred spirit.

It was Marcus, after all, who came forward with the tool Arch needed once again to hack away at a deficit which had begun to seem insurmountable.

We were listening to Walsh read down the day's agenda the morning after the first debate. Arch hadn't done poorly, exactly, but Baird had come off much better. The primary election was shaping up to be a referendum on poise and experience. Not only was Dan Baird a physician and a congressman, but he'd been a national champion in policy debate at Montgomery Bell. Arch did fine, but he looked like what he was: young, opportunistic, inexperienced. The outsider card didn't help him much, given that Baird had walked away from Congress to serve God and save Africa. Arch's charm and intelligence couldn't compensate for the facts.

Goldberg had been boiling his brains and burning up the phone, looking for some liability in Dan Baird, some soft underbelly where he could slide in a knife that might disembowel the good doctor's righteous image, but nothing had yet to yield. Dan Baird, it seemed, was that rarest of all things: an honest man, true to his principles. His only apparent shortcomings—being absurdly rich, detached from the reality of life for underclass and minority Tennesseans, lockstep alignment with GOP policies that favored the rich at the expense of the poor, etc.—were just as true of Arch.

Goldberg was lamenting this very fact when Marcus came in, holding a copy of the *New Yorker*. How many fifteen-year-old kids from the projects killed time reading the *New Yorker*? The question itself confesses the inherent bias which made us all so smitten with him.

"I was just reading Jeffrey Toobin's new piece," Marcus said. "Have you been following the Carrie Benvenuto situation?"

Who hadn't? These were the years before iPhones and Facebook and Twitter, when the lingua franca of populist outrage was still twenty-four-hour cable news. After O. J., there was JonBenét. Monica Lewinsky fed the fix for a while. The 2000 election had turned out even better than Fox and CNN could have dreamed, with the ludicrous recount controversy and made-for-TV characters like the cartoonish Katherine Harris. Then came 9/11 and "shock and awe" and "Mission Accomplished." But the public had wearied of the war in Iraq, which began as a patriotic movie with a happy ending but had turned out to be a depressingly long documentary series with no heroes or victories. The Benvenuto situation was a great way to give us all something else to argue about.

In 1996, Carrie Benvenuto suffered a catastrophic stroke. She was thirty-one years old, a dental hygienist in Fort Walton Beach, Florida, with a prescription for Xanax to treat periodic panic attacks and a serious drinking habit she had managed to hide from everyone who knew her, with the possible exception of her husband, Chris, who claimed ignorance but drank heavily himself.

When she came out of the initial coma, Carrie could not speak or respond in any way suggesting consciousness, but she could open her eyes and move her head. Her doctors determined that her brain function was nonexistent. After a year, her husband petitioned to have her feeding tube removed, in accordance with Florida law. Her parents, Bob and Marie Palacios, filed a motion of their own, insisting that Carrie be kept alive and signed over to their care.

The story should have ended there, but for one key complication: the Benvenuto and Palacios families were Catholic. The parents insisted that their daughter was still "alive"; that removing her feeding tube was tantamount to murder. The husband refused to relinquish responsibility for her care to the parents and would not agree to a divorce. He'd started dating again and wanted to remarry in the church. There was also the matter of a substantial life insurance policy that would pay out to the next of kin. Even after resolving medical bills, the husband would pocket close to half a million dollars.

The Palacios family did not seem much less craven than their estranged son-in-law. If he signed his wife's care over to them, they'd become the policy's beneficiaries. Furthermore, the right-to-life movement had been looking for a good cause to push back against the legalization of physician-assisted suicide.

"What's your point, Marcus?" Goldberg asked.

"Baird is a doctor," Marcus said. "I wonder what he thinks about it."

"Who cares?" Goldberg replied.

"Lots of people," Marcus said. "People who vote."

Goldberg stroked his chin.

"Goddamn, kid," he said. "You're a fucking genius."

"I don't follow," Arch said.

"Don't you see?" Goldberg said. "Baird is a man of science. He knows goddamn well that the woman is brain-dead. Keeping her hooked up to a feeding tube is just prolonging the inevitable."

"How does that help us?" Arch asked.

"We just need to force Baird to take a position," Goldberg said. "He's screwed either way. The doctors aren't on the fence. Any rational person can see that the law favors the husband. If he goes with the right-to-life crowd, he gets called out as a liar and a phony. The rubes might love it, but the press will murder him. If he says what he really thinks, he'll lose the evangelicals.

And Baird's Catholic. He'd be contradicting the motherfucking pope. Every mackerel snapper in the country will call him a traitor."

Bart Walsh reddened. "I'm Catholic, you foul-mouthed son of a bitch," he said.

"Sorry, Bart," Goldberg said. "But I'm right, yes?"

Walsh loosened his tie. "Yes," he muttered. "But it could backfire. Whatever Baird says, he'll most likely spin it as dirty politics. A desperation tactic. A distraction. You have a reputation for that, you know."

"He'll never know it came from us," Goldberg said.

"How are you going to pull that off?" Walsh asked.

"What you don't know, you don't have to deny, Bart," Goldberg said. "Leave it to me. Besides, at this point, we've got nothing to lose."

"Don't make me look like an asshole, Andy," Arch said.

"That's what you pay me for," Goldberg said. "And I'm worth every penny."

Arch clapped Marcus on the shoulder. "Well done, young man," he said.

Marcus nodded and slipped back out the door with his magazine.

"What do you think, Charlie?" Arch asked.

I thought the whole story was cheap and manipulative—pure exploitation by the cable news piranhas, shallow on the part of the politicians, tawdry and embarrassing for the families. But something had turned in me.

The shine had long since come off Arch. The facade of noble compromise—the notion that you had to do a few nasty things to be in a position to do good things—had given way to naked ambition. I no longer believed that Arch wanted to serve the greater good; he just wanted to win. Still, I couldn't stand Dan Baird.

Why did I loathe him so? He was what Arch was supposed to be. He loved his wife and appeared to be faithful to her. He had principles. He'd devoted his life to serving others when he could have simply enjoyed his wealth and watched it multiply. He went to church and never once looked like he was doing it to appear holier than the rest of us. He never said a cross word about anyone.

Maybe this was precisely why I despised him. If Dan Baird was what Arch was supposed to be, where did I stack up? I'd been given so much and done next to nothing of value with it. I lied when it suited me. I had no faith. My only guiding principles were self-interest and a remora-like devotion to Arch—a devotion that had not prevented me from coveting his wife.

"Well?" Arch said.

If Baird was truly as good as he seemed, I thought, then Arch was a charlatan, and I was a pig. Maybe this nasty little trap was the answer—the way to prove Arch's contention that no one could reach the pinnacle without compromising himself.

"Do it," I said.

THEY HELD THE last debate at Rhodes in Memphis. I stood with Marcus and Vanessa near Andy Goldberg, who watched the moderator's table the entire night, chewing on his nails, pacing occasionally. Perhaps he wasn't certain his ploy would come to fruition. He needn't have worried. The two moderators were both reporters from the *Commercial Appeal*, which had been hemorrhaging subscribers and advertising revenue for years. Neither one gave a shit about which millionaire ended up as the Republican nominee. No political beat writer would pass an opportunity to get national exposure on *Hardball* or *The O'Reilly Factor* or get a story picked up by the Associated Press.

With about thirty minutes to go, one of the moderators started in.

"Dr. Baird," he said. "You're aware of the ongoing controversy in Florida over the Benvenuto case, are you not?"

"I am," Baird said.

"Then you must also be aware that Congress has been called upon to intervene," the journalist said. "If elected to the Senate, where would you side on the issue?"

"Well, it's a complex case, Carl," Baird said.

"Yes, but you've seen the video of Mrs. Benvenuto, and you've followed the case. As a physician, you must have an opinion."

"I am a physician," Baird said. "But I'm not Mrs. Benvenuto's physician, nor am I a neurologist. Do I have an opinion? Indeed I do. Everyone has an opinion. You know how much those opinions are worth when you don't know all the facts? Squat."

"But as a celebrated surgeon," the journalist continued, "surely your opinion would matter a great deal to your colleagues in the Senate. So would you mind sharing it with the audience?"

Baird paused for a moment before answering.

"I have seen the footage," he said. "It's deeply touching to watch. Mrs. Benvenuto smiles. She makes noises, which sound like efforts to speak. She seems to respond as if she were conscious. But I've also read summaries of the reports on the tests of her brain function. These tests have been conducted multiple times in multiple facilities by multiple experts. Each time, they have been conclusive. In my judgment, this is not a right-to-life issue. Her heart is beating, but she will never recover consciousness. Her body will never be able to survive without the help of machines. By law, the decision to continue artificial life support or to cease falls to her next of kin. That person happens to be her husband, not her parents. There's no disputing this fact. Hence, the choice, however heartbreaking, belongs to him. As much as I may personally disagree with his choice, the law in this matter is clear."

"If she were your wife," the journalist asked, "would you do the same?"

"In my career, I've performed dozens of transplant surgeries," Baird said. "In almost every case, the heart that saved a life came from the body of a person whose loved ones had to confront these exact circumstances. This is why Eleanor and I are both organ donors, and why we have a notarized living will. So yes, Carl, I would do the same, and I know for a fact that, given the choice, Eleanor would also."

The audience did not react much one way or the other, but, next to me, Andy Goldberg swelled.

"I know I'm not an expert like Dr. Baird, Carl," Arch said. "But do I get to weigh in?"

"Absolutely, Mr. Creigh," the journalist said.

Arch placed his hands on the lectern. His smile closed into an expression of solemnity.

"I, too, have seen the video footage," Arch said. "I find it

hard to believe Mrs. Benvenuto has no brain function whatsoever. She certainly seems to be not just alive, but conscious.
But as I've said, I'm no expert. I am, however, a man of faith.
And my faith teaches me that all life is sacred, regardless of
whether it can sustain itself without assistance. That goes for
the unborn as well as for the sick."

I glanced over at Vanessa. Her eyes were locked on Arch,
her jaw set firm, her face calm and serene, unwavering.

"I believe our elected officials have a moral obligation to
protect those who can't protect themselves, even from their
own husbands or mothers," Arch said. "So while in principle
I believe we should defer to the judgment of expert medical
professionals, I don't think it's appropriate for Congress to just
stand aside and let such a sensitive matter be settled with cold
reason rather than compassion."

"Dr. Baird, fifteen seconds," the journalist said.

"You're right about one thing, Mr. Creigh," Baird said.
"You're not an expert."

"No, sir, I'm not," Arch said. "But I know what it feels like
to lose a child. And I know my wife and I would have given
anything for just one more minute with her. And I think if I
were Carrie Benvenuto's father, I'd prefer my daughter's fate be
in God's hands, not the hands of so-called experts."

Vanessa had disappeared. So I went after her.

I found her on the loading dock outside the theater, clutching herself, gazing out past the lights illuminating the parking
lot, watching the dark.

"Don't say it," she said.

"Say what?"

"That it's just politics."

"I would never say that," I said. "You know I wouldn't."

She sighed.

"Did you ever tell him?" I asked.

"Did you?"

"Of course not," I said. "I made a promise."

She turned to face me.

"That's right," she said. "You always keep your promises, don't you?"

"Not always," I said.

"But you'd keep his secrets," she said. "And mine."

"Yes," I said.

"Come here," she said.

I stepped toward her. She grasped the lapels of my jacket and pulled my face close to hers. When her lips brushed against mine, I neither expected it nor was I surprised.

"You've thought about that, haven't you?" she whispered.

"Yes," I said.

"I've thought about it too."

She let go of my jacket and stepped away. In the dim light of the loading dock, her eyes were without pity or anger or desire. "There's another secret for you," she said.

She returned in time to join Arch onstage at the conclusion of the debate, where she smiled and shook hands with Dan Baird and his wife and children.

In a little over six months, Carrie Benvenuto's feeding tube would be removed. Two weeks later, she would die, and an autopsy would reveal that she had, in fact, been in a vegetative state. But the special election for US senator from Tennessee would be long over by then.

THE EXCHANGE MADE the national news. Baird didn't help himself by backing away from his original remarks in interviews. Sound bites and pull quotes are not the ideal media for complexity of thought and reasoning. Right-to-life activists descended upon Tennessee to help get out the vote. By the Friday before the election, the polls gave Arch a slim lead.

I couldn't rejoice at Arch's good luck. I kept thinking of the look that had passed over Vanessa's face when Arch made those remarks about the rights of the unborn, and the words she'd said to me and the kiss we'd shared. Was it true that Arch didn't know? I had no idea. I doubted knowing would have changed anything. If Baird had supported the other side of the Benvenuto controversy, Arch would have argued for science and reason and organ donation and cast aspersions on Baird's fidelity to the code of medical ethics.

Arch must have sensed my disgust. Or maybe I just looked tired.

"You should take the night off," he said.

We were leaving in less than an hour for a rally in Chattanooga. There were lots of evangelicals and Catholics registered to vote there.

"I'm fine," I said.

"It's okay," Arch said. "I can take Marcus. I bet he's never stayed in a hotel like the Chattanoogan. We'll give him your room and let him order a shitload of room service. He'll love it."

"Are you sure?" I asked.

"Absolutely," Arch said. "Get some rest."

He didn't need to twist my arm. I left without speaking to anyone. I drove home in silence. When I went into my house, I walked straight into my bedroom without even turning on a single light and fell face-forward onto the bed. I woke a few hours later to a knock on the door. It was Vanessa.

"What are you doing here?" I asked.

She didn't say a word. She just walked right past me, straight to my bedroom. By the time I'd shut and locked the door, she was already slipping out of her clothes.

FIFTEEN

Arch was too preoccupied with his lunch meeting even to ask how I'd spent my night off. He immersed himself in the endless phone calls and the tension of a manic race sliding toward at least a temporary conclusion, buoyed by the growing promise of victory.

At the end of the day, we were huddled in the campaign office, drinking coffee and listening to Goldberg read off the agenda, when my BlackBerry buzzed. Jamie Haltom's name and number appeared on the screen.

"Hey," I said. "What's going on?"

"I need you to get over here as soon as you can," he said. "It's important." He didn't sound drunk.

"Who is it?" Arch asked.

I put my hand over the receiver.

"Fucking Jamie," I said.

No one seemed able anymore to speak of Jamie without prefacing his name with some profanity.

"Get rid of him," Goldberg said.

"I can't talk," I said.

"You need to come over here," Jamie said. "To the restaurant. Now."

"What for?"

"Just do it, would you? This is no joke."

"Don't fuck with me, Jamie," I said.

"Trust me, I'm not fucking with you."

"All right," I said. "Hold on."

I covered the receiver again.

"He says he needs me to go over to the restaurant," I said.

"Now?" Arch asked.

"He says it's really important."

"Go ahead," Arch said.

"I don't know how long I'll be."

"It's fine," he said. "We're almost done here. Go put Jamie's fire out and then get some rest."

"Sorry," I said.

"No worries, bud."

The drive took less than fifteen minutes. Jamie was waiting for me at the door.

"Come on," he said. "I put them downstairs."

"Who?" I asked.

"You'll see."

Jamie had converted the basement into a wine cellar, which also served as a private room for intimate dinner parties. I followed him through the dining room into a dark corridor and down a staircase lit with copper sconces.

"Go on in," he said. "I'll make sure no one comes down."

"Cut the cloak-and-dagger shit, Jamie," I said.

He shook his head. "I'll be upstairs," he said.

At a large table in the center of the room sat Nick Averett, an open laptop computer in front of him.

"What do you want?" I asked.

"Sit down," he said.

"I think I'll stand."

"You're going to need a seat after you see what I have to show you."

Averett turned the laptop around so I could see the screen. A grainy video was playing. There is no need to describe what it displayed.

"Who is that?"

"I assume you mean the one on top?" Averett said.

"You didn't answer my question."

"Todd is an old friend of mine from Chattanooga. Arch got his number from me, actually. The amateur photography was Todd's idea, but when he contacted me about how he might make some use of it, I thought, 'What an opportunity.'"

I felt dizzy.

"Turn it off," I said. "I've seen enough."

Averett closed the laptop.

"What do you want?" I asked.

"I want to go to Washington," he said.

"You're not happy in Atlanta?"

"Are you fucking kidding?" he said.

"It's a nice city," I said.

"Right," he said. "Don't you get it? Arch has a gift. He could go all the way. With the right people around him, of course. I tried to explain that to him before. If I'd been around, this would never have happened. He's very lucky it fell into my hands. I'd like to fix things for him. But it won't be cheap."

"Why are you telling this to me?" I said. "Why don't you just ask him yourself?"

Averett reached down under the table and brought out a folder.

"Arch never wanted me to leave," Averett said. "He knows he needs me. The lovely wife, on the other hand—well, let's just say she's not my strongest advocate."

"I don't like you much either."

"Why don't you open the envelope?"

"Why don't you fuck off and die?"

"Just take a look," he said. "For Vanessa's sake."

I opened the envelope and slid its contents out onto the table. Averett sat back and smirked as I numbly absorbed the evidence of my own recent indiscretion—so recent that I could still smell her on my fingers when I covered my mouth with my hand.

"I'd rather not have to share these with Arch," Averett said. "And I'd really hate if they got into the wrong hands. But as you know, people will do pretty fucked-up things for money."

I resisted the urge to lunge across the table and choke the bastard to death. For one thing, I was no fighter—not yet, anyway. For another, Averett had me; he had both of us. Attacking him wouldn't deliver me from the predicament, which was not mine alone to resolve.

"Would you mind telling me how you got these?" I asked.

"You should know, Boykin," Averett said, "that I specialize in opposition research."

I nodded.

"What do you want me to do?" I asked.

"Tell Mrs. Creigh about our conversation," he said. "As

much or as little as you see fit. Tell her I'm coming back. If she gets in the way, I'll be offering my services—and my resources—to the opposition."

"What should I say to Arch?" I asked.

"Tell him to call me at his earliest convenience."

"That's it?"

"That's it."

"He'll wonder why you didn't just call him yourself."

"No, he won't."

I sat dumbly as Averett put the envelope and the laptop into his briefcase. He stood and buttoned his jacket.

"Get yourself together," he said. "Have a drink. Then go back to the office. I'll expect a call by tomorrow afternoon."

He shouldered his briefcase. He paused as he walked past me.

"A word of advice," he said. "Next time, draw the blinds."

SIXTEEN

I left without bothering to find Jamie. My phone rang over and over. After the tenth call, I turned it off. I paid no attention to where I was going. I rolled down the windows and listened to the noise of the city as I smoked one cigarette after another. After a while, I stopped at a gas station and bought two more packs of Camel Lights and a tallboy of Pabst, which I drank from a brown paper bag.

I drove and drove, following the lines of the road without care or reason. I drove through East Nashville, down toward where Montague Village once had stood. I drove across the river, down West End and up Belle Meade Boulevard, slowing down but not stopping in front of the great house. I drove past the stone columns marking the road up to Yeatman. I drove across the bridge in Bellevue, along the Natchez Trace, back down and over toward Leiper's Fork. I was so lost in thought that it came as a genuine surprise when I found myself on the driveway in front of the farm, where my mother and Jim had spent their life together—where the first half of my life in Nashville had ended and the second half began.

I was turning around to leave when the porch lights came on and the door opened. Jim came out, peering down at me from the top of the stairs. I cut the engine, stepped out of the car, and walked over toward him.

"Charlie?" he said. "What on earth?"

What could I say? It was nearly midnight.

Jim looked me over. I must have looked ghastly.

"Come in, son," he said.

I SAT DOWN on the couch, in the same spot I'd sat when Jim and my mother informed me that they were going to have a child together. Jim went into the kitchen. A short while later, he came back with two mugs filled with coffee.

"How do you take it?" he asked.

"Black is fine," I said.

He handed me a mug, set the other on the table, eased into a chair by the fireplace, and waited for me to explain myself.

"I need your help," I said.

"I'll always help you," he said. "You know that."

"I don't know where to begin."

"Try this," he said. "Tell me about your day."

I must have been drunker than I realized; I told him everything. Not everything, of course—I left out the more graphic details—but I did not shy away from the facts, from Averett's unsavory home movie to my visit from Vanessa the previous night and the evidence of that encounter. He took it all in quite calmly.

"Let's take a walk," he finally said.

We went out onto the porch and down the steps and into the field. The only lights came from the house. The sky was brilliant with stars. It was beautiful enough to make me weep.

"You must feel pretty disgusted with me," I said.

He took a moment to consider before speaking.

"No," he said. "I'm not disgusted. Just a little disheartened."

"You're not surprised?"

"Not especially."

"You knew."

"Which part?"

"About Arch."

"I've known Archer all his life," he said. "You know how I feel about him. I love him as if he were my own. I know his strengths and his weaknesses. And I know Vanessa's as well. And yours too."

Despite the darkness, I could see his face well enough to notice a wistful smile.

"I never wanted Archer to go into politics," he said. "You know about his father."

"Yes, sir."

"That sort of thing runs in the family," he said. "You've seen it, haven't you?"

"Glimpses."

"Arch is stronger than his father. His need to prove himself always seemed enough to hold back the darkness. But maybe not strong enough. And there's the other thing. What's the old saying? Don't get caught with a dead girl or a live boy."

"Did you ever say that to Arch?"

"Of course. But Arch stopped listening to me a long time ago," Jim said. "Anyway, Arch made his own choices."

"Maybe that other thing isn't really a choice," I said.

"Everything is a choice, Charlie," he said. He looked up at the stars.

There was no point in disagreeing with him; he would never come around to understanding anything outside of what he'd always known. "What do you want me to do, Jim?" I asked.

"What do you want to do?"

"I don't want to do anything," I said.

"That's not an option, son."

"I know."

I tossed my cigarette on the ground and stamped it out.

"I just remembered," Jim said. "I have something for you."

I followed him back up into the house. I resumed my place on the couch. Jim went upstairs. A few minutes later, he came down holding a cardboard file box. He set the box on the table in front of me and sat back down in his chair.

"Go ahead," he said. "Open it."

Inside, I found stacks of letters, envelopes filled with photographs, and an old Zippo lighter, and a set of dog tags. I lifted the string up and held the dog tags in my palm. The name I saw was one I had not thought about for a very long time: John LaRue.

I looked up at Jim.

"That's right," he said.

I sat in silent astonishment, flipping through photographs of the father I'd never known.

"Five or six years after you left," Jim explained, "your mother received a letter on US Department of Defense stationery."

Jim went on. A group of widows had launched a project to connect Vietnam veterans with their lost comrades' families, with emphasis on MIAs. An attorney from Chicago named Norman Hatcher reached out to them, looking for my mother on behalf of his dear friend John LaRue, who, it turned out, was never missing in action, but in fact, had been killed in a covert operation in Cambodia. At the time, the Army was denying any activity across the borders of Laos and Cambodia, so the mission was kept a secret, and the KIAs were filed as MIAs until the Army could come up with a passable cover story. Norman Hatcher was with my father when he died, and promised him that he'd go back home and find his girl, Bonnie, and tell her that he loved her. The task turned out to be harder than he'd expected; he'd given up until he'd received word of the widows' project. The widows, it seemed, were much more resourceful and determined than the men themselves.

"We flew Norman Hatcher down here," Jim said. "He stayed with us for a few days. He was a kind man. He talked a lot about Jesus. He'd become a born-again Christian. I think that's why he'd wanted to find your mother, and you. That's right, your father knew about you. It's in the letters."

I struggled to hold the letters steady enough to read them. They were written in block script, surprisingly clear and nimble, given my impression of John LaRue. His words were not remarkable—plainspoken declarations of love, vows of devotion and determination to come home and rescue me and my mother, to live happily ever after and so forth. The sort of words any soldier in a combat zone would write to the girl back home, who had become the focus of all of his hopes in the midst of all of that terror and brutality. The thing that kept him going, perhaps even the thing that kept him sane. Nevertheless, they stirred in me a sensation too deep and powerful to name. For a short while, Arch and Vanessa and the quandary in which I had so foolishly implicated myself vanished from my thoughts. My father knew about me. I had existed to him before he died. Had he lived, I would have known him. Perhaps he'd have come home and married my mother. Perhaps I'd have lived an entirely different life.

"We showed Mr. Hatcher your picture, told him you were doing well," Jim said. "Your mother didn't want to say where you were. I think she was embarrassed. She thought it might hurt poor Mr. Hatcher to learn that his dead friend's boy had run away from home. She didn't think she could make him understand. So we told him you were away at school, but we'd tell you about him, and you'd write if you wanted to speak to him yourself."

"Is he still alive?"

"Norman Hatcher? I don't know," Jim said. "I imagine so. It wasn't that long ago."

I picked up one of the pictures: a color shot of two men sitting on a wall of sandbags around a foxhole. I didn't have to ask which one was John LaRue. I could tell by the eyes, and the mouth, and the crooked smile, which were mine as well.

"Your mother was waiting for you to come home so she could give you all of these things and tell you what she'd learned, and how she'd felt," he said. "But by the time you came back, she was too sick to remember. And I couldn't think about anything else but her. We just let it slip our minds. I had all but forgotten about these things until just a few weeks ago when I was taking boxes out to put into storage. I would have called you then, but you were busy with the campaign. Anyway, there it is. Your history."

I flipped through the pictures, studying my father's face, observing our resemblance and the differences between us, imagining how my mother would have been smitten to the point of recklessness with him.

"She never really talked to you about your father, did she?" Jim said.

"Not much," I said.

"She never told me much either," he said. "Not until we heard from the widows and Norman Hatcher. I have to admit, I was very jealous. I loved your mother as I have never loved anything else in this world. So much that it pains me to this day to think of her with anyone else, or worse, to think of her loving anyone else. I have to remind myself that if not for John LaRue, and you, your mother and I would never have found each other."

I put down the picture and picked up the Zippo. The brass was smooth and burnished. My father's initials—JTL—were engraved on its side.

"I was so jealous of you," I said.

"I was jealous of you too," he said. "You had her to yourself for so long. I think if I hadn't been so jealous, I'd have tried harder to bring you back. When you told me to go fuck myself, down in Mexico, I was relieved. I didn't want to share her with you. She loved you first, and best. Her heart broke when you ran away. She never got over it. Dolly helped, but that pain was always there."

"I am so sorry."

"Don't be," he said. "The past is as good as it's going to get."

We sat in silence. After a while, I set the lighter down on the coffee table.

"I think I could use a drink," Jim said. "Would you like a drink?"

"Oh, yes," I said.

Before long, I was good and drunk. I don't recall how much Jim had to drink; much less than I, presumably, as he was steady enough to help me up the stairs to my old room and into my bed.

The last hour or so was a fog, but I do remember this. After he'd put me in bed, before Jim left the room, he hugged me, and I reached up and held on to him. I closed my eyes, and I thought of my mother, and I knew Jim was thinking of her too. And as I held on to Jim, for a moment, I imagined that I was clinging not to my stepfather, but to my real father, John Truman LaRue, made flesh again, who had arrived at that precise moment, to tell me . . . to tell me what?

SEVENTEEN

When I came downstairs the next morning, Jim and Dolly were gone. So I sat in the kitchen alone, drinking coffee. A memory came to me. Royal Gorge, Colorado, near the end of a monthlong road trip with Arch and the twins the summer after he graduated from Yeatman. The trip had been my first experience of the vastness of this country: the desert and the plains and the great mountains of the West, the color and the light and the black depth of the horizon as the sky went from blue to pink and orange to purple to cobalt flecked with innumerable stars. The sweet scents of sage and fir, woodsmoke and black mountain earth.

Arch wanted us all to kayak through the gorge; he said the experience would be life-changing. Even then, he was always trying to change our lives for us.

We rented gear and arranged transportation at an outfitter in Salida. The night before the trip, Jamie ate a pot brownie and drank about fifteen Natural Lights; when we woke him up to leave, he barely made it out of the tent before heaving. So we left him at the campsite to sleep it off and drove to the put-in, about a quarter mile upriver from the first rapids. Arch left Vanessa and me with the boats and paddles while he drove to the take-out area, where he'd arranged for a ride back on one of the rafting company buses.

Early morning, June, Colorado. Infinite sky. The canyon downstream, rocks scattered along the hills around its mouth, scattered patches of sweetgrass and yellow and purple wild-flowers. The scent of piñon. Dirty-blond hair. Goose-bumped flesh along the slopes of narrow arms and calves. The faint trace of pale lip balm along the Cupid's bow of her lovely mouth.

Had we known the river was near flood stage, Vanessa and I would have been afraid. We should have remembered it was already Arch's habit to lead us into things for which we were not properly prepared.

A bus loaded with rafts pulled to a stop, Arch hopped out, and twenty minutes later we were on the river, speeding toward the mouth of the canyon, the sound of the rapids growing louder and more violent as the cliffs rose up and the shadows fell across the water.

We'd paddled kayaks in the gentler rivers of Tennessee and North Carolina, and thought we knew what we were doing. Arch had coached us before we put in, reminding us how to bail out and swim if we flipped (only he knew how to "Eskimo roll" a kayak back upright if it capsized). We agreed that Arch would lead, followed first by Vanessa, with me at the rear.

When we reached the first rapids, I didn't even have time to be frightened. The current took over. After maybe twenty or thirty seconds of pure terror, we poured out into the flat and looked around for each other, our faces blanched with awe and relief.

After that first drop, we settled into an easy, confident rhythm. The fear of disaster dissipated. Soon, the water picked up speed again as the channel narrowed and dropped between the rocks and turned to roaring froth. At the center of the run stood a large boulder almost obscured by the explosion of aerated foam and mist spewing up over it. Arch nimbly steered to the side of the rock and descended. Even if she'd been much more experienced, Vanessa wouldn't likely have had time to follow Arch's maneuver. The nose of her boat plunged over the rock, tilted up, and capsized, just as it sped toward a second, much larger drop. I had only a moment to look for her before I slid past the boulder and fell into the spume.

I eddied out at the bottom of the run, below what paddlers call a "hole," where the steepness of the drop causes the flow of the water to recirculate, creating a vortex capable of sucking a boat under. It was the only part of the river about which Arch had expressed any real concern. He'd urged us to paddle hard throughout and throw our weight forward at the bottom. Even though I was doing as I'd been told, I'd felt the hole sucking me down for a jarring, petrifying moment, grasping at the stern of the kayak before the current caught the hull and spit me out into flat water.

I turned and saw Vanessa's boat, still upended, bobbing in the shallows on the far side of the eddy. Arch was already ashore and running back upriver.

A lone paddler in a narrow kayak floated up the crest of the great wave crashing against the canyon wall and hurtled into the chute with practiced grace. He was a bearded man, maybe about forty, wearing a fiberglass helmet. He came up alongside the bank beneath me.

"Our friend swam," Arch shouted. "Did you see her?"

The man shook his head.

Arch took off running. The bearded man and I got out of our boats. He gathered a throw rope and a first-aid kit. We came up over the rocks and spotted Vanessa, floating against the far wall of the canyon, in the eddy. The cliff around her was vertical, featureless, far too slick for her to climb out. Her face was frighteningly pale.

Arch mounted a large boulder jutting out over the current. I thought he meant to hurl a rope to her; instead, he leapt into the air and disappeared into the river. A moment later, he surfaced and swam toward Vanessa. He wrapped his arms around her and spoke close to her ear. Vanessa nodded, her own face mirroring Arch's fixed determination.

Arch pushed off the wall, holding Vanessa from behind. They hit the chute and disappeared. Their heads popped up just as they descended into the current, hurtling toward the hole below. Just before he went under, Arch pushed Vanessa forward, flinging her past the danger and out toward the gentle water as he vanished beneath the roiling foam.

The bearded man tossed his throw rope to Vanessa. I stood at the edge of the bank, searching for Arch below the surface of all of that noisy, bubbling water. The seconds stretched on. Counting aloud, I realized with mounting dread that he'd been down for close to a minute. For an instant, I tried to fathom the unthinkable. And then he popped up, gasping for air, some sixty feet beyond where he'd gone under.

"Hot damn. He swam right down into it, below the

current," the man said. "Down's the only way out. Smart kid. That hole's a killer."

As soon as the water was shallow and gentle enough for him to stand, Arch went straight for Vanessa. She sat with her arms wrapped around her knees, holding herself. Her whole body shook, her face a blank mask of fatigue—what soldiers call the thousand-yard stare. Arch sat down behind her, covering her with an emergency blanket, enclosing her in his arms.

I felt a tap on my shoulder. When I turned, the stranger was pointing up into the air over my head. There it was—the Royal Gorge Bridge, a thousand feet above us. From that distance, the center of it looked like a black thread stretched taut across the sky.

The sun glinted off the windows of a train as it passed over. In the distance, we heard a long, lone whistle. I looked back at Arch clinging to Vanessa, her eyes cold and emotionless, her body warmed by his imperfect devotion, Arch chastened but also exultant.

Recalling that moment years after, I might as well have been standing there again, only now able to describe what I felt then but could not express, even to myself. I knew that no matter how I loved them, however close I might wish to be, I would always remain on the outside of that circle. I knew that theirs was a charmed existence, in ways that went far beyond their privilege. And I was quite certain that Arch would never die.

I CALLED VANESSA before I left to go into the office. I wasn't confident she'd answer the phone. She picked up on the first ring.

"Where are you?" she asked.

"At the farm," I said.

"Are you okay?"

"Fine," I said.

"Why didn't you answer your phone?"

"I turned it off."

"Why? What were you doing?"

I told her what I had found waiting for me in the cellar at Jamie's place, what I had heard.

"That's unfortunate," she said.

"Unfortunate?"

"Yes," she said.

"Is that all you have to say?"

"I don't know what you mean."

I listened to the silence on the other end of the call, trying to imagine what Vanessa was doing, what she was thinking.

"I'm going to tell him," I said.

"No, you won't."

"Why wouldn't I?"

"Because you love him."

I drew in a breath and let it out slowly.

"Let's just go," I said. "You and me. We can go anywhere you want."

I hadn't given the words a single thought. They just spilled out.

"I'm not going anywhere," she said. "Neither are you."

"Vanessa," I said.

"Don't say it, Charlie," she said.

"Don't say what?" I said.

"That you love me."

"I do," I said. "You know I do."

"I know," she said. "And you know too."

"What do I know?"

"That it isn't enough."

I wished with all my heart that I could prove her wrong.

"I have to go," Vanessa said. "Goodbye, Charlie."

I put the phone down. There was nothing else to do but go find Arch.

When I reached the office, he was in a meeting. I sat in front of his desk until he came in.

"What the hell, bud," he said. "We've been worried about you."

I shut the door behind me. Arch sat down behind the desk. I told him everything Nick Averett had told me, what he had shown me on his computer, what he wanted. Arch crossed his arms behind his head. I thought I detected a hint of worry in his expression. It might just as likely have been a projection of my wish to see him squirm for once.

"I need to tell you what I did while you were in Chattanooga. Do you want to know what I was doing?" I asked. "Who I was with?"

He shifted in his chair. A look of mild contempt came over his face. I took out a cigarette.

"Don't smoke in here," Arch said.

"You'd better call Averett," I said. "The clock is ticking." I took a long drag and let the smoke trickle out through my nostrils.

"There's something else," I said.

"Do tell."

"I went out to the farm last night."

"You told Jim?"

"Yes."

"Jesus Christ," he said. "What the fuck is wrong with you?"

"I wouldn't know how to begin to answer that," I said. "But that's not why I mention it. Jim gave me something. Something of my mother's." I took the lighter out of my pocket and handed it to him.

"That belonged to my father," I said.

I told Arch about the widows and Norman Hatcher and the pictures and the letters.

"I'll be damned," he said.

He eased back into his chair and fondled the Zippo just as I had, flipping the lid open and closed, and then placed it on the desk. He slumped back into his chair. I slipped the lighter back into my pocket.

"Arch," I said. "I think I'm done."

"You're just hungover."

"No," I said. "Really. Consider this my resignation."

"Oh, come on," he said. "We can get past this. We love each other, right? All of us. We'll figure it out."

"Not this time," I said.

"What are you going to do?" he said. "Go back to painting portraits?"

"There's a war going on, you know," I said. "Maybe I'll follow in my father's footsteps and be all that I can be."

Arch laughed. "What, you're going to join the Army? You? You're not your father, Charlie. You're an artist. Besides, you're too old."

"I hear they'll take anyone these days."

"Now I think you're still drunk."

I doused my cigarette in a half-filled Styrofoam coffee cup.

"Come on, Charlie," he said. "I need you. Now more than ever. We're going to win, you know. It'll be over soon, and we'll go to Washington, and it will be better, for all of us."

Arch stood and rounded the desk. "Come on, brother," he said.

He almost had me. Then I remembered something Vanessa had told me long ago. "Arch doesn't love anyone as much as he loves being loved," she'd said. Was that true for Vanessa too? I wondered. For me?

"I do love you, you know," I said. "And I will miss you."

"You just need a good night's sleep," he said. "You'll feel better after. We're going to win, and then we'll all go to DC, and we'll start over. All of us. It's going to be fine. You'll see."

I dropped the cup into the wastebasket and walked out the door.

A YEAR LATER, Arch and Vanessa were in Washington, and I was on the other side of the world, consumed by heat and long hours of fear and dread and suffocating silence between eruptions of violence and the calls to prayer pealing out across the rooftops.

In time, Arch and Vanessa left my dreams, replaced by the faces of dead soldiers, and, sometimes, of my mother, young again, with Sunny and the other women by the pool at Montague Village, and the father I never knew.

Epilogue

The Spirit and the Flesh

The place had been dead when we arrived. It was the sort of joint Mike and I both liked: old and dark, a bit grungy, a single television behind the bar, a string of colored Christmas tree lights strung above the shelves of bottles.

"You never spoke to him again?" Mike asked.

"Not once," I said. "He kept calling me for a while, but I never answered. I never even listened to the messages. Eventually, I threw the phone away. Everything I knew about him came from what I saw in the news."

"And her?"

"The same. Or almost. She never called."

"And you never tried to reach her?"

"I didn't think I could bear it," I said. "I wrote her a letter once, in Iraq. I was feeling the way I think my father must have felt when he wrote those letters to my mother. I never sent it. I read it over and over. Then I burned it."

Mike emptied his drink.

"Another round?" he asked.

"I'd better not."

A waitress appeared beside the booth. She pointed at the plate between us.

"You want a box for that?" she asked.

We'd ordered food so as not to look like we were just getting loaded: stale tortilla chips smothered by cheese, pickled jalapenos, and watery salsa. The menu called the dish Freedom Nachos.

"No, thank you," Mike said. "Just the check."

I emptied my drink.

"Do you still paint?" he asked.

"I haven't touched a brush in years," I said.

Mike pointed at my father's lighter, next to my cigarettes and the overflowing ashtray.

"Can I see that?" he said.

I slid the lighter over to him. He flipped open the lid before setting it back on the table and pushing it back toward me.

"Last week, when I came into the chapel in the morning, there was a boy there," he said. "A private, about the same age as the kid whose parents we just left. He was standing in the pulpit holding a revolver in his mouth."

"Jesus," I said.

"Do you know how many times I've seen things like that? And it's not all combat trauma. A lot of these men had never been deployed. Why do they do want to take their own lives? Why would anyone?"

At the bar, an old man sat on a stool at the corner, his face lit up by the blue screen of a video poker machine.

"What did you do?"

"I talked to him. I told him how when Christ hung in agony on the cross, he cried out, 'Why have you forsaken me?' I think hell happened in those five words. Why have you forsaken me? In that moment, Jesus was in hell. Not the physical agony, but the death of the spirit. But he overcame death. Body and soul. He showed us the way out of hell."

"Did that work?"

"Enough to calm him down and get him into treatment."

"How's he doing?"

"I don't know. I was planning to check in on him this afternoon."

"I'm sorry," I said. "You have more important things to do."

Mike reached across the table and grasped my hand.

"You're not going to pray for me, are you?" I asked.

He smiled.

"The thought never crossed my mind," he said.

IN THE NEXT six months, I delivered two more casualty notifications, one in Goodlettsville, the other in Murfreesboro. Mike Bailey was not with me; both boys were Baptists. After the second, I put in for my discharge.

For a while, I lived with Sunny and her husband—they'd been married for eight years—while I looked for a new place of my own. I'd kept my house in East Nashville when I enlisted; Sunny suggested that I sell it. Gentrification had made it worth more than triple what I'd paid. But I liked the tenants—a high school biology teacher and a midwife with two straw-haired children, one a kindergartner in the neighborhood school.

Dolly was living in New York, working at an auction house.

I wrote her long letters narrating the history of our mother's life as I remembered it. I flew up one weekend on the pretext of visiting the museums and galleries and took her out to lunch at a bistro on the Upper West Side, near her apartment building. She had grown lean and leggy, like Vanessa, but with my mother's chestnut hair and eyes. She spent most of our time together looking at her phone. But she met me, and she didn't tell me to fuck off and get out of her life. I left feeling more hope than regret.

Another year passed. I never tried to reach Vanessa and had stopped wishing she would try to reach me. So the day she called, the sound of her voice hit me with the same force I'd have felt if it had been my mother's.

"Where are you?" I asked.

"Home," she said.

The last time I'd seen her, she was on television, next to Dan Baird when he announced his intention to run for Arch's vacated Senate seat. She stood there looking as stoic and serene as Baird, who had every reason to spit on Arch's grave, talked about the tragic loss of such a promising public servant and vowed to continue the good work Arch had begun for the country and for the people of Tennessee.

The next morning, I drove across Nashville and into Belle Meade. A fog had settled overnight across Middle Tennessee, thinning with the rising sun into a misty vapor. I turned off West End, onto the Boulevard, and steered up the long pebbled driveway. She met me at the front door.

For years, I had seen Vanessa only on screens and in photographs, where she looked more or less unchanged by time. Face-to-face, I could see the lines around her eyes, worn deeper, no doubt, by sadness as much as by the years. This is not to say that she was not as lovely as ever, or that I did not feel seized by the old yearning. I mention it only to observe that those little signs, visible only at close range, reminded me how far removed we were from that first sun-drenched afternoon by the pool, and that heartbroken drive on the Natchez Trace, and that last night when she arrived at my house unannounced and I followed her back to my bedroom.

"You're out of uniform," she said.

"That's over now," I said. "Trying to get used to being a civilian again."

"Good," she said. "I'll have one less thing to worry about."

"You worry about me?"

"I never stopped worrying about you."

Behind her, the walls of the great room were bare, much of the furniture gone, the rest draped with white covers.

A tray of fruit and scones sat at the center of the kitchen table, along with a set of fine china dishes and cups on saucers, one cup half full, a faint lipstick stain on the rim.

"Will you eat?" she asked.

"Just coffee, please."

We carried our coffee out to the table on the slate patio behind the kitchen. The mist had burned off. The grass was still long and green in the sunshine, but scattered with fallen leaves as the trees turned red and gold and yellow with the coming of fall. We sat down at the patio table and sipped our coffee, neither of us wishing to waste time with small talk but unsure what to say.

"I thought I might see you at the memorial service," she said.

"I didn't want to be a distraction."

"I could have used one."

"I'm sorry. To be honest, I didn't think I could bear it."

What couldn't I bear? Listening to a naïve priest try to pin a happy ending on the tail end of a tragedy? Seeing all of those people I'd run away from once again? Being just another face in the crowd, somewhere in the back of the room, inauspicious, anonymous, unrecognizable?

"The news said something about a note," I said. "What did it say?"

"He said he was sorry. He told me where to find him and that I should send someone else. That's pretty much it."

"There must have been something."

"There is always something."

"Enlighten me."

Vanessa took in a long breath and let it out slowly. She pushed her hair behind her ears. I noticed her pearl earrings—the same, I assumed, as the ones she wore on the day of Arch's first election. They had belonged to Arch's grandmother. Heirloom jewelry. Who would wear them next? Dolly, no doubt. Things go on, as they must.

"Do you remember Sandy Hook?" she said.

"How could I forget?" When it happened, I was still in Iraq, where over the course of the war I had seen so much of man's inhumanity to man that I had nearly lost the capacity for pity. There had been times when I'd heard or read of some fresh atrocity back home and observed the horror and indignation flowing forth on television. Only in the United States of America, I thought, does anyone still feel that such things are not as predictable as the sunrise. But none of the horrors I had witnessed could harden my heart against what had happened in that school.

"He was at the Capitol when the news broke," Vanessa said. "I was at work. When we got home, Arch and I made a drink and turned on the TV, and it started to sink in. We cried—oh, how we cried. But the next day, the NRA lobbyists were lining up outside his office doors. Arch went in that day ready to break ranks. But his name was already on the short list for vice president. He didn't need much persuading to accept that taking on the NRA would put a swift end to that possibility."

"Maybe it would have been brilliant," I said. "Maybe he would have looked like the most principled Republican in the Senate."

"This is Tennessee, Charlie," she said. "Half the people who voted for Arch are stockpiling ammunition and watching the sky for black helicopters."

Vanessa set her coffee down at the table and gazed off at the yard.

"Did the other thing have any influence on his decision?"

"I don't know."

"You don't know, or you don't want to know?"

"We never talked about it. After the scare he'd had before, I assumed Arch was discreet. Still, it's possible. Nick swore to us that he'd taken care of it for good, but it's hard to make anything disappear anymore. Arch would hardly be the first member of Congress who cast a vote to protect a secret. The big lobbying firms have a file on every one of them."

She crossed her legs and smoothed the hem of her dress. "The bill never had a chance anyway," she said.

I stamped out my cigarette and watched the glint of the sun-light on the morning dew.

"About a week after the gun bill died, Arch got a letter from one of the Sandy Hook moms," Vanessa said. "He let me read it. I think I have it somewhere. I don't ever want to look at it again. I guess that was the killing blow. Did you see the news about the walking tour?"

It had been a big story. During a Senate recess, Arch had grown a beard and gone undercover, hiking and backpacking around East Tennessee, visiting little towns and farms while pretending to be a vagabond traveler so that he could get to know the good people of his state up close.

"That was nothing but a big charade," she said. "Andy Goldberg and Nick Averett orchestrated the whole thing. The beard was real. Arch grew it because the treatment center wouldn't let him have a shaving razor, for fear he might split it open and use it to slit his wrists."

"What about all of those farmers and store clerks he became so friendly with?"

"All very well compensated, carefully coached, and required to sign agreements that would all but doom them to a chain gang if they ever told anyone the truth."

Vanessa's phone buzzed on the table. She picked it up, glanced at the screen, silenced it, and placed it facedown next to her coffee.

"I guess the treatment didn't take," I said.

"Maybe it did, maybe it didn't," she said. "Maybe Arch thought he was acting honorably, like one of those ancient Romans Walker Varnadoe tried to make you all worship back at Yeatman. I'm tired of being expected to excuse everything with illness."

It didn't seem a good time to note the irony of a powerful man secretly afflicted with depression shooting himself out of shame over voting down legislation designed to deter the mentally ill from having access to guns.

"I'd like to see the garden again," I said. "Will you come with me?"

"It's not much to look at anymore."

"Just the same."

"Okay."

We followed the path leading around the house to the rose garden, its heirloom vines pruned and winterized, the leaves already yellowing, a few red scatterings of new growth coaxed out by the variations in temperature so typical of the change of seasons in Middle Tennessee, where summer seemed always to tease with the possibility of return before the first frost.

"I'm selling the house," she said.

"I thought when I saw all of the furniture covered that you might be," I said. "When does it go on the market?"

"It's already under contract. I just have to sign some paperwork. Mother and Daddy have already come through to mark what they'd like to have. Jamie didn't want anything except a share of the equity. I'm not keeping much myself. There's no room for any of it where I'm living now. The closing is in a month, but I won't need to be here."

"You're staying in Washington?"

"I'm with a nonprofit," she said. "We raise money and lobby for women's health care and education in the developing world."

"That sounds like a noble calling."

"It's hard to feel sorry for yourself when you're holding the hand of an Afghan woman who has had her nose and ears cut off for trying to escape slavery."

"It's good that you're helping her."

"She's helped me far more. As have many others. Isn't that always the case with people like us?"

"In my experience, people like us do more harm than good, despite our best intentions. But I understand what you mean."

She stopped and faced me. A wistfulness came over her. *How strange,* I thought, *to feel at once so close and so distant.*

"Have you found someone yet?" she asked.

"No," I said. "Have you?"

"I have. A man I work with. We didn't start seeing each other until Arch was gone, but the feelings began before. We're keeping it under wraps for a while longer. But I thought you should know."

"Did you think I thought you had called me for that?"

"Didn't you?"

I looked back past the roses toward the long yard.

"I thought I loved you once," she said. "I think now I was using you to love myself. Or maybe it was something else. I don't know. Besides . . . you loved Arch first. So did I. We both know that's not something we could ever get past."

There was so much I wanted to say to her. Instead, I just smiled—that sad, sweet smile they say makes me such a comfort to the bereaved.

"I have one last favor to ask," she said.

"Anything," I said.

"The new owner has hired an architectural engineer.

There's structural damage in the walls. They're going to keep the bones, but it won't look the same. I want to be able to remember it the way it was."

"I'm out of practice," I said. "I've only just begun to try again."

"You're the only person I'd ever ask," she said.

I RETURNED A few days later with an easel and a stool and a box of oil paints in the trunk of my car. The house and grounds were still and silent. I walked down into the yard, found a spot in the shade of the red oaks, set up my easel and board, and prepared the pallet. The air was cool and redolent with the scent of the oils and the late blooms in the gardens and the coming of fall.

I sat down on my stool and glanced across the yard. As I studied the house, I thought of the first time I'd visited it on that summer day when I was boy—how grand and glorious it had seemed; how I could hardly believe anyone might actually live in such a place. I thought of walking up the driveway with my mother heading toward the kitchen, and Jim calling out to us, desperate not to let my mother enter through a door meant for servants. I thought of our years in the carriage house, and how I had been lulled into believing that my time in that place and that world might be more than temporary— that I belonged there. I thought of the day I returned after my sojourn in Mexico, of how much my absence had altered my view of the things that had not changed and seemed as if they never would. I thought of how, soon, the house would look so different—how, at that very moment, it already belonged to someone else, someone who knew nothing of what had taken place there, just as I knew nothing of what it had meant to others who had known it before me. Those people were long dead, the moments of joy in which they delighted and the sorrows for which they suffered now forgotten. Or perhaps they were sealed away somewhere, in lost letters or old diaries moldering in a box somewhere to remain unread, unknown, unremarkable, just as mine were destined to be, but for whatever trace of them might flow from my heart to my hand onto the bare white canvas over which I gazed as I prepared to make my final offering at the temple in which I and those I loved best were formed.

The sun lit up the facade of the house. A breeze whispered through the trees, sending golden leaves cascading around to rest, suspended, on the tips of the long blades of grass. I bowed my head and cast up a silent prayer. A deep calm came over me. I opened my eyes and picked up the brush and began.

ACKNOWLEDGMENTS

DEEPEST THANKS TO Gail Hochman, for your faith, your wisdom, and your inestimable kindness. Thanks to the good people at Algonquin, past and present, especially Betsy Gleick, Michael McKenzie, Lauren Moseley, Stephanie Mendoza, Brunson Hoole, Elisabeth Scharlatt, Craig Popelars, and Andra Miller. I am so very grateful for Kathy Pories, the kind of editor that isn't supposed to exist anymore.

Many thanks to Maria Browning, Tim Henderson, and all the good people of Chapter 16 and Humanities Tennessee, stalwarts of literary life in Nashville and beyond. Thanks to my dear friends at Parnassus Books for providing a home away from home and a place of belonging to my family and so many others. To the American Booksellers Association and to all the independent booksellers: thank you for keeping the culture of books and ideas alive and thriving.

To everyone at St. Augustine's Episcopal Chapel in Nashville, especially Scott Owings: thank you for, among many other things, reminding me occasionally to take a few deeper-than-normal breaths and teaching me to listen in both the silence and the storm for the still, small voice.

To Peter Taylor: thank you for helping me remember why stories and language still matter, and for prompting me to write the letter that changed the course of my life in the most unexpected and beautiful way. To all of my family—Pettyjohns, Webbs, Lees, Stevenses, Hearnes, Spencers, and Hoods: thank you for your steadfast love and support in this and all things. To Izzy and Trent: let's gooooo! To Mary-Randolph and Lettie: this whole world is yours and mine.

Finally, to Helen—first and last, forever and ever, Amen.